the RESOLUTIONS

Mia García

KATHERINE TEGEN BOOKS
An Imprint of HarperCollins Publishers

Katherine Tegen Books is an imprint of HarperCollins Publishers.

The Resolutions
Copyright © 2018 by HarperCollins Publishers
All rights reserved. Printed in the United States of America. No part
of this book may be used or reproduced in any manner whatsoever
without written permission except in the case of brief quotations
embodied in critical articles and reviews. For information address
HarperCollins Children's Books, a division of HarperCollins
Publishers, 195 Broadway, New York, NY 10007.
www.epicreads.com

Library of Congress Control Number: 2018952187
ISBN 978-0-06-265682-7

18 19 20 21 22   PC/LSCH   10 9 8 7 6 5 4 3 2 1
❖
First Edition

"Tell me who you walk with, and I'll tell you who you are."
—Esmeralda Santiago, *When I Was Puerto Rican*

NEW YEAR'S EVE

NORA

THE ORIGINAL RECIPE called for three dollops of Nutella in the batter, but Nora placed five. With a knife she swirled the chocolate into the brownie batter, making complicated patterns that would mostly disappear as the mixture baked and rose. But still she felt quite calm doing it. When it was nice and swirled she placed the pan and its peanut butter counterpart in the oven, set the timer on her phone, and wrote out the adjusted recipe in her notebook.

Already her mind wondered what other alterations she could make. What would the brownies taste like with swirls of guayaba? Or a gooey layer of dulce de leche? Her mouth watered, and she sighed as she closed her overflowing recipe notebook and placed it back on the cookbook section of their bookshelf. She loved how baking made her mind tumble with new ideas. How even as she whisked flour, sugar, and chocolate her mind offered her a dozen other options and variations to try.

Too bad they rarely found a home outside of her circle of friends and the odd customer. But that was the way it had to be; Nora understood that. She and her mother spent years cultivating the classic Puerto Rican cuisine they served at their small restaurant (could they call it that when they only had one tiny table?), La Islita del Caribe, and many of her recipes simply did not fit the bill. Though they still brightened her heart, and that was good enough for her. She wouldn't have notebooks filled with recipes if they didn't.

She ran her finger across the spines on the shelf. They contained various histories of Puerto Rico (where her mother was born) and Cuba (where her father's parents were born), biographies about fancy superstars like Rita Moreno, and some of her mother's favorite books. The baking and cooking section was by far the largest and featured two copies of her mother's favorite Puerto Rican cookbook. Its classic recipes were the basis for their first menu. She still remembered her seven-year-old self stretching until she could see over the counter as she helped her mother serve out containers filled with arroz relleno to their first customers.

As Nora grew so did her role in La Islita, until she was head of the dessert menu. Though she'd love to add her newer recipes, Nora was proud of her work and the trust her mother placed in her. Eventually Nora would run La Islita herself, but that was far off in the future, regardless of how many times her mother reminded her of it.

Dropping all the dishes in the sink, she filled it with water and let them soak while she decided whether or not to make a third dessert for Jess's New Year's Eve party. Could it still be called a party when it was just Jess, Lee, Ryan, and Nora? Either way, Nora couldn't wait to see her friends. Between school and work at La Islita she rarely had time to just sit and hang out. She missed Lee dragging her to whichever latest sci-fi or superhero movie was out that week. Or just talking with Jess and Ryan over a hot cup of café she hadn't made herself.

She eyed the oven and the two baking sets of brownies trying to remember last year's sugar consumption.

Though Ryan was in charge of the candy for the party, Nora was in the charge of the dessert—and the two should never be confused. Pulling out the notebook again she flipped through the recipes, not finding anything she could whip up with what was left in the fridge. She eyed her mom's recent yard sale purchase and leafed through a cookbook that looked like it was from the nineties, landing on a recipe for vanilla meringues. It was kind of perfect since they reminded her of the lemon meringues her abu used to bring with her whenever she visited. Though the ones pictured in the book were perfectly shaped, while her grandmother's were dyed a wicked green color and were shaped by however they landed when the spoon slapped down on the metal sheet.

The recipe called for four egg whites that have been separated from the yolk for at least twenty-four hours. Who had time for that? Nora was pretty sure her grand-mother didn't keep random egg whites in her fridge for no damn reason, so fresh ones it would be. She filled a small bowl with warm water and set the eggs inside to lose some of the cold while she washed the dishes. There were only so many mixing bowls in the apartment.

The recipe called for regular sugar and powdered sugar. Got to love a recipe that calls for two types of sugar.

Her phone buzzed.

Ryan: As usual, I never learn from my mistakes and am helping Jess set up.

Jess: You love it.

Ryan: Do I?

Lee: Are you guys texting while in the same room?

Ryan: . . . No.

Jess: Yes.

Lee: Dorks.

Ryan: So, that's TWIX for Nora, Peanut M&M's for Jess, and a hot bag of dicks for Lee. Did I get that right?

Lee: HEY.

Nora: ☺

Lee: Rude.

Ryan: ☺

Lee: But for serious, you got my Starburst, right?

Ryan: I'm not an amateur.

Lee: I never doubted you.

Nora smiled and shook her head as she dipped her hands into the still-warm water. Finding the sponge hiding at the bottom she got to work dislodging the chocolaty sweetness from the bowls. She was lost in the task when the sound of jangling keys came from the door.

"Nora!" her mother called from the entrance, dragging out the O in her name.

"¡Aqui!" she answered, not that there were many places she could be in their tiny apartment.

Her mom tossed her keys into a small bowl by the door and struggled to pull off her snow boots. "Why did I even put these on today? You'd think after years of living here I could figure out Denver weather, pero no."

Free of the bulky shoes, she came around the kitchen counter and gave Nora a big hug. She smelled of frying oil, cumin, and garlic; remnants of a long day at La Islita. Most days Nora smelled like café, vanilla, and sugar. Beth often said she could taste the sugar on her skin.

"It's easy," Nora said as her mother slumped on the couch. "It snows for one day then it's gone the next, and it's always bike-riding weather por alguna razón."

"Today sucked."

"Did the order get out okay?" Nora felt a pang of guilt for taking the day off.

"Sí. I just don't understand how some people always find something to complain about, coño." She peeked at

Nora from the couch. "Por favor dime we still have some of the café your tía sent from Puerto Rico."

"We do." Nora pulled a glass container from the pantry and measured coffee grounds into the moka pot. "What was it this time?"

"Why don't we put olives in our piñon? We don't, that's why! My mother didn't like them, I don't like them, Dios. If you want one with olives make it yourself, Doña Claudia."

"She's a good customer though."

"Yes, and she knows it, la vieja." Her mother shrugged the day off like a coat and slipped on a smile. "We missed you at the store today."

"I know." Nora pulled out a rag from a drawer and concentrated on drying the bowl, ignoring the guilt that threatened to mess with her stomach. She knew her mother hadn't meant to tap into the guilt, but dammit if her heart didn't fall for it each time.

"It's never the same without you," her mother said, staring at Nora for a beat longer than necessary.

"What?"

Her mother shrugged.

Nora wasn't buying it. "What's that look for?"

"Just being sentimental." She tried to wave Nora away, but now she needed to know.

"About?"

"You."

"Me?" What would make her sentimental about me?

8

"Sí, tu. I'm proud of you, you know that?"

Nora cringed, feeling a flush starting along her neck. "Mami . . ."

"I know, I know! I was just thinking of how lucky I am to have you. Today was a very good day at La Islita, and it wouldn't be where it is now without you. And you know what?" She looked away from Nora, like she could see something Nora couldn't. "I see big things for us, Mija. Just you wait. It's going to be our year. La Islita's year. All because of you."

Nora shook her head. "You're just exaggerating."

"I never exaggerate."

She did. She really did.

Nora pulled the now room-temperature eggs out of the bowl, setting them on top of the rag. She shook off the tendrils of guilt that still clung to her heart. Tendrils that told her she could've gotten up earlier and helped at the store while making the treats for tonight. She would've been tired, yes, but wasn't she always tired?

"¿Qué haces?"

"Meringues."

"¿Ay, guárdame unos cuantos?" She patted her stomach. "I need a treat."

"Claro."

"You know." She looked pensive for a moment. "We do need a new dessert for the spring catering menu. Meringues would be easy-ish, and your abuela would've loved to see

9

them on the menu. ¿Qué crees?"

Nora could see herself piping thousands of tiny little meringue kisses over and over again, waiting hours for a batch to dry out so she could pack them up for whatever wedding, cumpleaños, or party they were preparing for. Her back ached already.

"I don't know—they do take a lot of time in the oven to make them light as a feather."

Her mother shrugged. "Piénsalo and let me know; you're the boss."

Nora could hear the water start to steam, traveling up the pot, and she thought back to an article she'd read yesterday about how you could never really catch up on sleep, which somehow made her more tired.

"Excited for tonight?" Her mother pulled off the hair ties that held the tangle of black hair atop her head, letting the curtain of black cascade along her shoulders. Nora's hair was almost as black as her mother's, but instead of straight it was a mass of tight curls that she usually kept back in a professional bun.

"Yes, it's been so hard to get everyone together, especially Ryan." Nora didn't fight the smile that crept on her lips.

"Is he still . . . ?" her mother asked as she came around the kitchen counter to help her.

"Heartbroken?"

Her mother nodded.

"Yeah."

"Bueno, maybe tonight will be good for him?"

"I hope so."

Nora slid two small bowls between them. "This one for yolks and the other for egg whites. Don't dump the whites into the mixing bowl until you make sure there are no yolk bits in them."

Her mother bumped her butt against hers. "You trying to show me my own moves?"

"Technically these are Abu's moves."

"Oh I see." Her mother cracked an egg on the counter, dropping the contents on her cupped hand. "Let me show you mine, then."

Nora reached for an egg, concentrating on the feel of the whites as they passed through her fingers, coating her skin, then dropping the yolk in the waiting bowl. She smiled as she watched her mother do the same. How many times had they stood like this, side by side, tinkering with recipes? Hundreds? How many were still to come? The thought made her stumble like a crack on the sidewalk, and she stopped, the egg yolk close to slipping between her fingers before she pushed past it and kept going.

RYAN

JESS WAS ON Ryan's bed, and she wouldn't leave. If he
wanted her out he'd have to extract himself from the sheets
that his sleeping self had wrapped so meticulously around
his body and push her off from his side. That felt like a lot
of work for this early in the morning . . . or was it afternoon? She bounced on his bed with such force she'd almost
bounced him off it.

"Jessica Marie Agüedo, don't do this."

It's not that he didn't deserve it. He'd been a shit friend
for the past several weeks, ever since he'd broken up with
Jason. Again.

He felt Jess still and imagined her trying to figure out
which part of the talking bedsheet blob was his face.

"Whoa, full name! Well, fullish. You're missing like
three more last names. Anyway, you promised you'd help

me prep for New Year's."

"That was Past-Ryan. Past-Ryan was still in a relationship and much happier." Not entirely true, a part of him whispered, but it was not the time to get into the nuances of Ryan and Jason's failed attempt at saving their relationship after their first breakup when Jason left for college. Their reconciliation had lasted right until Thanksgiving, just in time to go to the TAA's (Taiwanese Association of America) Thanksgiving celebration. Perfect. "Past-Ryan says a lot of shit Present-Ryan regrets. Present-Ryan cannot be held accountable for Past-Ryan's promises."

Present-Ryan could not actually be found, as his heart was shattered into a million pieces, and who are you without a heart?

"Come on," she pleaded. "You can't stay in there all day."

What was left of the day, anyway. "That sounds like a challenge."

He should get up. He should help his friend like he'd promised, but it was so damn hard to move, to think. He was stuck in place, and it was simply easier not to try.

"Come on! No one else helps set up."

"Have faith! You never know, just because no one ever has . . ."

"You miss us, I know it." Jess shifted and lay down next to the cocoon, poking the fabric with her finger.

He did miss them; of course he did. Jess, Nora, and Lee had been nothing but supportive since the breakup. Lee had even offered to kill Jason and hide the body if needed. Ryan had politely declined, unable to manage even a split second of anger to consider it. All he could manage was self-doubt. To be fair, he'd gotten rather good at self-doubt.

Jess's finger poked through a fold in the fabric, searching for a shoulder to nudge.

"Stop that, it's creepy." Ryan closed his eyes and when he opened them again they focused on the thread inches from his face. Faded tones of blue weaving in and out of each other. How quickly would they come apart with one snip? He imagined pulling one thread until flecks of light dotted the blanket, then another, his hands working across, forming patterns. He could see them, pinpricks of light, Morse code across the fabric, until his mind stumbled, the threads snapping, leaving nothing but blinding light. Scrunching his eyes, he turned back to Jess.

"We miss you." Jess paused. He heard her take a deep breath.

"I'm here," he said, though he knew that's not what she meant. "Sort of."

Ryan curled into himself. He pulled the blankets closer to his body, the fabric felt itchy across his newly buzzed head. It seemed like a good idea at the time, now he had to stop his hand from reaching for the strands. Instead his fingers reached for a broken thread in the fabric and pulled.

He felt Jess shift closer to him, and he wondered if she was also remembering when they were kids and would hide beneath his bed to scribble all over the boards under his mattress. It felt good to have her near, and he thought maybe he should tell her, but she probably already knew.

"You know, I have so much to do, and if you came with me you would be super busy."

"I'm confused by this tactic." He pulled the blanket down just a bit, uncovering one eye, looking at Jess through the fuzz of his sheets. Hazy and softly colored Jess blended into the fabric like he'd taken a dry brush to an oil painting just as it dried.

"I'll make sure you're so busy, you won't have time to obsess over Jason."

"I'm not obsessing. I don't obsess. I'm sulking, I think . . . or . . ." He sighed. If only words were like paint, maybe he'd be better at saying what he felt. If Ryan were a painting at this very moment he'd be a canvas covered in charcoal. The charcoal would rub off on your hands—even if you swore you never touched it. Etched into the center of the painting would be a speck of white that echoed like a light in the dark. And depending on which way you looked at it, it was either getting brighter or dimming.

For a moment he itched to pick up his old sketchbook to paint the thought out, but as quickly as the image came, it drowned under a wave of doubt and paralysis.

"Well, sulking it is. But think about how much you won't have to think about with all the shit I'm going to make you do!"

He pressed his hands against his eyes, waiting for the little pricks of light to appear, but he knew there was a smile on Jess's face just now. It's comforting to know your friends so well.

"I promise you," Jess's voice was clear and warm and just what he needed. "You won't have any other thoughts aside from how annoying I am."

It was his turn to smile. "You aren't that annoying."

"Is that a yes?" she asked, hopeful.

He could say no. He could. Staying in place felt like a relief and exhausting at the same time, but Jess felt like a tether, a way out if only for this one moment. What would happen if he didn't take it? Would he ever have it again? "I need to shower."

"Yes, you do."

"Rude," he said, finally butting her off the bed, just a bit satisfied at the thump she made when she hit the ground.

"I'll wait for you downstairs. Ten minutes?"

"What? Thirty at least."

"Fine."

Ryan untangled the fabric from his body. He pictured a majestic unveiling like a butterfly from that chrysalis thing, but in actuality it was a lot of muffled grunts, eventually falling off the bed. The sun greeted him with the same cheerfulness that Jess had—not caring whether he was ready or not. He dropped the tangled bundle on the floor, which fit in with the rest of the mess in his room.

How Jess had managed to stop herself from organizing it while he was cocooned, he had no idea. But then there in the corner of his room he spotted the pile of small boxes— gifts from his grandmother's many travels (travels he'd one day be a part of when schedules and budgets aligned). Previously an unruly mountain—now sorted into three small piles and tucked against the wall. Could be worse.

Down the hall he could hear Jess chatting with his parents. Any delay now would come at a cost. He fished his towel from underneath a pile of possibly clean clothes and crossed the hall to the bathroom. He made the water scalding hot and hopped in. The water circled down the drain as he closed his eyes and imagined his sadness as tones of gray circling down and away. When he opened his eyes, he could still feel it clinging to his skin, which was just as well. Without his sadness, would there be anything left of him?

LEE

LEE HAD REACHED the end of the internet. She knew it was the end because it featured a rotating ice cream cone that did most of the work for you, and that surely signaled the end of humanity. How lazy did you have to be to need a rotating ice cream cone?

And the fact that she was on the verge of even considering buying the thing meant it was time to step away from her laptop. She still had several hours until she needed to be at Jess's and the possibilities were endless: she could pretend to clean her room again, but since the accidental result of pretending to clean one's room is actually cleaning your room, it was already annoyingly put together. She should finish the last volume in the graphic novel series she was reading, but that meant the series would come to an end and she wasn't ready for that.

Her pile of unread film magazines on the floor next to her desk toppled over as if on cue. She was sorting them into keep and toss piles when there was a knock on the door.

"Lee?" her father called from the other side of the door.

"I'm decent," she replied, eyeing her solar system jammies.

Her father popped his head in, an easy smile on his face for a man who looked like he could bench press a small car. Her dad had always been muscle on the outside and marshmallow on the inside, but not that many people saw past the six-foot-tall, giant-of-a-man part. Where her father was an open book, Lee kept her emotions close to the chest as much as possible. It was safer that way.

He settled by her desk, noticing the video she'd left up on her screen.

"What's this?" Her father's face was an inch from the screen. Lee made a mental note to remind him to make an appointment with an eye doctor. His eyesight was getting worse and worse.

"The greatest invention in mankind's history."

His smile took over his whole face. "I thought that was penicillin?"

"Common mistake."

"That so?" Her father chuckled before his eyes started to wander around her room as the pause in conversation extended.

Lee sighed, knowing what was coming next. When

things got uncomfortable between them it was always about her mother. Paula Maria Perez-Carter. Careful how you pronounced Paula, of course, making sure to stretch out the *u* until it carried with it her bilingual tongue and brown skin that absorbed the sun deep into her heart. Her mother's memory carried a weight, even three years after her death. It was unfair to her memory, but it was the truth.

"What's up?"

"I wanted to make sure you were okay missing those school days for the trip to Virginia for your mother's birthday?"

"I don't think you ever have to ask if I'm okay with missing school," Lee said. "It's always okay."

"Just making sure. In case you might have any plans. You never know."

Lee shook her head. Her mother's birthday would be forever marked in her calendar along with the day of her death. But their trip to Virginia in April would be to celebrate her birthday as they had every year, come rain or shine, as her mother would've wanted it.

What she wouldn't have wanted was the ripple effect of the trip. Each year leading up to it her father would run around finding ways to keep busy until April, to keep his mind from wandering over to how much he missed her. Last year it was starting a community garden in the middle of winter. This year it was tackling the guest room—or what was supposed to be the guest room—but was really a room for what Lee called the "too hard stuff." Anything that was too hard to get rid of: certain items of clothing, jewelry that Lee didn't want to go through, medical bills, photos, all connected to Lee's mom.

"No plans. Are we staying with Auntie Rose?" She smiled, slipping her hand into his; brown skin against brown skin.

"I don't think we can get out of that one." Her dad smiled, placing his other hand over hers.

Lee always thought her hands were big like her father's until moments like this when she felt five again, holding his hand as they crossed the street.

Lee was somewhere in the middle: short like her mom but strong like her father. Blunt like her, and soft like him. Though she hid that softness as much as she could.

He pushed himself off the desk, and within two steps he was at the door, taking up the whole frame. It always made Lee smile, like they were living in a dollhouse her dad had outgrown. "When you heading out?"

"Probably around eight. You have your office shenanigans?"

"Shenanigans require a degree of fun that my coworkers know nothing about."

"Sounds like a rager," Lee said.

"I don't think we have the same definition of rager."

"Didn't you fall asleep at last year's party?"

He shook his head. "Power nap."

Lee winked. "Right."

Closing the door behind him, Lee heard her phone buzz somewhere below her pillows. Jess had managed to pull Ryan out from under his comforter. Good. She'd missed annoying him these last few weeks.

She sent out a quick group text confirming that the drinks were taken care of before tossing her phone back on the bed. Going into her closet she searched for her comfiest sweater for tonight—Jess's basement was freezing in the winter—when her eyes landed on the small beat-up box she'd stuffed in her closet.

The guest room wasn't the only place they'd stashed the "too hard stuff." Maybe she should do a little cleaning herself before the trip? Pulling the box down, she fiddled with the tape sealing it shut, which was slightly yellowed now and peeling off the sides.

She jostled the box, hearing the familiar clang of a wind chime, lifting the memory up from the fog—yes—she remembered tossing it on top of other things.

A notebook, an album, everything else was frayed; there might be other things, but her memories cracked under the scrutiny.

Her phone buzzed again.

Whatever else was in the box had waited this long so it could wait another day, and another. She dropped it next to her shoes, grabbed her sweater, and closed the closet door.

One thing at a time.

JESS

ACCORDING TO TRADITION, the four of them would gather in Jess's basement every New Year's Eve.

Lee always took possession of the sofa, if it could still be called that, while deciding on the order of the evening's entertainment. She had the most opinions on what they watched, so it was better to let her pick. Ryan and Nora plopped down on the mountain of pillows Jess arranged on the floor, discussing what color Ryan would dye his hair once it grew back. Because Nora couldn't dye her own hair (as it didn't fit La Islita's image) she lived through encouraging others to do so.

This was how it was supposed to be, all four of them together. And tonight would be a New Year's Eve to remember, she was sure of it.

Jess felt like they'd all been drifting apart these last few months. Between Ryan's broken heart, Nora's schedule picking up at La Islita, and Jess's own list of commitments, the four of them had barely any time for each other. (Lee was just increasingly withdrawn—but it was hard to get her alone to ask why.) A part of Jess wondered if they felt the same way too. Sometimes she felt like she was the only one trying to coordinate plans—and most of the time, only one or two of them would be free on the same night. Would she one day be one of those people with just fond memories of her high school friends?

No—that wouldn't be them, not if she could help it. She shook off the thoughts of college breaks filled with awkward, forced conversations and sat down next to Lee on the couch, her notebook tucked under her arm. She knew it wasn't possible, but the notebook felt warm, like it, too, was excited for what was to come.

All the food was laid out on the floor in front of the TV, a giant spread even for a group double their size: Nora's three desserts, a pile of candy, three boxes of pizza, popcorn, and as many sugary drinks as Lee could carry.

"What are we watching first?" Ryan slapped Lee's leg.

Lee returned the smack with a pillow. "I keep going back and forth. It's between this movie about some white people finding an ancient artifact, which of course, they take home. It doesn't end well for them. Or option two, which is about some white people moving into a creepy new house . . ."

"Let me guess," Ryan said, reaching for the popcorn. "It doesn't end well. What else do we got?"

Lee nodded, reaching for option three. "Classic sci-fi, which could use a little more color, but it's still good."

Ryan shoved a handful of popcorn in his mouth. "That one!"

Lee handed Jess the DVD, and she dutifully hopped off the couch toward the TV set, accidentally dropping her notebook.

"Please tell me you aren't doing homework, Jess." Nora pointed to the notebook before flipping open the first pizza box. Jess's mom had blessedly kept the pizzas in the oven to warm while they were setting up, which meant the cheese was melted enough for those gorgeous cheese strands to appear. Nora picked up a piece and did a little shimmy as the cheese stretched and stretched.

"Nope!" Jess dropped the disc in the player and turned around. "It's something I wanted to talk to you guys about before we dove into Lee's movie marathon."

The door to the basement opened, and Jess's twin brother, David, peered down, the sound of several acoustic guitars following after him. "Can I join you?"

Ugh. "Weren't you going to a friend's party?"

David shrugged. "Grounded."

"For?" Jess couldn't believe she hadn't noticed David was grounded, but she'd been so preoccupied with the plans for this evening it was entirely possible she'd missed it.

"Uh." David smiled. "Language."

Lee shifted to face David, craning her neck. "Language?"

"I may have been playing one particularly intense *Warcraft* raid and said a few things in the heat of the moment."

Yeah, that made sense. Whenever David had a free moment he spent it battling . . . Orcs? Was it Orcs? Lee would not approve of Jess's lackluster fantasy vocabulary.

She heard Ryan whispering to Nora, "What's a *Warcraft*?"

Nora didn't answer.

"Sooooo?" David waited as a *tap, tap, tap* of a tango started behind him.

For a second her mind was a jumble of annoyance, but she quickly tucked it back. "Sure, can you give me a bit, though? I need to talk about something . . ."

Lee turned at that, her eyes narrowing. Jess narrowed hers right back, making sure there was a smile along with it.

"What kind of something?"

"Stuff."

Jess grinned. She and David had never really had that so-called twin sense or anything. If they did, then maybe this would be easier.

"How long does 'stuff' take?"

"Like an hour."

"An hour?" David was about to ask why when Jess heard her mother call for him. He sighed and headed up the stairs. "An hour it is, but if Mami tries to dance with me I'm hiding here." He slammed the door behind him.

Lee's head was cocked to the side, eyeing the waiting movie behind them. Maybe even wondering what Jess was up to.

"So," Jess said, her mind focusing on the task at hand while her stomach did a little dance of excitement. "I've been thinking that this year should be different." She paused, waiting to be interrupted, but no one did. She took a breath, pressing the notebook against her chest before exhaling. "I want us to do the resolutions again this year, but this time I want to do them right."

"This sounds ominous," Lee quipped.

"Oh!" Nora said, beaming. "I like the resolutions. They're fun."

"Yes!" Jess returned Nora's smile, nudging the Nutella brownies toward Nora, who was trying to reach them by using her foot to kick the container closer. "Last year was . . . actually, I don't remember what happened with our resolutions last year."

"We didn't do them," Lee said, rolling her eyes.

"Right! Which is why I think this is the perfect year to do them as they're meant to be done."

"Which is . . . ?" Lee asked. Jess knew she was waiting for the other shoe to drop.

"To do the things we always talk about but never do."

"How so?" Ryan gathered a blanket around himself.

"Well, skipping things like pass the driver's license exam after the third try."

"Hey. Rude," Lee grumbled, accepting a brownie from Nora.

"Or attempting to be less of a slob." Jess jerked her head toward Ryan.

"I've decided I'm just artistic . . . it's really in the way you see it," Ryan said. "One person's mound of junk is another's MoMA exhibit."

"No, you're a slob," Nora chimed in.

Ryan stuck out his tongue and grabbed the meringues. He popped two in his mouth like popcorn.

Jess continued, putting every nervous but excited beat of her heart into her words, hoping that it would convince her friends. "Think of all the stuff we've always wanted for each other. All the things we might not see in ourselves, but that the rest of us can," Jess said. "And also, a bit of tough love. A little 'put your money where your mouth is,' if you will. Time to stop talking a big game and . . . I can't remember how that one ends, but you get the point!"

"Is this about Jason and me?" Ryan said midchew.

"It's about all of us." She looked at each one of them, hoping her love for her friends translated through everything she was saying. "Listen, I miss you guys. I know we all have our shit to do and we're midway through our junior year. There's a ton of stuff coming our way, but I really want us to look back on this year and know that we made the most of it. And our time together."

That drew a smile from Lee. Maybe her plan would work after all. "Okay, so how do we do that?"

"Well," Jess replied, grinning. Lee would love this part, she was sure of it. "You tell me. I want you to write them for me."

Lee sat straighter, a quirk at the corner of her mouth. "You want us to handle your New Year's resolutions?"

"We'll all write them for each other. But really think about it! Nothing silly or jokey like jumping off a bridge. Real resolutions. Think of it as a friendly push down the path to awesome."

Ugh, she needed to work on her motivational speeches.

"And we have to do them?" Ryan asked. "Do we, like, pinkie promise or something? We did zero of our resolutions last year. I don't know . . . ," he said, scratching his head.

Jess picked up a pillow and chucked it at Ryan.

"Oh no." Nora giggled. "She means business."

Jess picked up another pillow, aiming it at Nora who covered her mouth. "I'm serious. I want us to do this." They needed to do this. In the fall they'd be seniors. They'd be applying to schools in different cities—maybe even different states. These last few months had felt like the beginning of the end. She waited, wondering if she should simply tell them everything. How she worried they would drift apart and they were moments away from being that person they used to hang out with a while ago . . . but in the end there was only one thing her mind could settle on: "Trust me. We need this."

"We?" Nora chimed in, looking at Jess like she was understanding something for the first time.

"Yeah. We." Jess nodded.

"So we get to write yours?" Important details needed to be double-checked.

"Yes. That's the point."

"I might be up for that." Lee seemed to think about it.

"So that's a yes for Epic New Year's Resolution Time?" Jess hopped on her toes, her energy rising.

Nora cheered and shook Ryan by the shoulders until he cheered as well.

"Are we really going to call it that?" Lee said.

Jess rolled her eyes.

"Okay, so what now?" Nora said.

Jess pulled the notebook from under her arm, ripping three pages and handing them out. "I figure we can huddle three at a time and think of two resolutions for each person. We can trade off so the person doesn't see their resolution until the end."

"Oh, like a surprise!" Nora bounced up and down.

"I've already got one." Ryan's smirk was way too wicked as he jotted down a resolution.

"Cool, who for?" Jess asked.

"You."

Jess's stomach did a little worry dance, but she willed it to stop. This is what she'd wanted.

"CAN I SEE?" Lee said, smushing against Ryan. Nora looked over their shoulders. They conferred for several minutes.

Jess tried to hide her smile, but it was hard to. She scrolled through Instagram to give them time to finish.

"Can we have the official notebook?" Nora walked over, tapping Jess on the shoulder. "We want to make a clean page for everyone. Ours are full of scratches."

Jess tore out the page she was working on and handed the notebook over to Nora, who passed it to Lee. "You have the best handwriting."

When Lee was finished writing, she closed it up and handed the notebook to Ryan, then it was time for Jess, Nora, and him to confer.

"Can we get this over with?" Lee said. "This is far more intense than I was anticipating."

Jess couldn't help but agree a little bit—even though it was her idea, she couldn't help but squirm a bit in anticipation of what her friends had in mind for her. But this was the point, she reminded herself, and you can't escape this either.

"Who's first?" Ryan said, just as Lee shouted, "NOT IT." Then Nora, and Jess, until Ryan was the only one left. "I hate all of you." Nora tossed him the notebook, and he stared at it for a good hard minute before opening it. "You are all a bunch of heartless jerks. Is it cool to throw the notebook across the room?"

Jess tried to look encouraging. This couldn't fall apart after just one resolution.

"Read it out loud!" Lee shouted from the couch with a grin.

"Karma," he mouthed then read from the page aloud. "Number one—"

"Just one thing"—Jess raised her hand—"numbers aren't meant to show importance."

"NUMBER ONE." He eyed Lee, who had clearly contributed the first one. "Kiss someone wrong for you." He frowned. "Not sure I appreciate my friends trying to pimp me out. It's only been—"

"Three months," Lee said.

"No, it's been—"

"A month if we count from Thanksgiving."

"Well, I really loved him," Ryan said. "So it's going to take however long it takes."

Nora stood to wrap her arm around his waist. Jess and Lee joined her on his other side.

"We know it still hurts. We're not asking you to fall in love with someone! It's just a kiss. Nothing more," Jess said. A kiss might just be another push out of his funk, one more step toward getting Ryan back.

"Yeah! Get out there and get out of your head!" Lee

added, squeezing his shoulder.

"Keep going," Nora said.

Ryan took a deep breath, glancing up at Jess. "Show your work and don't apologize for it." He rolled his eyes. "What work?"

"That's the point."

Ryan sank down into the pillows. "Maybe I don't want to paint."

Jess knew it was a lie even now as his finger traced shapes on the ratty couch cushion. Jess's hand reached for his, and he curled his around it.

"Okay, that one isn't so bad, I guess," Ryan said. "Don't they say you do your best work when you're miserable?"

"I'll go next," Nora said, and Ryan passed the notebook.

Lee curled deeper into the couch now that only she and Nora were on it. She pulled the fuzzy blanket tighter around herself. "Why is it always freezing down here?"

"Heater problems," Jess said, nudging closer to Ryan. He wrapped his arm around her shoulder.

Nora cleared her throat. "Okay—here we go! Number one: put your feet in the ocean. Uh, not sure if that's possible, guys. The closest beach is fourteen hours from here."

"The fact that you know how long it takes to drive to the nearest beach," Lee said, "is why it's on the list."

"And," Ryan added, "it's your recurring dream for a reason." For years—since she was eleven or so—Nora had a recurring dream about walking along the beaches of Puerto Rico. She swore it was tucked-away memories from her childhood trips, but Jess wondered if it was something more, a way of her telling herself there was something else out there.

"True . . ." Jess could already see Nora trying to figure out how her schedule at La Islita would ever allow her to take such a trip.

"Keep going," Lee said. "It gets better."

"Number two." Nora scanned, her face scrunching up. "Choose your own adventure?"

"That was a group effort, by the way," Ryan chimed in.

"What does it even mean, though?"

"It means," Jess started, "think about what you really want and need this year."

"But I thought the point was—"

"I know." Jess smiled, hoping that Nora would understand. She wondered if Nora didn't understand how the world held more options than she allowed herself to see. "Choose your own adventure, Nora."

"Okay, but when you say it like that it feels like I'm going on some quest or something."

Lee laughed, and Jess nodded. "You kind of are."

Lee was next, and she took a deep breath before asking Nora to toss her a few meringues for courage.

"Number one: relearn Spanish."

Jess knew deep down Lee had been expecting that one.

Out of the four of them, Lee rarely spoke more than a word of Spanish here or there, claiming it never felt right or she was tired of the old ladies at the Latino Community Center telling her the pronunciation was off.

"Lee?" Jess put a hand on her shoulder. Lee hadn't seen her move to her side and jumped. "I figure I can help you after school."

"You have track."

"After track," Jess said, already calculating how to balance practice with a new lesson plan. Jess had tutored before so that wasn't a big deal, except classes were getting harder, and she did need to keep her spot as valedictorian (if Nora's girlfriend, Beth, didn't knock her down to salutatorian) . . . but that shouldn't matter, she reminded herself. This was for Lee.

"We'll all help," Nora added, "even though my Spanish is not that great."

"Best Spanglish in all of Denver, though!" Ryan said.

"I'll take that." Nora smiled and nudged Lee.

Lee nodded, going over it one more time. "Yeah, it actually feels like I wrote this one myself."

"So you'll have no one but yourself to blame," Jess said. Lee rolled her eyes. "So . . . good?"

"Yes. I like this one."

Jess hugged Lee, toppling them both over.

"Okay! Okay! Stop attacking, you're like a giant Puerto Rican puppy or something."

"Right." Jess hovered nearby, bouncing on the tips of her toes, just a hint of worry on her face. Because, really, if anything could piss off Lee it would be this next resolution. "One more."

"Number two: decide." Lee looked up at her friends. "Decide what?"

Nora cringed, and Lee understood. "Wait, really?"

Jess jumped in. "You can be pissed."

"Oh good, because I am pissed."

Jess had to get this out as quickly as possible. "We know it's a big one, but we thought we had to. We aren't trying to be insensitive or anything. We love you."

"So you say." Lee held up the notebook. "But do you have any idea?"

"No," Jess jumped in again. "No, we don't, not even a little." Her heart was beating faster now, and she swore she saw tears at the corners of Lee's eyes. Shit, what had she done?

"It's just you talk about it sometimes like you don't care, but we know you do. And I can't imagine how scary it is to know, or not know, so we thought that if you needed or wanted a push to get tested, we could be that for you. Do you . . . do you want a push? So the decision isn't hanging over your head?"

Lee was quiet, and Jess held her breath. Had she gone too far? It felt like an eternity passed before Lee answered with just the slightest nod.

"I don't know," she said, then, "Maybe."

"Maybe is a start." Jess wrapped her arm around Lee.

Lee nodded, and though she didn't look up to meet any eyes, she didn't pull away from Jess. Jess tore off the notebook page and tentatively handed it over. She worried Lee might not take it at all, but she did.

Finally it was Jess's turn.

"Too late to back out?" she joked. Her fingers itched to turn to her page, to read what her friends wanted for her.

"Too late now." Ryan shrugged. "Box opened. Worms out."

"Now you have to lie in it," Nora added.

"No, honey." Ryan patted her shoulder. "No. That's not the saying." Nora rolled her eyes.

Jess held the notebook, thoughts swirling in her head. With a breath she cracked it open and turned to her page, and there she found the same sentence written out twice:

Say YES to everything.

Huh?

She read it again.

"Everything?" she said.

"Everything," her friends responded in unison.

"'Within reason,'" Nora added. "Like don't kill anyone or have an orgy or something, unless you want to."

"Just like—" Ryan started.

"Loosen up!" Lee finished with a flourish. "Go on dates. Cut class. Um . . . go skinny-dipping. Be spontaneous!"

"Jess?" Nora pressed.

Everything was silent, which was weird because Jess could swear her heart was kicking it up a notch. Why did it feel like an insult? Jess didn't think she was so uptight. In fact, she made a constant effort to be outgoing and engaging. She did like to schedule and organize, but she didn't think she was excessive about it.

She read the sentences. Don't shake, don't shake, she thought. She was fine. This was fine. She would handle this like she did everything else.

With a flip of a switch, sound rushed in.

"You okay?" Lee reached over and touched Jess on the nose.

Jess shook off the worry and put on a quick mask. "I'm good. Sounds like a piece of cake."

"You sure?" Lee asked, her expression soft. "You didn't look so sure a moment ago."

"Oh, you know," she tuned her voice, adjusting the strings until it reflected none of her worry, her fear. "Just total regret," she said with a laugh.

"I mean, if you want to back out . . . ," said Lee.

"No," she added quickly—this was just the initial flash of panic before the start of a project. She could do this.

She always did.

"Okay then, this is going to be great. Just you wait!"

They each tucked the resolutions into their bags or pockets. There was an awkward pause as Jess pressed play and the sounds of a galactic universe invaded the basement. She worried that the awkwardness would not fade and she'd ruined their night, but it wasn't long before she saw Lee relax into the couch and Nora munch down on some double peanut butter brownies.

Jess released a breath, letting a smile fall on her face.

She felt Lee nudge her from behind. "Sheesh, stop smiling so much," Lee said, but she hid her own smile behind her blanket hoodie. Jess joined her on the couch, turning up the volume, the movie's soundtrack mixing with the thoughts inside her until her own little movie played in her mind. It starred Jess, Lee, Ryan, and Nora. And it featured the amazing year they were sure to have.

SPRING SEMESTER

NORA

DOS CAFÉS CON leche y una tostada para Carmen. Un café negro for the guy with the Broncos cap, but only one quesito for Doña Iris, who usually had two; she's starting a diet today so it's best if she only has one . . . and on and on Nora went. Pouring café into cups and buttering the delicious pan de agua, covering it in foil and setting it on la plancha until the bread was warm and the butter melted. Taking order after order, every day different but every day the same.

When and if there was a lull she would crouch down, moving her muscles in different ways, tricking the ache in her calves and feet even for just minutes at a time. She tried to wake up early every morning to do a few minutes of yoga, preparing her body for the long day ahead. It wasn't much, but it kept her back from killing her later in the day. Nora worked most mornings or afternoons (depending on the day) at La Islita and all day Saturday. Blessedly, they closed on Sundays.

Lulls were also filled with homework and finishing whatever reading she needed to do for the week. She hid her books and notebooks behind the pastry display, pulling them out whenever there was a free moment.

She was a chapter away from finishing *The Grapes of Wrath* when one of La Islita's regulars, Doña Rodríguez, walked in. Nora slipped the book back behind the display and started working on Doña Rodríguez's usual order. By the time she'd arranged her giant purse on the ground, Nora was already pressing down the pancito until it was warm and buttery.

Doña Rodríguez cooed when Nora came around the counter and placed her order down. "Mil gracias. Como lo necesitaba hoy."

Nora smiled. Doña Rodríguez said that every day. Nora helped her tuck her giant purse under the table before someone tripped on it and returned to her place behind the counter and the awaiting chapter.

Ednita Nazario hit her note and sang about heartache. She was one of her mother's favorite singers, so her music was usually blasting through the speakers. The music welcomed one customer after the other. Nora's hips swayed as she turned pages.

When Nora picked the music, La Islita's rhythm shifted from Latin ballads and merengue to a fusion of beats: rhythms that made you hop up and down, and songs that made you struggle to sing along if your lips didn't move fast enough.

La Islita might not look like much from the outside—just a small storefront with a bright yellow awning crammed into a busy street in downtown Denver, but on the inside La Islita was always dancing. Along the yellow walls hung photos and local articles written about La Islita, praising its signature café made from Puerto Rican beans, or its work in the Latino community raising funds for hurricane relief. There were three stools by the window and one wisp of a table that was usually occupied by Doña Rodríguez until around two in the afternoon. When they got busy the store was a mess of elbows and awkward shimmies, but still, people endured it for a taste of medianoches, quesitos, and cups of piping hot asopao.

She leaned against the counter, removing some of the pressure from her feet as she waited for Ryan, Lee, and Jess—they'd texted earlier that they'd stop by to hang for a bit, as Nora would be working at least until six.

As she waited she reread through their endless group chat all the way back to Ryan's step-by-step recap of TAA's Lunar New Year celebration and how all his grandmother's friends seemed to be updated on his love life.

It felt so good to roll her foot a bit; she really needed to get new shoe insoles. She went through them so fast now that the catering side was really taking off. Nora would have to talk to her mom about setting limits on orders and widening the overlap time between them. She couldn't keep convincing Beth that boiling giant calderos of rice was a super-sexy-date activity. And as much as La Islita was a part of Nora's life, she was starting to worry about how much of her life it required of her.

"Nora!" her mother yelled from the back.

Nora sighed. "¿Qué?" She popped her head through the door separating the kitchen from the front. The customers didn't need to hear whatever back-and-forth this would be.

Her mother came forward with a metal baking pan. "Mira." She turned the pan toward Nora. "¡Mira este desastre!"

No wonder her mother was yelling. It was the tres leches they'd asked Rosio to make. They'd hired her two weeks ago. Half the cake was sunken, not spongy and light like it needed to be so it could soak up the cream. Then there was the meringue on top. Usually a small amount of weeping in a meringue is passable, but the cake looked like it was caught in an egg white downpour. Rosio hadn't cooked it long enough.

"Well . . ." Nora tried to find something good to say, but it was pretty hard.

"No trates. There's nothing good to say about it." Her mother threw the contents of the pan into the garbage can. "This is why I only trust you with the desserts. Rosio is lucky she only made one batch—can you imagine if all of the tres leches were ruined?"

She could. It would involve Nora staying late again and making up the work.

"She'll get better." Nora had hoped Rosio would be able to take some of Nora's responsibilities, allowing her to concentrate more on schoolwork and leave La Islita at a decent time.

"Ay, nena, I hope so." Her mother handed her the pan, placing a hand on her cheek. "But for now, just handle it yourself, okay?" She tucked several strands of Nora's hair behind her ear. "Y arréglate el pelo, we always have to look professional."

Her mother turned, leaving Nora with the empty tres leches pan. Astrid and Hector, who'd worked with her mother for years, offered her sympathetic smiles before getting back to work.

Nora dumped the pan in the sink and headed for the bathroom. She took a moment before turning on the light, standing in the pitch-black listening to the whirr of the AC and rhythmic clanging of pan against pan.

One breath.

Two.

Three.

On four she closed her eyes and flipped on the light, squinting until her eyes adjusted. Her flushed reflection stared back at her. She ran a napkin under the faucet and washed her face. Still pink, but less shiny. She gathered the messy tendrils of her hair and tied them back into a neat ponytail.

There was a lull in the music, and then the upbeat tempo of her mom's favorite Marc Anthony album started up. The familiar jingle of the front door followed.

And on the afternoon went. Nora finished her chapter, and as she closed the book, she felt a gentle touch on her shoulder. Doña Rodríguez leaned across the counter with her empty coffee cup.

"Si no te molesta," she motioned to the cup. "I think today is a two-cup day."

Nora smiled and reached for the cup and saucer, placing it in the bin and grabbing a clean set.

"Was it good?" Doña Rodríguez asked, pointing at the book.

Nora shrugged. "It was okay." The truth was she barely remembered any of it, the result of reading it in twenty-minute intervals over the course of the week.

Doña Rodríguez nodded, reading the back of the book. "There's sugar in some of the pages."

"Oh." Nora laughed. "That's normal for me. I take La Islita with me everywhere."

Doña Rodríguez chuckled. "A good place to take with you."

Nora heated the milk and dropped a tablespoon of brown sugar in the cup before pouring the café over it.

"How is school?"

Nora shrugged. "School is school."

"You're a senior, aren't you?"

"Junior." She waited until the sugar dissolved a bit, then poured the milk in.

"Ah, gracias." Doña Rodríguez smiled as Nora passed her the steaming cup. "Are you excited for your senior year?"

"Slightly more excited for the summer." Nora tucked the book away and leaned across the counter. Summer meant she didn't have to worry about balancing school, La Islita, and friends. Just the last two.

"Claro." Doña Rodríguez sat back at the table, which now included the daily newspaper open across it—should anyone try and share the table with her. "That's only a few months away, so it's not far."

Not far indeed. Sometimes it felt like days passed by in a series of cafecitos and baked desserts.

"And any plans after that?"

"Plans?"

"College?"

"Oh," Nora said. "Yes, there's a plan."

Doña Rodríguez nodded, taking a sip of her café, clearly waiting for Nora to continue. Sometimes Nora forgot how nosy she could get and how good she was at pulling secrets out of people. Whatever you told her, you had to be fine with being public knowledge days later. It was how the entire neighborhood (including her ex-boyfriend) had found out Nora was bisexual about two days after her mother did.

"Uh, well." Nora sighed. She could already hear her mother telling her to be nice to her elders. "It's not that interesting. My mom and I talked about it and figured that once I graduated I could go to school part-time at a local college. That way it wouldn't interfere with my work at La Islita, which can get a bit overwhelming. I'm not sure what classes or subject I would study yet, most likely business, but I'm not worried about it."

They'd also spoken about not going to college and simply working at La Islita full-time—after all, it wouldn't be long before she'd manage everything herself. But Nora convinced her mother it might be useful to take some business courses for the future of La Islita. So at least now she'd have the semblance of a life until after college.

"Well, you seem to have things figured out."

It did read that way, didn't it? Her postgraduation plans and her career at La Islita were squares on a board game with just one path. There was nowhere else to go, was there?

"NORA!" RYAN PULLED out the *A* in her name, smiling as he said it, until Nora smiled too. Since the New Year's Eve party weeks ago, Ryan had made an effort to unslump himself and reach out more often. It was his idea to visit her today.

Next to him, Beth leaned over the counter and waited for a hello kiss. It was quick and sweet. Nora clung to her smile as they separated, then wondered if her mother would consider PDA unprofessional as well.

Behind them Lee and Jess had snagged Doña Rodríguez's empty table.

"How's it going?" Ryan asked.

"Going."

"Freedom still at six?"

"Sí. Movie still at eight?"

"Yep," Ryan said. "Figure we can pop in for some pre-movie burgers at the diner."

Yes. Pre-movie food was good, and food made by someone else was always preferable.

"Sounds good." Nora rested her hand on top of Beth's before Ryan nudged her out of the way.

"Not to be rude," he said, "but you're going to need that hand to make me a cafecito and grab Jess a Malta, gracias."

Nora gave Beth another kiss before flipping Ryan off.

"Did you hear about the party?" Beth said as Nora prepared the coffees. Lee hadn't asked for one, but it was just a matter of time. No one could resist the smell of La Islita's café.

"Tonight?" A party would be good. Loud music. Beth in a dark corner, her smile, her lips. Yes, a party would be good.

"No, end of March, I think. Beth is throwing it. I mean, Liz," Beth said.

"Why did she change her name again?" Nora said, passing the first cafecito over to Ryan, who passed it to Lee.

"On account of there being, like, five Beths in our class," Jess said from the table. "Our Beth is the best, of course."

"Thank you," Beth said with a smile. "It's a bonfire. It's supposed to be end-of-winter themed but like in March."

"Pretty sure that's called spring," Ryan replied.

"That already sounds amazing. We're going," Nora said with a smile. It would be the perfect thing to look forward to.

"All of us?" Lee sipped her café. "Why is this a group decision?"

"Lee, you know you get one party veto a semester," Ryan reminded her. "Do you really want to use it now?"

"Ugh, fine," Lee grumbled. "I'll bring a book."

"Do not bring a book!" Ryan shouted. "Parties are for mingling, or so I'm told."

Nora giggled and remembered the party freshman year when Ryan spent the entire time sketching random strangers and not interacting with anyone at all.

When the time came to finally close the café, Nora linked arms with Beth and headed out into the night. After dinner they bought tickets for a high school comedy starring people in their twenties pretending to be eighteen. It was the summer after senior year, and the main character had no idea what she was doing in the fall—let alone the rest of her future.

Nora thought back to the conversation with Doña Rodríguez and wondered what that could possibly feel like. Nora's future was simply waiting for her to get there. What would happen if she didn't? If she changed course in the middle of the path?

The audience erupted in laughter at a joke she'd missed, and Beth giggled and leaned her head against Nora's shoulder. She pushed any thoughts about the future away.

JESS

JESS WAS TIRED, but she rallied. It had been a long week at school, including covering for the student aide at the front office who was sick with the flu. It wasn't much, just helping with filing and photocopying.

Another yes for the resolution, and not bad overall.

She yawned but caught herself, slapping on a smile as they walked into Liz's backyard for the end-of-winter party. People had clustered off into groups surrounding the crackling fire pit and the keg. The brisk night air was perfectly accented by the strung-up fairy lights along the trees. The music was blaring from somewhere in the distance, and Nora was already bumping her hip against Beth.

"Drinks?" Ryan asked. They all nodded. "Cool, let's go snag some."

They turned to head for the keg, but Nora and Beth broke away and beelined for the group of people dancing. Nora had been looking forward to dancing away every exhausting hour of La Islita, so Jess wasn't surprised she headed straight to it. How Nora managed to have any energy at all impressed her.

"What was that, like, five minutes before she abandoned us for the dance floor? A new record, I think," Lee said. "I'll scope out a place to sit while you two grab drinks."

Jess and Ryan were weaving into the crowd toward the keg when Liz stepped in front of Jess, separating her from Ryan.

"JESS!" Liz was all smiles and bear hugs, which meant she had already visited the keg at least once. Jess couldn't help but smile back; Liz after one beer could brighten even the grumpiest of people. Jess always left their chats feeling like she could conquer the world.

"Hey, Liz." Jess pulled away from the hug, and strands of Liz's hair clung to her lip gloss. Behind them Ryan slowly tiptoed away, motioning in the direction of the keg. Jess nodded to let him know she was fine with being abandoned; uplifting Liz conversations tended to run long. Liz squeezed her shoulder.

"It's so good to see you."

Jess smiled. "Liz, you saw me this morning at school."

They were in most of the same classes and usually

ended up partnered up because their last names both started with *A*.

"Right—duh." She giggled. "I'm just really happy you came."

Jess lost sight of Ryan in the crowd gathering by the keg and some guy's particularly broad shoulders. Meanwhile Liz had not stopped talking and Jess had no idea what she'd been talking about, so she did the only thing she could: smile and say "totally" as often as needed.

"So I figured why not, you know?" Liz said.

"Totally."

Liz squealed. "I'm so glad you agree, like, I really respect your opinion."

On what she had no idea, but it was lovely to hear. Liz was the kind of person who seemed to like everyone, which in turn made everyone like her. Including Jess.

"Thanks."

"I'm thinking I won't have as stiff competition for vice president of the Student Council, but you never know. Plus, if you believe in me I can totally do it!"

"Yeah—you can totally do it." Jess turned, hoping this would be the perfect time to exit the conversation. "I should go help Ryan." She'd almost succeeded when Liz snagged Jess's hand and pulled her back.

"Oh my God! I just thought of something!"

"Yeah?"

"You should run for president! YES, you would be

perfect! You are, like, made to run for office one day."

"Oh, hmm."

Jess had thought about it before—in fact, during her freshman year, she vowed she'd run for Student Council president in two years. But now it felt like a bigger commitment; it would be a lot more time spent at school, and though it was good for college applications, she'd read in a college-prep blog that it wasn't as important anymore, which meant it would take away from things that would help her.

"I don't know, Liz." She really needed to get out of here.

"Nooooo," Liz continued, being a bit more forceful than Jess was anticipating. Insistent-Liz usually happened around beer two or three, so Jess had been off from the beginning. "Please, you have to. YOU HAVE TO. You would be so good at it, Jess. It's like you're made for it. And of course with me as your VP, we could actually make a difference."

Everyone said that. No one actually made a difference.

If Jess were president she'd love to introduce more diverse volunteering programs at the school, but, again, not something she had time for.

"Please say yes."

Jess squirmed—did this count as something she had to say yes to? It probably did. It had been something she was thinking about and it was far away.

She wouldn't need to deal with it until senior year. Plus,

she'd just need to run. There was no guarantee she'd win.

"Okay. Yes."

A few minutes later, Jess was still recovering from the high-pitched squeal that had come out of Liz's mouth. It had possibly shattered her eardrums. She saw Ryan talking to the broad-shouldered guy while in line for the keg and decided to leave him there while she looked for Lee. She spotted her just as David did—and before Jess could call out, Lee was helping him with his drinks and heading out into the darkness behind Liz's house.

Great.

She could stand around and wait for Lee to get back. Jess doubted it would take that long to help David carry drinks.

"Damn, girl, you're tall." Jess didn't turn to see who'd said it, not that it mattered. She'd heard that stuff before. "I'd let you wrap those legs around me any day."

She'd heard that before too. Time to move. She walked away, weaving through classmates and trying to shrug off the male laughter that had followed the commentary.

She thought back to her second yes of the resolutions and all that would come of it. More work, but she could handle it. Wasn't she supposed to be putting herself out there more, after all? And what of the other resolutions? Would they really help?

They hadn't really talked about it much, aside from the occasional joke and acknowledgment that the resolutions existed. What if it failed and this was just a horrible idea that wouldn't help their friendship at all? Maybe she shouldn't have convinced them to do this in the first place.

Ugh. Her mind was not being helpful.

What she needed now was to sit with her friends and just enjoy the night. Since Lee had left they needed a new spot to sit, so she decided to scope out the party instead. She sent a group text that she was looking for a new place to sit and that Lee should meet Ryan by the keg to help him with the drinks.

With that she looped around, searching for free couch space or walls to lean by. She smiled and said hello to class-mates, and each time the conversations were the same. Could she believe that test on Tuesday? Had she started thinking about schools? Was she freaking out that the SATs were so close?

After the third surface conversation like this, Jess started to feel a bit unsettled. Was this all her classmates thought of her? Test and scholarships and SATs? The reso-lutions themselves were supposed to loosen her up, right? Did everyone think she needed to loosen up? Her thoughts were a mess in her head, and her muscles felt like they needed to move, to run.

The dark behind the house looked inviting. Liz's house was set on five acres of land, and if Jess walked out far enough, she could be alone. She pushed through her class-mates until the music was just a far-off echo, the lights from the house casting a dim glow over the grass.

When she took a breath she was startled by her own heartbeat. How did it get so fast? She glanced back at the party and inched farther away; with each step it felt like she could breathe a bit better.

When she was far enough she searched for her favorite constellation: Orion's belt. She liked it the best because of how well she could find it on a clear night. "There you are," she whispered, her mind hers again.

RYAN

RYAN'S DUMB EYES kept zeroing in on every damn couple in the place, no matter how hard he tried. It not only made him think of Jason, but also the resolutions. Maybe they were meant to be inspiring, but right now, they were just annoying.

There was another couple making out under a nearby tree. Did they think no one could see them, or did they just not care? His body ached, remembering what it felt like to be so consumed by someone that the rest of the world disappeared.

He hated how quickly his mind turned back to how it felt to have Jason's hands running down his back. How easily he gave away his smiles, like they were just as easy as breathing. Ryan's phone was burning a hole in his pocket. Earlier he'd untapped a like on one of Jason's Instagram photos. He didn't want to look too eager—but now he was wondering if the unliking would say more than the actual liking?

He really should have unfollowed Jason a couple months ago, but he couldn't bring himself to do it. Every time he almost bit the bullet, a new picture popped up like the one he saw today. Jason looked so cute, even though the flash had bleached out his face. He was wearing the shirt that brought out the blue in his eyes. If Ryan had to justify it, he'd say he just liked the composition of the photo and not Jason at all.

A lie, of course, but he'd still say that.

Ryan took out his phone, going back over the photo, noticing the blur of faces in the background. The caption read: *Michael throws the best parties! Happy to be back with my best people!!!*

He rolled his shoulders. Don't you DARE relike this, he told himself sternly. Taking another look at his surroundings, he flipped his phone camera into selfie mode and waited until his face came into focus. Behind him dozens of bodies were dancing, drinking, laughing. The top of someone's purple-dyed hair stuck out over Ryan's head. He snapped the picture, messing with the colors until it felt like the breath of a flash, the memory of colors. He posted it with the caption: *New Party. New Year. New Me.*

He waited a minute before tucking his phone back in his pocket. No, he wasn't going to spend the entire party waiting for Jason to like it. And only three people to go before he got to the keg.

There was a tap on his shoulder.

"How'd I look?"

Ryan turned around and found himself staring at a pair of brown eyes that could pass for black, but for the slightest hint of umber.

"Excuse me?"

"In the photo," the guy said, then motioned to his hair, faded at the sides and long in the middle but styled back. It made Ryan miss his own hair. "Did I look okay?"

"Oh . . ." Ryan shrugged. "I think I only got your hair."

"Of course." The guy smiled. "It doesn't like to be ignored."

"Your hair is sentient?" Ryan looked up at the strands of dark purple.

"Feels like it sometimes." He paused, taking a moment to look at Ryan a bit closer. "My name's Blake. I figure we should get to know each other since we'll be in this line for at least a year."

Checking the line again, Ryan realized that somehow three new people had cut in front of him. And now Karen from Bio was trying to fill at least eight cups.

"What the fuck?" Ryan said out loud. "Where the hell did they come from?"

Blake was still talking. "Do I know you from somewhere?"

"Smooth." Ryan rolled his eyes and went back to watching the line.

"I swear," Blake continued. "You just look familiar."

Was this guy hitting on him? He felt a bit of flush of excitement that was quickly stamped down by the thought that it wasn't the guy he'd want flirting with him. "'You just look familiar' is the grandfather of all lines."

Blake smiled again, and even Ryan had to admit it was a nice smile. "You aren't going to share your name?"

"My name is not-in-the-mood-to-flirt-Ryan."

"One, that's a long name. Two, who says I'm flirting? Maybe I'm just being nice?" Ryan's stomach did a little flip of embarrassment but quickly recovered.

"That's true. Sorry I assumed."

Blake leaned toward Ryan—the twinkle lights hanging from the trees above them complementing the olive in his skin. If Ryan wanted to paint him he'd use acrylics layering the hints of light so they felt like they were reaching out to the observer.

"I am though," Blake said. "Flirting."

He felt his cheeks warm for a second and turned away to stare out in front of him. Where was Jess when you needed her?

"Looking for a way out?" Blake said.

Ryan wasn't sure how to answer.

"I'm sorry. I was coming on strong." Blake took a step back, physically giving Ryan more space. "I thought you were cute and thought I should give it a shot. Plus, my friend dumped me for a girl he just met in line, and I thought magic might strike twice." Blake shifted so Ryan got a full view of the couple; they were one deep breath away from inhaling each other. "Sorry."

"Holy shit."

Blake sighed. "We used to date too."

Ryan scrunched up his face, looking from Blake to one half of the kissing couple. "Him?"

"Yeah," Blake replied. "Still best friends though. Otherwise I would not be at this party with no one else I know while he makes out with someone who is either his soul mate or his only source of air . . . not sure which."

Ryan wasn't sure what he was surprised by more: Blake's honesty, or the fact that he was totally okay with his ex making out with someone new right in front of him? Would he be that okay if Jason did the same? It might just break his heart even more. What would Jason think of his resolutions? Would it bother him? He knew he shouldn't care, that the resolution was about him and not Jason, but the two felt so intertwined.

They finally reached the keg as a text from Jess came in:

Out among the stars. Take a right at the patio, past the weed clouds, and keep going until you trip over me.

"Need help?" Blake motioned as he handed Ryan a few cups.

Ryan nodded. He'd read his mind.

"It doesn't bother you?" Ryan asked, pointing to Blake's ex. "To see your ex like that? I mean . . ."

Blake balanced two cups in each hand as Ryan filled them as high as they would go without spilling the head all over Blake's hands.

"You just broke up with someone, didn't you?"

It might as well be written on every part of him.

"Obvious?"

"The question gave it away." He waited for Ryan to fill a fifth cup. "We were best friends before and sort of slipped into the making out shit. We didn't really call it dating, just . . . I mean, we trusted each other a lot and wanted to figure things out together."

Not at all like Ryan and Jason. They hadn't accidentally slipped into their relationship. Ryan had crushed on Jason for almost a year before he had the courage to ask him out. "And then?"

"Then it swung back to friendship. It was gradual, really."

Ryan nodded, snagging two of the four beers Blake carried. Blake made it sound so easy, like heartbreak was just like falling asleep. For Ryan heartbreak was like falling and not knowing when you would land. It was the wind knocked out of you until you forget how to breathe.

"I'm guessing from the look on your face that's not what you wanted to hear." Blake followed him out into the crowd. "When did you break up?"

"Six months ago," Ryan said. "Well, also four months ago." Blake cocked his head to the side even as they weaved around people. "We broke up because he—we—didn't think we could handle—" Ryan stopped suddenly, stomping his foot down. "You know what? Fuck it. HE didn't think we could handle the long distance. But we missed each other, so we got back together for a month. And then we broke up again right before Thanksgiving."

Ryan took a deep breath and apologized to the random guy he almost spilled all his beer on.

"Where's he studying?" Blake asked when they reached the edge of the house and the clouds of weed smoke. Instead of heading out to find Jess, Ryan found the nearest empty wall space and leaned against it. He placed the cups to the side as Blake joined him on the floor.

"Boulder."

Blake tipped his head, probably wondering if he'd heard right. "Boulder?"

"Yeah—I know."

Denver and Boulder were only thirty minutes apart, maybe an hour if the traffic was bad.

"Do you still like him?"

Ryan took another deep breath, feeling the wall at his back. It had soaked up the cool night air, and he flushed himself against it, feeling his shoulders unknot.

"Yes."

Jason was his first love—the first time he'd ever felt like

his heart would burst from his body. The first time his skin needed someone else's touch that much. It felt so good to be with him and even better to be wanted by him. Ryan had tangled so much of himself up in their relationship that now that it was gone, he wasn't sure what was left. Who was he now?

Above them faded pinpoints of light dotted the swath of black.

"That's rough." Blake nodded, unzipping his jacket and slipping it off, revealing a series of tattoos along his upper arm.

"Your parents let you get those?"

"They have their own."

The tattoos looked like a tangle of paint, but he couldn't see them with detail without getting closer.

"Can I see?" Ryan asked.

Blake inched closer until their legs touched and he could angle himself so Ryan could get a clear view of his arm.

"Paintbrushes?" Ryan reached out, fingers hovering just over the ink. Blake's muscle flexed, but Ryan didn't think he was doing it to show off, rather to keep his arm up so Ryan could see clearly.

"Had it for a year now," Blake said, "and planning my next one."

"You paint?" Ryan traced the two paintbrushes running along his arm; from the brushes' bold strokes of red paint wrapped halfway around his bicep.

"I do."

"I used to." Ryan used to muse about getting some of his old sketches tattooed, but he could never decide on one.

"Did you? Wait—" Blake stopped midsentence, staring at Ryan as the smile grew on his face.

"What?" Ryan turned his head to look behind him, then down at his shirt. Had he spilled something?

"I figured it out! I remember where I know you from. I took an art class at your school over the summer and one of your paintings is still displayed in that room. It's gorgeous—a split portrait of your parents, I think, and there's a photo of you right by it."

That was still up there?

"Fuck, that's embarrassing—that painting is two years old."

Blake shrugged. "Still a great painting. Why did you stop?"

Why had he stopped? Why had he truly stopped, if he loved painting so much? It was one of the thoughts that bothered him the most—that echoed when he wondered if he should pick it up again. Ryan thought back to the resolutions and begrudgingly admitted that maybe they would be more useful than he wanted to admit.

"Sorry—that's none of my business."

"It's okay."

"Have you thought of starting again? They teach classes every season—I think some of the spring classes start up in two weeks." When Ryan didn't answer right away, Blake looked down at his lap. "Sorry—I'm being pushy again."

"No, I'm just, it's funny you say that because it's one of my New Year's resolutions to start back up again, sort of. Not exactly, but . . . never mind, just, yes, I've thought of it."

"What's the other one?"

"Other what?"

"You said it was one of your resolutions, so there's clearly more than one."

Oh boy. Ryan reached for one of the cups. The beer was warm, but he wasn't sure it had ever been cold. "Um, the other one is kind of silly. My friends wrote them for me. And the second one is to kiss someone wrong for me." He winced as he said it, waiting for his reaction. "I know how it sounds."

"Doesn't sound so bad," Blake said. "Plus you could kiss anyone and check it off the list."

"What?"

"Well—you said you still had a thing for your ex, so technically anybody is going to be wrong for you. Even me," Blake said.

"That's true," Ryan said, unsure if Blake had just volunteered to be kissed or not.

Then Blake leaned in to whisper, "I'm saying you can kiss me if you want to."

Ryan was suddenly aware of Blake's closeness, the way his hand was just inches from him, how his lips were flushed and quickly turning up into another easy smile. "I . . ."

Blake smiled, and for a moment the butterflies in Ryan's stomach kicked into gear. Damn, he's really good at this flirting thing, he thought before reminding himself that this was just part of his resolutions. "Don't worry. I know you aren't interested, but I figure since we're friends now . . ."

"We're friends?"

"Well." Blake smiled. "We had a pretty good conversation, shared woes, and had a drink. I think we are."

It would handle one of the resolutions, even though Ryan still didn't understand why they'd picked it for him.

"Okay. Yes, uh, thank you?"

"Yeah, it is a bit like a business transaction, isn't it?"

Blake moved closer, waiting for Ryan to close the gap between them. He shifted until they were flush against each other and Ryan wondered what Blake saw in his eyes. What would be written across them? Could he see the heartbreak?

He closed his eyes and kissed him.

Ryan expected to hate it; after all, it wasn't Jason. Instead it was nice and sweet and made him feel like he wasn't just made up of gloom and the jagged pieces of heart. Like somewhere inside, a part of him still ticked. Ryan's hands traveled up to Blake's cheek as he moved into the kiss, their legs shifting toward each other as they continued. Blake's lips were soft, tasted of beer, and were well versed in kissing.

When they pulled away fireworks hadn't littered the sky, proclaiming it true love. Instead, Ryan smiled, still tasting the beer on his lips, relishing the flush that traveled up his skin.

"That's the most chaste kiss I've ever had," Blake said. "I feel downright angelic right now."

Ryan arched a brow. "Compliment?"

"Yes." Blake cleared his throat, then reached for his jacket. "Tonight was unexpected. And I'm kind of bummed I need to go, but I need to go."

Ryan nodded, feeling like he should say something, not leave it here as semi-strangers who shared a kiss.

"Can I have your number? I mean, if we are friends, I should have your number." Then Ryan quickly added, "Plus I need to know where to take this art class. I'm already on a roll with the resolutions after all."

They exchanged phones, each adding their numbers in. "Sure—for the art class." Ryan tossed the phone back, and Blake disappeared into the crowd. Ryan balanced the beers in his hands and passed the clouds of smoke to find Jess. One resolution down and another almost started. Not bad for someone who could barely leave his bed a few months ago.

He'd make sure to gloat.

LEE

IF LEE COULD disappear deeper into the patio sofa she would, but what if it turned out to be a wormhole to another dimension or universe? She'd be stuck in another universe and would probably be asked to rule it or some shit because of some dumb prophecy. Mystical worlds would be so much better without prophecies.

Ryan and Jess were still not back, and Lee had lost all but one of the seats she'd tried to save. They should just claim some square of grass in the darkness out back—it seemed to be what everyone else was doing. Lee stared into the fire as she attempted to pull a braid out of the ballerina bun on her head—anything to keep her hands busy while she waited.

Off in the distance she caught sight of Ryan and Jess,

each stuck in place talking to different people, their faces flipping between mild annoyance and actual interest. Jess was much better at the interested face than Ryan.

Then she saw David weaving around the crowd by the bonfire, three cups of beer in his hands, perilously close to soaking anyone who might shift as he shimmied between them. Lee glanced back to Jess, then again to David, thinking how they made such an interesting pair of twins. The Amazon and . . . well, David.

Lee had nicknamed Jess the Amazon after she'd seen her jump over hurdles in practice. If anyone would fit in on an island of warrior women, it would be Jess. But where Jess was powerful, David was . . . what was David?

As she thought about this, David made his way toward her. He beamed when their eyes met, and it made Lee sit up straighter.

"Thank God," he said when he reached her. "I'm so happy to see you!"

"You are?" Lee said. They hadn't ever really hung out on their own before.

"Sí," he said, a smile still on his face. As he shifted closer to her his mop of curls fell into his eyes. He tried to push it back with the hand holding his cup and some beer sloshed over the side and onto his jeans. The scene made Lee smile.

"I need your help," David said. He turned to reveal two bottles of beer tucked into his back pockets and a pair of jeans close to falling off his—rather cute, Lee thought—butt. "I'm one accidental shove away from being an unfortunate teen movie moment, and I am so not wearing the right undies for it."

"What are the right undies for it?"

"Not the ones I'm wearing."

"So what undies are you wearing?"

WHY DID YOU JUST ASK THAT?

His lips quirked, and he stepped closer to her. "You first."

Fair play.

Lee cleared her throat and nodded, reaching out to grab the cups from David. As he passed them, she looked down to the white fabric peeking above his jeans.

"Thank you, thank you, thank you," David said, not noticing her wandering eyes.

They barreled through the crowds, and Lee mumbled at least a dozen sorrys on the way to a small group huddled on the lawn.

"Finally," one of the boys said, walking toward them. He wasn't very tall and wore a long black duster. She thought his name was Derek but wasn't sure enough to say it out loud. "Thought you were lost."

"Needed saving," David replied, handing out the beers. "Thankfully Lee was there."

"To Lee," possible-Derek said while lifting his beer. Next to Derek was Audra of the nose ring, who was dating possible-Derek—that, or they just liked making out in the halls at school.

"Jess's friend, right?" A short black girl with a pink pixie-cut nodded at her, and Lee's stomach felt a little pang as she had no idea who she was. "I'm Anna. I'm new, so don't worry about forgetting my name."

"You look like a fairy." It tumbled out of Lee's mouth before she could stop herself. When Anna didn't seem to mind, more words came out of Lee's mouth. "In like a classic, like, Seelie Court way with all the fancy colors. I like your hair."

"I love you," Anna said. "And thank you, that's kind of what I was going for." If Nora were here she'd be peppering Anna with questions about her hair. For as long as Lee had known her she'd wanted to dye her hair bright pink, and Lee could see why. Anna looked super cute and it must be fun changing up the color every now and then.

"So what's your thing?" Anna said.

"My thing?"

David leaned in, bumping shoulders with Lee. He kept his eyes on her as he sipped from his beer. Her mind flicked back to the hint of white fabric she'd caught earlier. "Anna was homeschooled before now, so she has no social skills."

Anna pursed her lips. "I like to get to know people, thank you." Anna turned back to Lee, waiting for a response.

How did this turn into one of Lee's nightmares so quickly? Was she in fact stuck in the same teen movie she'd saved David from just moments ago? "Just your average nerd with obsessive tendencies."

"Join the club," Audra smirked, before adding, "though, seriously, there is a club."

"I should explain." David moved until his shoulder rubbed against Lee's just a bit, making her a lot warmer than she'd been a second ago. "We are all gamers. *World of Warcraft* specifically, and a couple others. It's how we all became friends. Plus some random people from Virginia, but I think they're, like . . . fifty or something."

"I know," Lee said. David's obsession with gaming was not a secret by any means. "It's hard to miss it when you play with your door open during finals week."

"Oh." He laughed a bit. "Yeah, sorry about that. It helps me destress."

"It doesn't sound like destressing." There was usually a lot of yelling and ordering people around at times. It was no surprise that he'd been grounded for it.

"You should come play it one day, you'll see."

God, his smile was so inviting, Lee found herself smiling back. Did he always have those dimples? He must have.

"I don't play video games." Something about the hand-eye coordination didn't work with Lee at all.

"No big." Audra smiled, her nose ring catching the light. "Not a rule that all nerds have to like the same thing. I totally hate board games. Could give two shits about them."

"That's because you don't focus," Anna added, taking

a sip of her beer. "You would rock Settlers of Catan if you gave it a chance."

This must have been a previous debate because it wasn't long before Anna and Audra were locked into a heated debate about the virtues of Settlers of Catan, and something called "Eldritch Horror." It was the perfect time to slip away and rejoin Jess and the others, but she didn't. Next to her, she felt David shift toward her.

"What floats your boat, Lee?" David turned to her, and she wondered if there was something more in what he was asking . . . or if she just had a dirty mind. Probably that. "Jess says you like comic books."

"Yeah, I like comic books or graphic novels, whatever you want to call them," she stammered. "I'm not, like, an expert."

"Who is?" David shrugged. "I don't read much, but if I wanted to . . ." He paused, his eyes flicking down to Lee's lips for a moment before quickly looking away. She hadn't just imagined that, had she? He recovered and continued. "If I wanted to read something good, what would you recommend?"

Recommendations Lee could do. In fact, she preferred it to actually talking about herself. Top Ten Horror Films? Check. Actually talking about her life? Not so much. She started listing them off: "Well, it's a lot. *Sandman*, *The Wicked + the Divine*, *Captain Marvel*, *Ms. Marvel* . . . oh man . . . *Saga*, the new *Black Panther*." She made it a point to ignore the way David was looking at her right now. "I'm missing so many now. Um, *X-Men*."

He nodded at that.

"Storm all the way, baby," Anna said, coming back into the conversation. "Oh, and Rogue, love a southern twang on a lady."

"I have a soft spot for a planet-consuming Dark Phoenix force. I feel like Jean gets a bad rap," Derek replied.

"I blame Scott," Lee started. Once her nerd activated it was hard to stop. "Jean is a total commentary on how we view women's ability to hold power. Why can't she just be a badass and stay alive?"

"I mean, technically you could say it's implied in the name Phoenix that she needs to die and come back," Anna replied.

Lee nodded. "True, but once in a while you just want her to have a couple of good days, you know? Go out with Storm and Rogue for a ladies' night or something."

That part made Anna spit out her drink. Lee laughed.

"I can never keep the timelines straight," Derek added.

"No one can," Lee said, "not that it matters, they just retcon it anyway, then pull some Cap-Hydra bullshit, then retcon it again."

"Exactly." Derek nodded. "So friggin' confusing."

It was nice to talk with fellow nerds. Usually when Lee went on about her opinions about comics or horror films she'd have to stop and explain to Nora that "retcon" meant adding new information to a story to reframe a current plot in comics, or how Lt. Ripley in *Alien* was originally written as a man's role and what that meant for the character, or that Ororo Munroe was never meant to be a side character and that's why they could never get her right in the X-Men movies.

David nudged her on the shoulder, offering up his beer. Lee hesitated at first, then accepted. It would be nice to have something to look at when she wanted to avoid eye contact.

"I hope we aren't being too pushy?" He motioned toward his friends, who had started talking about some new game she couldn't keep up with.

"No, no." Lee hoped she hadn't said that too quickly, but she'd been pleasantly surprised at how easy it was to talk to them. "This is okay."

"Good. Glad." He dropped his voice to a fake whisper. "I can't stand these nerds, so . . ."

"Hey!" Audra said. "Not nice, Aguedo!"

"Agüedo, Audra, Agüedo. You pronounce the *u*."

Audra slumped. "Why couldn't you pick an easier name?"

"Blame the ancestors." David shrugged.

"Everyone else can pronounce it, Audra," Anna teased.

"Really?" Audra challenged.

"Agüedo," Anna said, a slight bump as she reached the *u*, like her tongue wanted to skip over it but knew better.

David was smiling into his beer when everyone turned to her.

Oh.

Her heart skipped, and cold pierced her skin. Which was odd because her tongue knew how to shape the sounds to pronounce her best friend's last name. It did, really, but what if it chose now to stumble?

It hurt that sometimes her Spanish came with a doubt. Was that the word? Was that how you said it? Was it? She sipped the ice-cold beer and cleared her throat. "Agüedo," she finally said, trying to hold on to the name, to check it back and forth for defects.

"See?" Anna said. "Not so hard."

"No fair." Audra huffed, the cold picked up her breath, taking it up and out. "You guys know my tongue doesn't do what I want."

"Your tongue is perfect, babe." Derek leaned in for a kiss.

"Gross." Anna rolled her eyes. "PDA on your own time. Not sacred friend time."

Lee smiled to herself. Her tongue had not let her down.

She took a sip of the beer as a text came in from Jess. Perfect timing. She gave David back his beer and excused herself to find Jess.

NORA

NORA WAS IN the middle of it all, teaching the white people how to dance to reggaeton. It wasn't her favorite music, but her mom liked to blast some Wisin y Yandel whenever a bout of spring-cleaning hit, so dance parties always followed. You'd think her mom would be embarrassed to teach her kid how to grind, but it's super hard not to let the beat take you away.

She felt Beth's arms around her waist and leaned back as the song turned from the repeating thump to a quicker beat. She turned, she and Beth raising their hands at the same time as they hopped up and down. Nora tossed her hair back, the curls going everywhere, expanding, sucking up the volume in the air. She would need multiple hair ties to pull it back after this. Beth was effervescent, her smile bright as she leaned in and out of Nora's embrace.

Whatever worries Nora's body still clung to after a long day at La Islita eased and melted with each beat. Louder, she wanted to yell till each thump of the music drowned out her thoughts, drowned out the memory of the day.

Her hands could still feel the weight of the caldero in her hands, the resistance of the thick platano soup that she'd stirred all damn day—she needed to get rid of that memory. She reached out for Beth, holding strands of her hair along her fingertips, relishing the feel of them.

Remember that, she told her hands. She had always made herself pause to savor a moment with Beth since their first kiss.

They'd met through Jess in a way—both runners on the same team. Beth was one of the best, and Nora loved to watch her run, her long legs as commanding on the track as when they wrapped themselves around Nora. She'd come into La Islita almost every day for a cafecito or pastry at the beginning, and Nora had such a crush on her. It was one of Nora's favorite parts of the day to see Beth's smiling face at La Islita. She'd thought it was the coffee and sweets that lured her in each time; after all, Beth had said she couldn't resist them, but it was Lee who figured it out.

"She's totally flirting with you!" Lee said after each of Beth's visits, until finally Nora was brave enough to make a move. The next time Beth asked her what she recommended that day, Nora said, "Me."

They'd shared a first kiss on the longest workday ever. Nora had had to cancel their date, and instead Beth showed

up to help her close and walked her home. She still remembered the way Beth had shuffled her feet before stepping
forward and bringing their lips together.

Remember all of that . . .

Nora pulled Beth toward her, her heart beating against
her chest, a sheen of sweat on her face.

They reached for each other, lips colliding in an explo-
sion of warmth, of a thousand fireworks. Beth was her
warm sunny day in the winter. Nora's other hand was at
Beth's back, itching to lift her shirt and touch the skin
underneath. When Beth pulled away her cheeks were pink.
"We aren't alone, you know."

She gave Beth her best puppy dog eyes. "Everyone else
is making out too."

Around them their classmates danced, each in their
own world of hips, bodies, lips, and beat.

"Still." Beth gave her a quick peck.

"Okay, okay," Nora said, the music picking up again.
"One more dance and we'll find everyone."

Beth nodded as Nora leaned in for a kiss, teasing Beth's
bottom lip.

The beat slipped around their bodies and they obeyed.

Lee: What's his name again?

Ryan: Blake.

Nora: Blake of the nice ass.

Ryan: How do you know he has a nice ass?

Nora: Beth and I can spot a nice ass from miles away.

Lee: And he knew you BJ?

Ryan: BJ?

Lee: Before Jason . . .

Jess: We aren't using that.

Lee: Boo.

Ryan: Yeah no. And he didn't know me, just recognized my photo.

Jess: More importantly, how was the kiss?

Ryan: Fine.

Lee: Stop. You're killing me with the details.

Nora: TELL US.

Ryan: FINE. It was . . . good. Happy? Sheesh. It was nice, and he was a good kisser. So was I.

Nora: Yes you are!

Ryan: MORE IMPORTANTLY, one resolution down! Does that mean I'm winning?

Jess: Not a competition.

Ryan: . . . So yes?

Nora: No.

Ryan: Taking that as a yes. ALSO, turns out the art class he mentioned is still taking students, so I'm on my way to resolution 2! Jealous?

Nora: A bit.

Lee: You'll figure it out, Nora. We promise. Right, Madam President?

Jess: Very funny. At least the party was fruitful for Ryan.

Lee: It wasn't a bad party.

Jess: It was fine—I guess it wasn't for me.

Ryan: Wait, Lee thought the party wasn't bad? Who are you, and what have you done with Lee?

Lee: There is no Lee, only Zuul.

SHE'D HIGHLIGHTED THE entire page of the SAT workbook.

The entire page.

Across from her Beth studied her own workbook, oblivious to the blatant waste of highlighter ink. Nora quickly turned to a random page and vowed to study the contents instead of just highlighting words to pass the time.

The library was especially quiet today. Usually there were one or two groups talking in whispers, but this time all her classmates seemed to realize what loomed just months away because everyone around her had their noses stuck in a similar workbook.

Nora should be studying. The SATs weren't going to take themselves, and according to Jess it was better to stagger the prep rather than cram the week before like Nora had wanted to. Still, as soon as Nora turned to the problems on the page her mind glazed over, unable to keep much of anything in except for one recurring thing.

Her resolutions. One in particular.

"What would you choose?" Nora whispered to Beth across the table.

Beth looked up from her workbook. "Hmm?"

"If you had to choose your own adventure—what would you do?"

"It's your resolution, not mine."

"I know. I just want to know." So I can steal it, Nora thought for just a second. Beth scrunched her nose as she thought.

"I would travel," she finally said, the start of a grin on her face. "Or I would ride a motorcycle. Or . . . I would steal you away more often."

"Steal me for what?"

"Wicked things." Beth touched the tip of Nora's lips, lingering on them long enough for a flush to travel up Nora's neck.

Under the table their shoes touched, pressing against each other.

After a moment of watching Nora's cheeks get pinker, Beth said, "You already know it, you know?"

"Know what?"

"What your adventure is."

Nora looked down at the test questions. Her resolution might as well be one of them for as much as she knew the answer to it. "Doesn't feel like it . . ."

Still Beth nodded. "It's in here." She touched Nora's temple, brushing her fingers down her neck to her chest above her heart. "And here. Everything else is just too loud. Eventually you'll hear it, it'll be the loudest thing in there."

A hand slammed against the table making them both jump.

"Shh!" the librarian said in the loudest whisper ever.

"Sorry," Nora mouthed, but Beth stared back at the

librarian with a simple smile on her face.

Nora spent the rest of the study period trying to listen, to hear the answer, but all she got was the steady beat of her heart and the shuffle of passing pages.

Not loud enough yet.

LEE

THE DAY HAD cleared up at least, but the grass was still wet from the rain the night before. Or was it the morning dew soaking Lee's shoes?

"Just in time," her father said, looking up at the sky. The sun hid behind giant clouds of white.

"April showers," Auntie Rose said, turning to give Lee a soft smile.

Lee nodded, following Rose and her father down the rows of plaques and tombstones of Columbia Gardens Cemetery, the orange tulips shaking their heads as she walked. She read the names as she passed: Douglas. Anderson. Buchanan. The closer they got to her mother's grave the more familiar the names were. Lee didn't think she would remember that Richard Addams died in 1985, but she must have stored that information somewhere. She nodded to Richard's stone as she passed.

"Well then." Her father took a deep breath. Lee took a moment before looking up. She knew where she was. Between Angela Rowe and Eugenia Moore at Paula Maria Perez-Carter's grave.

"Hola, Mami," she whispered, watching her father place a hand on the granite, dusting off dried leaves stuck on the stone. Her aunt came up to help before taking a step back, giving her brother room. He turned to Lee, reaching out a hand. It took Lee a moment to realize he wanted the potted tulips she'd carried all the way here.

They always brought potted flowers, not cut ones. Flowers that would continue to grow long after they left. One time her cousin told her they threw those pots in the garbage after the visitors left but she was sure he was being cruel when her aunt wasn't watching. Cameron barely knew anything at all, so how would he know the ins and outs of cemetery business? Lee liked to imagine that the caretaker would gather all the potted plants and dried flowers, taking them off into a big field to plant. There they would flourish, wild and free, in whatever patch of earth they found.

Maybe her mother could see that field from wherever she was.

He placed the tulips by her headstone, his long robin's-egg-blue tie flapping forward as he did. It had tiny Easter eggs on it too, but you had to be pretty close to see them. "Happy birthday, amor."

90

Lee's father didn't speak much Spanish, and most of the words he knew were endearments he'd learned from her mother. He rarely spoke them except here.

Her auntie Rose took another step back, extending her hand to Lee. They would give her father time alone, then it would be Lee's turn. Together they walked back through the path; not that far off in the distance Lee recognized the tree she'd sat below time and time again. She sat beneath it.

"The ground is dry," she said to her aunt, waving her over.

"Surprised they haven't put a bench here yet," Auntie Rose said as she sat down. "Seems like the perfect place for one."

Lee supposed so. From where they sat they had a good view of the rest of the cemetery. Above them the leaves still carried the day's rain, and gentle drops peppered the ground around them.

Her father leaned down by the grave until he almost disappeared behind her mother's tombstone. What was he saying? What did he ever say?

She imagined he spoke about the time passed and maybe even updated her on the last year like she'd just gone on vacation. You would've been forty-six today, he would say. Happy birthday.

Lee shook off a shiver that came with a thick drop from above. Her cousins always asked why they came on her mother's birthday and not the anniversary of her death.

Because, Lee always said with a shrug, but she could never finish the sentence.

"Because it's better," her father had said once. It was better to remember her on this day, but Lee still didn't understand.

Her aunt held her hand, giving it a gentle squeeze every now and again. A reminder she wasn't alone. It made Lee slightly anxious, like she should be thinking about what to say to her mother. They'd come all this way.

When she tried to pull out the words, all that came were strangled cries. Her mind was not a blank—she wished it was—instead it was a mess, nothing coming forward as a single thought.

"Lee." Her father hovered above her, his hand ready to help her up.

She looked up, up, up to his face, the crinkle in his eyes. She placed her hands in his and let him tug her up until she was folded into one of his classic hugs.

When he released, she knew it was her time to walk over to her mother. She still didn't know what to say. The wind picked up around her almost like it was pushing her toward the grave. Behind her, her father took her place below the tree.

A faint trace of water soaked into her tights as she knelt down.

"Hi," she said, already disappointed in herself. "I don't know what to say."

The tulips bent with each gust of wind. Lee watched, realizing she was avoiding her mother's name on the stone as if it were her mother's eyes.

"I'm taking out my braids." She tugged at her hair, wrapping a braid around her finger before dropping it. What a silly thing to talk about, but it was the closest thing her mind could latch onto. "It's time, and since I'm here with Auntie Rose . . ."

She let out a breath. Here with Auntie Rose. As if she was here for nothing else. Just a visit. All her mind wanted to scream was: I miss you, I miss you, I miss you. Why did you leave? Why did it take you? Will it take me?

"I found my notebook yesterday," she started, searching for her next sentence. "'Found' sounds like I'd lost it, except that it's been in the same box for the last three years, but yeah. I found it."

Lee sank back down on her feet. "It's blank. I know what should be on it—what was supposed to be on it. I remember getting it"—she took a breath—"the therapist wanted me to write out my feelings. I never did." The rain had soaked into the granite, making her mother's name stand out much more. "I never did. I'm sorry. I was supposed to write you, but every time I tried all that came out was . . . it wasn't nice."

She brushed the tear from her cheek. "There's a brochure too—between the pages—I even remember getting it. When we went to the doctor for a visit and they had these bright and shiny brochures out. Newly designed. All about testing your kids for Huntington's. I don't know if you remember that waiting room, but it was always too cold and it had these ugly brochures, but this one, you could tell it was new. I grabbed one. Stuffed it in my jacket and brought it home."

Each time the wind kicked up, it sent a shiver down her back. "I remember that brochure was the scariest thing in my room. Like it already held the answer. I never read it, then you got sick again and we were all so busy. . . ."

They'd watched her mother like a hawk those days. Any change in temperature, prolonged cough was monitored.

"It was easier to stuff it away," Lee said, remembering how she'd hidden the brochure between the pages of the notebook, knowing she would not look at it again. "It's always easier to put things away, Mami. I'm really good at it."

Now both sat at the bottom of her suitcase waiting for her to have the strength.

"Did it feel like your whole future disappeared when you found out? Dreams just snuffed out of existence? I know I haven't gotten tested yet, but sometimes it feels like I already know. Deep down. That I can hear the clock ticking down the days." She let out a shaky breath. "It's pessimistic and I know you wouldn't like it, but I have to think you felt it too."

Her body felt heavy and she leaned a bit till her hands

rested on the grass. "You won't like this, you won't, but I thought of not applying to college." If she closed her eyes Lee could almost imagine her mother gasping at the thought. "I am, but it crosses my mind, what the point of it would be if . . .

"You should be here to yell at me about this. To tell me . . . tell me what to do."

Lee took one deep breath and looked back to the tree, signaling her father and aunt. They would come join her and take one more moment together before leaving. "I'm sorry, Mami, this is not the happy update you deserve. I miss you, and I love you."

THAT EVENING AUNTIE Rose and Lee's father shared cooking duties. They opted to make some classic grilled cheese, because nothing warmed you in cold weather like grilled cheese. Lee watched them shuffle around each other in the kitchen, coating bread with slabs of butter then hearing it sizzle when it hit the pan.

"What are you putting on that grilled cheese?" Auntie Rose peered over her brother's shoulder as he layered two different cheeses on the sizzling bread.

"Gruyere and another cheese I picked up at the market."

"What's wrong with American cheese?"

Her father sighed. "Nothing is wrong with it, I'm just trying something new. You'll like it."

"Hmm." Auntie Rose went back to coating the slices of bread with butter. "Don't ruin those grilled cheeses."

"You'll like it!" her father repeated, then turned to Lee. "Back me up here."

Lee raised her hands. "Don't bring me into this, I have no idea what this Gruyere grilled cheese is all about."

"My own daughter."

The cheese oozed out of the sandwiches as Lee, her father, Auntie Rose, and Cameron simultaneously reached for a triangle. Auntie Rose's husband worked late, but still, they'd made enough to feed the neighborhood if they needed to.

"Well?" her father asked after they'd all taken a bite.

The cheese was still warm and gooey, complementing the crunch of the buttered bread.

"It's delicious," she said, taking another half.

"See?" he said, satisfied that he'd proved his point. "A friend at work is a bit of a foodie and gave me the recipe."

"Lot of foodies in tech?" She imagined it was easy to get hungry if all you did was stare at a screen all day. Or at least that's what she imagined they did all day.

Her father nodded. "We all have our hobbies."

"Well, I approve," her aunt said, reaching for another half of grilled cheese.

"Told you to trust me."

Later, when everyone's bellies were filled with cheese and bread, Lee snuck back to the room she was sharing with her dad and pulled out the notebook, the brochure still between its pages. It was dated now. The shiny graphics that made Lee grab it in the first place felt cheesy and childish. Turning it to the back she recognized the website at the bottom.

One her fingers had typed many times before, and she was surprised when her computer didn't autocomplete the address.

Huntington's Disease Society of America.

It was still as plain as she remembered it; the first thing to draw your eye was the giant *What is Huntington's Disease?* right at the top before giving the visitor the lowdown:

Huntington's disease (HD) is a fatal genetic disorder causing progressive deterioration of nerve cells in the brain.

Yep. Her stomach hurt.

It deteriorates a person's health and has no cure.

No cure, so that was still the same then. Of course it was; if they'd discovered anything new since her mom died, her father would've told her. That, and it would be all over the news.

Lee hovered over the menu, seeing: "Genetic Testing and Family Planning." With reluctance she clicked on it.

People at risk face a difficult choice. . . .

She scoffed. *Difficult* felt too light of a word.

There is no "right" answer.

Then how would she do this?

Did she really want to know? Part of her screamed YES,

the other simply screamed, feeling like a deer caught in the headlights as a truck headed straight for her. She clicked on other pages that reminded her she had a fifty-fifty chance of inheriting HD, and if she did the following would await her:

Changes in coordination, involuntary movements, mood changes, irritability . . . and those were just the early stages. The stage where they still had hope, where they wondered if something was happening or if her mom was just getting clumsier, overworking herself, just having a bad day, week, month, year.

It was a thought that bothered Lee—did she accidentally drop that cup or was it something inside her? Was everything a sign, or was it nothing?

Then came the middle stage where movement becomes more of a problem. Where you add medication and go see specialists to help with involuntary movements and speech problems. Where you fight and fight and fight to keep going. Then there's the late stage where her mind was still aware, where she smiled when Lee walked into the room. But where she couldn't walk and couldn't speak. Where they fought in different ways.

Her fingers hovered over the *Where to Find Help* page when she heard the creak of the stairs and her father calling for her.

She closed the laptop, placing her notebook on top as her father came in.

"Where did you go?" The bed creaked from his weight. He tossed his slippers by his open suitcase and stretched out on the twin mattress. It was comically small for him, but he might just pop the air mattress if he tried sleeping on it.

"Just . . ." Lee stared at the blank page. Was it waiting for an answer too? "Writing to Jessica about our lessons."

Her father smiled. "You know I'm so happy about the Spanish lessons, right?"

Lee nodded, finding she couldn't keep her father's gaze.

"Did you tell your mother?"

"Oh." Lee deflated for a moment. That would've at least been something positive. "I forgot."

"Don't worry, baby." He stood, placing a hand on her chin, lifting it until their eyes met. "She knows."

THAT NIGHT AS her father slept, Lee read over the information once again, not any closer to figuring anything out. She picked up the phone and texted Jess.

Lee: What if this resolution thing doesn't work? Like . . .
there's a reason why I haven't done it yet.

It was probably too late for Jess to respond, but within minutes a message came in.

Jess: Tell me about it.

Lee: ?

Jess: Work it through with me. Word vomit it all out, it
might help.

Lee didn't know where to start, it all felt overwhelming and complicated. How could she write it all down for Jess to understand?

Jess: Let's try something else. Close your eyes.

Lee: Uh.

What the what? The phone buzzed, it was Jess calling.

"Okay," Jess said on the other side, "I realized if I asked you to close your eyes how would you ever read the messages? Now close your eyes."

Lee sighed and complied. Even if Jess wasn't in the same room, somehow she would know that Lee wasn't following instructions. "Okay. Eyes closed."

"Imagine a road."

"Jess, what is this?" she whispered, not wanting to wake anyone up this late.

"I'm trying to see what you see. Now imagine a road."

Lee pictured the road ahead of her covered in gravel and extending far beyond her.

"Done."

"Now," Jess continued, "picture a fork in the road. The fork is taking the test. The right side is you don't have the genetic markers for HD, and the left is that you do. Now what do you see?"

"What do you mean?"

"Close your eyes and look to the right," she said. "What do you see? What does the road look like? Is it long? Is it difficult?"

"It's—" Lee pictured it, focusing on the right side of the fork. The road went as far as her eye could see. The grass around it was green and filled with flowers. There were things off in the distance, too far for Lee to see. "Long, green, like I could walk on it forever."

"Okay." Jess's voice carried Lee. "Now turn to the left. What do you see?"

The image shifted to an uneven road that stopped abruptly at a dead end, nothing after it but darkness.

"Lee?" She heard Jess's voice on the other side of the phone. "What do you see?"

"Nothing." She swallowed. "There's nothing there."

Lee waited for Jess to say something, exhaling when she finally heard her voice on the other side. "That's the problem, isn't it? You aren't going to take this test until you change the way you see the road."

And how exactly was she supposed to do that? And how did you change a road that wasn't wrong? Huntington's was a dead end, and lying to herself wasn't going to help that.

"Lee?"

"I'm gonna go. Just need to think about some stuff. Thank you for calling, though."

When she hung up she drew out the roads in her notebook, extending the left one till it reached beyond the page, but it bothered her. That wasn't real. She scratched out the image and turned the page and went back to the website, writing down the information on the *Where to Find Help* page. When she was done she turned the page and wrote: Getting Tested: Pros & Cons.

Below pros she wrote: Knowing.

Below cons she wrote: Knowing.

RYAN

"JIA BA BUE? Did you eat?" were the first words out of Ryan's grandmother's mouth when she came on-screen. No matter what time of day it was his Taiwanese grandmother always made sure to ask. She wore a bright-blue hat twice the size of her head, her favorite travel hat, key in keeping the sun from her eyes. She had two of them in the same color to be safe.

"Yes, I ate, Ama." Ryan balanced his little sister, Katie, on his lap, who was ready with her portraits. She was the perfect distraction from his haircut that was not growing fast enough for his grandmother's liking. He received weekly email forwards on how raw eggs or this vitamin or that extract was the key to hair growth and was he taking them? Even now he could see her eyes travel up to his scalp.

He gave Katie a squeeze, and her five-year-old self jumped right in.

"Look, Ama!" She pushed a paper up against the screen until all you could see was splotches of color. "It's you."

"Is it?"

Katie nodded, and Ryan pulled the portrait back so she could see it more clearly.

"That's nice. I look happy. How's school?"

"Good!" Talking about her day was Katie's favorite subject, though truthfully most things were. "I hit Michael Wallace in the knee on Tuesday because he pulled my hair."

"Zuò de hǎo." His grandma nodded. "Always go for the knee like Ama taught you."

"Ma!" Ryan's dad popped in behind Ryan. "That's not funny."

"It wasn't supposed to be." She shrugged and smiled at Ryan. "When are you going to do another portrait of me? The old one needs a friend."

His grandmother never failed to ask him this since he'd gifted her with a portrait several birthdays ago—it was the final push she'd needed to accept that her eldest grandson was going to be a painter, not a doctor. After that she'd insisted she always knew he would be a painter and that it wouldn't be long before his art was famous all over the world like Cheng-po. Even when he thought he'd never draw again, his grandmother was right there to remind him: once an artist, always an artist. He wished he had her faith.

Ryan saw his dad slink off screen, returning to the

chaos of the kitchen. Nice. He'd have to change the subject on his own. "How's Florence?"

When Ryan's grandfather had passed away four years ago, his grandmother decided she couldn't bear to stay at home and mope. In addition to her biennial trips back to Taiwan, she now traveled in the winter or spring (whichever was cheapest) to someplace new for a month. So far she'd been to Thailand, New Zealand, and now Italy.

"I've had three gelati already! And joined a local protest for student rights!" His ama always reminded him you had to fight for the equality others took for granted. Growing up she'd been part of many civil rights marches and was the main reason Ryan knew anything about politics. She giggled, suddenly looking years younger. "I'm sending you some supplies I bought at a store called Zecchi. An art student recommended it. He was sketching at the Uffizi—not as good as you—and I just walked up to him and asked. Small store. Those are always best, don't you think?"

"You don't have to spend your world travels—"

She waved the complaint away. "I sent the package already, you'll need them for your class."

Of course she would know. "Dad! You told her?"

"Of course he told me," she huffed. "You're my grandson." She smiled, leaning into the phone camera. "I told you it was still there."

Ryan nodded, and his ama smiled back. "You'll see," she said. "You'll see. Now thank your ama and put your father on."

"Xièxie nǐ sòng wǒ zhè me bàng de lǐ wù, Ama," he said. His grandmother nodded, happy he was practicing his Mandarin. Her own tongue was accustomed to slipping between Mandarin, Taiwanese, and English.

"Can I stay on?" Katie bounced up and down, waving at the screen. Ryan passed her to his father, who took his place in the chair.

"What are you making?" his grandmother asked.

"I'm going to try the flan," his father replied.

"Again?" She looked disappointed at the strategy.

Ryan's parents had been involved in a sort of food war for as long as Ryan could remember. Every two weeks one of them tackled a dish from the other's family recipes. If they pulled it off they got bragging rights for two weeks. If they didn't, well, his dad still brought up that time his mom screwed up youfan (sticky rice), even though she killed the pork dumplings weeks before.

This week it was his dad's turn, and he made a second attempt at a flan made with evaporated milk—which should've been easy (his mom's words, not his), but it didn't set in the middle.

"Did you wiggle it?" he heard his grandmother say.

"Of course I did!"

"It looked funny," Katie volunteered.

"It doesn't have to look pretty," his father said, hurt that the simple dish had bested him.

"Tasted funny too." Katie erupted in a heap of giggles.

"Katie," he warned.

"Don't listen to your dad, Katie. Always speak your mind."

They kept chatting, his mom popping in to the conversation to throw some shade. Later they signed off as his grandmother was heading out for another walk and a gelato or two.

"You really going to try this flan thing again?" his mom smirked.

"I will not let the flan win, Sandra."

His mom laughed, sitting to watch her husband tackle the recipe. It was an old recipe from her mother that she'd translated into English—most of it—but if he needed any help translating, that's what trilingual children are for.

Ryan loved his parents during these times. Usually they were busy lawyers spitting out jargon over the dinner table, but on these nights they were just two silly, still very much in love people, having fun.

He didn't notice he was pulling out his phone, but before he knew it he was looking through his old photos again. Ryan and Jason kissing at a party (Lee had snapped that one), making faces at the camera, Jason on his bed, asleep—he hadn't noticed when Ryan had taken that one.

For a moment Ryan swore he could feel Jason's hand in his, remember the first time he felt his fingers curl around his. Jason had looked at Ryan like it was the simplest thing in the world to hold his hand, but for Ryan it felt like the world was going to burst. He didn't know that feeling would echo again when they shared their first kiss just moments later.

"What?" Jason had said, the goofiest grin on his face as Ryan had stared at their hands intertwined.

Ryan shook his head, a bit embarrassed. He should be playing it cool, shouldn't he? But he couldn't, not when Jason's hand felt so good in his. "Nothing. Just . . . this feels good."

Jason squeezed his hand. "It does." Then he leaned closer. "But you know what feels even better?"

Damn that was a good first kiss. Jason's hand traveled to Ryan's cheek, deepening the kiss and Ryan flushed up against Jason, his own hands grabbing the waist of his jeans. Jason walked Ryan home after, hand in hand, identical grins on their faces.

His father dropped a metal pan, and the clatter brought Ryan back from the past, phone still in his hand, looking through Jason's social feed. There was nothing new, and the last photo Jason had put up was a stack of books with the caption: *Essay due tomorrow. Please kill me.*

Did Jason look at his feed like this? Did he obsess over every dumb photo Ryan put up? It was all that damn party photo's fault—the one from Liz's party, where Blake's hair had peeked through. Ryan's heart had leapt a thousand feet when Jason liked it, and more than that, commented: *Looks like fun! I like the purple hair on you.*

It was the first time he'd messaged since the second breakup, and maybe he should take advantage of it?

Ryan: How is the essay coming along? Still alive?

He hit send before he could stop himself. It was a harmless text, after all. Nothing would come of it.

Moments later his phone buzzed.

Jason: Ha! Almost. You know me, I do my best writing the day before anything is due.

Ryan still remembered the late nights talking on the phone as Jason rushed to finish one more page.

Ryan: Good to see some things never change.

Jason: If it works, it works! I'm really happy you texted, talk to you later if this essay doesn't kick my ass too much?

Ryan: You know I'm always up late.

Was Jason hurting like Ryan was? Or was he just hiding it very well?

Because Ryan wasn't hiding it well. And he was trying to. He knew his smiles didn't reach his eyes, and he knew he should be able to go five minutes without thinking about Jason. If his resolutions were meant to distract him, to force him out of his funk and into the world, they weren't working yet.

Yes, he'd felt good for a second after kissing Blake—he was outside his own head, at least—but that momentary spark didn't last. By the end of the week he'd been back to moping and worrying that all the second resolution was going to prove was that he truly had nothing left.

What if he was the exception to the rule that misery produces good art?

He felt his mom move closer to him, and he stuffed the cell phone into his pocket and tried to look less depressed. "Don't tell him he needs to put the pan in the oven before the water or else it will be a splashy mess again." Her smile made her eyes crinkle.

"What was that?" His dad looked over to them. "Sabotage?"

"Just talking to my son."

"So you say." He cracked a smile. "Get ready for the best flan of your life."

"I've been ready for several weeks now," his mom countered, arching a brow.

"Patience is on my side. Before I didn't give it the time it needed in the oven; it was a mistake. I was lulled by the simplicity of the dish, and I won't make that mistake again."

He brandished the whisk like a sword, pointing it at the two of them before tackling the mix. He brought the caramel-coated metal mold closer to him and was about to pour the mixture in it when—

"Sieve," his mother whispered under her breath, and his dad course corrected, grabbing the sieve from the utensil drawer and pouring the mixture through it into the mold. "Looking good, mi amor!" She gave him a thumbs-up before turning to Ryan. His parents' banter had lifted enough gray clouds that his smile almost reached his eyes. "Nervous about the class?"

"A bit." Blake had come through with the information, and he'd signed up for a beginners' class called "Faux Beginners" for people who had let life get in the way of their art. Which was apparently so common it had its own class. "Not looking forward to getting up early for two classes on a Saturday." His art class schedule fit in perfectly with his Mandarin classes. Yay.

"Ay, nene, ten a.m. is not early." She smiled. "You used to get up at six when you were a baby. We still can't get Katie to sleep past nine."

Hearing her name, Katie smiled then went back to whatever was going on between her dolls and ponies. "It's a pincer move," she provided, showing how the My Little Ponies surrounded the dolls on all sides. "Right, Mami?"

"Exactly!" She beamed at Katie before turning to him; she was already bringing out her patented backrub move. "But that's not it, is it?"

He shrugged, resting his head down on the countertop.

His mom rubbed his arm, and he felt the anxiety try to hold on but lose against his mom's moves.

"Losing your first love is tough," she said.

Ryan lifted his head, finding her eyes. "You've said that before."

"I know. It's still true. Why don't you try and tell me what you're feeling?"

He dropped his head again. "I don't know what I'm feeling."

"I think you do," she said quietly as she leaned down

so only he could hear. "Whatever it is, I promise you it's not silly or dumb or whatever you think I'm going to say, okay?"

She squeezed his shoulder until a breath released.

"What if there's nothing left of me?"

His mother sighed, and he felt her hand reach for his. "I remember that feeling."

"You do?" He lifted his head.

"I do." Her smile was soft, and her hand reached out to touch his cheek. "Heartbreak will do that to you. And I know it feels like you think there's nothing but an empty hole in there, but I promise you, you will mend it."

He felt his face prick a bit, the beginning of tears. "But Jason."

"Mira, listen to me. I want you to remember what I'm saying because it may not mean much right now, but eventually you'll know. Relationships, love, they are extensions of you. They are not all of you. You do not cease to be when they are over. Ryan is still in there, even if he's a bit hard to find right now."

"How do you know?"

"I'm your mother." When Ryan rolled his eyes, she slapped him on the shoulder. "And the fact you are taking that class means something."

He couldn't take credit for that. "That's all Jess's fault."

She shook her head. "Jessica is persuasive, but you made the choice to do it."

"But . . ." Doubt still clung to Ryan like honey; he'd felt

it coating his body since the breakup, sticky and impossible to ignore. He paused and took a breath, feeling his mother's steady hand in his. "What if it just proves that's gone too?"

"I don't think it is."

"What if I suck?"

"We still ate that flan even though it was horrible, didn't we?"

His father finished loading the flan into the oven, splashing water on the floor. "Now you're being mean."

"You put three times the right amount of vanilla in it."

"I did not." He laughed, then paused. "Did I put vanilla in it this time?"

With a sigh his mother dipped her finger into the batter-coated bowl. "Yes."

"Oh good." His dad smiled and turned to Ryan. "Your doubt will always be there, and it will be the hardest thing to fight because it knows you so well. But there's no better feeling than proving it wrong."

"You won't believe us now." His mother nodded. "But just keep going. I promise you, you are not gone."

The hole in Ryan's heart begged to differ. It was wide and gnawed at his chest. It screamed that the class would be in vain, that he'd put aside his art for love and now both were gone. He was alone.

"You know what also helps?" his father added. "Sometimes when I'm feeling a bit off, I think, 'What would Ma do?'"

What would his grandmother do? Hadn't she lost the

love of her life? And look at her now, conquering the world. The thought brought a spark of life to Ryan's frame. What would his grandmother do? She'd shake a finger at him and tell him to go paint! That spot on the wall wouldn't fill itself. She would know all along that Ryan was still in there. She wouldn't have any doubt.

Ryan clung to that, hearing his grandmother's voice in his head over and over again. Do it for her, he repeated until it was enough.

Behind them Katie had already massacred the doll army and headed toward the Palace Pets nation. She took no prisoners.

NORA

NORA'S EYES NEVER left the oven as the little macaron domes rose, acquiring their signature crinkled feet. This batch would turn out much better than the last. Though the previous one had tasted delicious, the macarons didn't rise properly—she'd mixed the batter too much. Not that Hector cared, as he'd already eaten half of the first batch and was dipping the second half in Nutella.

"Nena, tienes un don." He reached for another misshaped shell before returning to the front of the house. "A gift."

Nora waved him away, making sure not to take her eyes away from this latest batch. She would not mess this recipe up again! When the timer dinged her heart skipped a beat as she rushed to open the oven door and gently take the macarons out. This batch looked great, perfectly domed tops, cute wrinkled feet, and more or less evenly sized. It felt a bit like cheating to use a paper outline when she piped, but she reminded herself she was still learning.

Reaching for the one closest to her she pulled it off the Silpat, holding her breath because if it stuck it meant she'd taken them out too early, but it quickly came right off. As did the next.

Nora couldn't help but do a little dance as she set each shell aside. Now it was time to make the filling. It should be Islita inspired, of course. Maybe a creamy dulce de leche buttercream or a papaya puree? She'd made the shell with vanilla extract so it would go with most flavors. She walked around the kitchen, fingers traveling over the stocked ingredients. Should she do a savory macaron? No, macarons weren't overly sweet, but no one wanted a salted cod one. She could keep it simple and stuff Nutella between the shells, but that would be too easy and her body ached for a challenge.

She hadn't spent hours making another batch to go simple now.

"Nora." Hector popped his head through the doorway.

"¿Sí?"

"Do we have any more pastelitos de guayaba y queso back there?"

Nora nodded, knowing exactly where she'd shoved the last tray. She was handing the golden pastries to Hector when she had an idea.

With a turn she flew to the shelves, gathering the guayaba paste and digging out the white chocolate from the pantry.

She set the chocolate to melt and dropped the guayaba in a pot with a shot of vinegar and water to cut the sweetness. To the chocolate she added sugar and cream cheese until it mixed to fluffy buttercream-like peaks. The guayaba took longer to get right. She needed it to be the texture of jam, but she'd added a bit too much water to begin with and had to balance it out with more paste. Then of course, she had to cool it down in an ice bath.

Around her Bomba Estéreo blasted.

It was time for assembly. She held the little cream shell in her hand and piped the white chocolate and cream cheese mixture around the edges, leaving a hole in the middle. There she dropped a bright-red dollop of guayaba, sealing it with another shell. She continued until every shell had its match and filling.

"¿Listos?" Hector waited by the doorway.

"How long have you been standing there?"

"Long enough!" He held out a hand for one of the finished macarons and Nora obliged. Instead of simply popping it in his mouth like he usually consumed most food, Hector paused and took a small bite. The guayaba leaked a bit, and she made a mental note to fiddle with the recipe.

With another bite he finished off the macaron, and Nora waited for a verdict.

"Well?"

Hector sighed. "It's a sin."

Nora shuffled. "Huh?"

"To keep all that talent locked up!" he followed with a smile.

Nora let out the breath she was holding, feeling the grin engulf her face. "Really? You liked it?"

"Dangerously good."

Behind Hector a voice came. "Lo que sea dangerously good," Doña Rodríguez shouted. "I better get a try."

Hector ducked back to the front, leaving the decision up to Nora. Usually she kept her experiments to herself and her friends, but those adorable little treats made her so proud she couldn't say no to the request.

She arranged them neatly on a plate, making sure to snap a photo and send to the group along with a message saying:

You better come by before these are all gone!

Nora brought the macarons and her notebook up to the front counter to where Doña Rodríguez waited for her chance to try them. Nora wrote down the recipe for the filling along with a note to try for a thicker guayaba center as she waited for the verdict.

"Bueno, niña," she started, her face grim then quickly cracking a smile. "¡Esto esta de show! I love them."

Nora could feel the blush on her cheeks and the swell of her heart.

"How long did these take you?"

"All morning," Nora replied.

She'd started off the day researching new compostable straws for her continuous crusade (her mother's word, not Nora's) of turning La Islita into a more eco-friendly store, when she'd gotten distracted by someone's post about the new fancy patisserie just a few blocks away and the bright pastel macarons they sold.

Nora had always wanted to retry her hand at macarons. She'd made them once for Jess's birthday a year ago and not since. Before she knew it, she'd piled the compostable straw samples on her mother's desk and was pulling out ingredients and tracking down the saved recipe in her notebook.

Now that she thought of it, she hadn't finished typing up the vendor analysis she'd promised her mother, who would not be swayed by graphic videos of plastic straws jutting out of adorable animals' bellies. This was business and facts were what mattered, which meant cost analysis. Nora printed out the final breakdown as her mother burst through the door.

"Nora!"

"Hola, Mami."

Nora waited by the counter as her mother chatted with Doña Rodríguez, then quickly popped into the back to drop off her purse. When she came back Nora had the analysis sheet waiting for her.

"If we can do the individually wrapped one that would be great, plus hygienic."

Her mother sighed but took the papers. "Not bad."

"Plus they look fancier but are still cheap. . . ."

"That I like."

The next chart showed their current orders and how the change would balance out with enough units. The final paper was a photo of a bird with a straw jutting out of its mouth.

Her mother gasped and held it up. "¿Y este? What's this for?"

"Efecto."

Her mother rolled her eyes then smiled, which meant Nora would get her straws, and all those little birds that didn't end up in her mother's asopao would be safe. She handed back the papers and was about to turn around when she stopped and looked over Nora's shoulder.

"What are those?" Her mother walked around her, plucking one of the macarons from the plate.

"I made quesito and guayaba macarons." Nora stood straighter, unable to hide the smile from her face.

"What for?" she said as she took a bite. "Though they are delicious."

Nora shrugged. "I just wanted to try out the recipe."

Her mother nodded, finishing up the macaron. Behind them Doña Rodríguez piped up, always willing to offer an unsolicited opinion. "You should sell them! They are perfect."

Nora beamed. "They still need a little work." But the

thought had crossed her mind; it always did when she tried new recipes. Nora had always wanted to debut new recipes at the store. To update their chalk menu with *Nora's Postres of the Week!* in a bright yellow chalk design.

"You should sell them!" Doña Rodríguez repeated.

It made Nora think back to the photo that had started it all. "You know, they sell them for two dollars at the patisserie a couple of blocks away."

"That's indecent," Doña Rodríguez said, then added, "You should sell them for two-fifty!"

Nora laughed, turning back to her mother. "And you can pretty much keep the shells the same but with different colors and just switch out the insides all the time! We can do a dulce de leche one or a Nutella one."

Her mind raced for new flavors; she should be writing these down.

"Or flan on the inside." She closed her eyes as she imagined the delicate custard inside the chewy shells. There were so many possibilities.

"Nora." Her mother reached for a napkin to dust off the sticky guayaba from her fingers. "You know what I'm going to say."

She did, but her heart still hurt when she said it.

"It's not our style." She placed her hands around Nora's shoulders. "I love that you're trying new things, but they're not for La Islita. We have to keep our style classic. Things your abuela would make."

Her abuela would make the macarons though; she loved to learn new things. In fact, you could probably go to Puerto Rico and find delicious macarons there, so why couldn't they experiment a bit?

"Macarons are French cuisine." Her mother touched her chin. "You understand?"

"Yes," she said, the lie bitter on her tongue.

The music shifted as Marc Anthony came over the speakers singing about living your life.

Nora continued the afternoon, the conversation still heavy on her shoulders. She put away the macarons after one too many customers asked if it was a new item on the menu, then followed it up with a confused "Why not?" when Nora shook her head. What felt like eight hundred cafecitos later her mother grabbed her by the shoulders.

"Niña," she said, a giant smile on her face. "No lo vas a creer."

"What?"

"Guess."

She didn't have it in her to guess. "Another quince-añera?"

"No."

"Well." She wiped down the counter as La India shouted about mi mayor venganza over the radio. "That's all I got."

"The convenience store next door is closing."

"Rogelio's?"

"Of course, claro, what other convenience store is there?"

"Why?"

"Well, apparently he's divorcing, and also he's a horrible business owner."

He really was—the store was barely stocked, dirty, and dingy. She rarely saw anyone go in there and usually warned people not to bother and just go to the much better family-run store up two blocks.

"Who's moving in?"

"No one yet—they haven't put it up on the market," she replied. "But . . ."

The pause made Nora turn, dropping the rag on the counter.

"¿But qué, Mami?"

She came up next to Nora. "What if we bought the store ourselves?"

Nora paused. "Like move?"

They were a little tight, that was true, but the thought of moving made Nora dizzy.

"In a way." Her mother smiled, eyes dancing with big dreams that always made Nora sigh. "More like an expansion!"

"An expansion?"

Oh no.

"Piénsalo—we combine both spaces, tear down the walls, expand the kitchen, and add more tables. We can be an actual restaurant, even expand the catering!"

Her mother kept talking, ideas for space, branding, and eventually her future. Nora's future tumbling out like it was the most natural thing in the world.

"Amor, imagine how much we could grow!"

Grow? She wasn't sure if the "we" meant La Islita, or she and Nora, or both. And could they grow if Nora couldn't even bring up new recipes? The tucked-away macarons said otherwise. La Islita would grow, her mother would grow, but would Nora?

She imagined the long nights fixing up another place, falling asleep in class, trying to cram in everything into the small pockets of time she had. Asking her friends and Beth to revolve all hangouts around the restaurant. She saw the time to try out new recipes dwindling more and more until no new pages would be added to her recipe book.

"What do you think?" Her mother's face was filled with so much hope that it drowned out everything else.

No, was what she thought, as a pit of worry settled in her stomach. But no would bounce off her mother and roll down the gutter. People telling her no was how she got where she was. No was a challenge—Nora needed facts.

"Quizás," Nora started to say, "pero . . ."

"¿Pero qué?" Her mother's shoulders straightened, preparing for the discussion.

"We don't have the money."

She waved the comment away, expecting it. "We don't know how much they will value it for."

"True, but based on size alone we can guess. It's twice the size of our store."

"Three times at least!" Offered Doña Rodríguez, living up to her notorious eavesdropper status. She motioned for them to continue as if someone had paused her favorite telenovela.

Nora sighed but kept going. "Three times, then, so we can calculate how much it would cost, not to mention repairs. The place is a dump. I would honestly feel bad for whoever ends up with it."

A frown started to appear.

YES, it's working!

"We can repair it!"

Nora shook her head. "Not to our standards, Mami. It's not like a paint job. We would need all new flooring, what's in there now is torn and disgusting. I saw someone drop five dollars there once and just leave it."

"Que exagera."

"I am not. You know I'm not!" She couldn't stop now. "We'd have to remove all the institutional lighting, probably exterminate, who knows what's died there. We might even find a dead body—okay, now I'm exaggerating." Then she smiled. "Or am I? Not to mention tearing down the walls—do we even know if that's possible?"

Her mother was smiling, and Nora wasn't sure what that meant.

"Where did you learn all this?"

"You . . . and HGTV."

"Bueno. I'm disappointed, but proud."

"Proud?"

She came closer, placing her hands on Nora's shoulders and giving them a squeeze. "All that off the top of your head means you're really getting it, Mija. La Islita will be yours in no time."

Nora's heart lurched as her feet shifted toward the door.

"It was just a thought—but you're right, we probably can't afford it." Still, her mother paused again, not quite deflated. A pause that meant the idea still clung to her mind, not ready to let go.

A pause that made the pit in Nora's stomach grow and her eyes drift down to the hidden plate of macarons.

"¿Mami?" she asked again, hoping to shake the pause loose and send it on its way.

Instead her mother straightened, rubbing Nora's shoulder. "¿Qué haría sin ti?" Then she returned to the kitchen to finish an order.

JESS

SHE'D SPENT TWO hours helping her mother reorganize the community center library, sorting out damaged books and jotting down which ones needed replacing. The "library" was only two bookcases long but a popular part of the center, next to the activity room. There was even a smaller library for picture books closest to the kids' area, which would benefit from the Clorox wipe down Jess would give it in a few minutes.

The creation of the library had been her mother's idea, and even though it was only two bookcases long, you could tell as she dusted and sorted through old copies it still gave her a sense of pride. Her mother had loved working at the Latino Community Center of Denver so much she made it her full-time job, handling the budget and overseeing center activities. She saw it as a place to bring the Latinx community together to grow and support each other.

A message that maybe not everyone in the community got. For example, the pair of chismosas that made sure to—loudly—comment on Jess's tight jeans like they'd never worn a tight skirt when they were seventeen. Was it some weird rule that as soon as you turned a certain age you needed to judge other people for everything you did as a teen?

"¿Se cree Jennifer Lopez?"

That one was new.

Jess almost turned around when she heard her mother next to her.

"Ignore them, Jess," she said. "They have nothing better to do." Then her mother turned and addressed them like she hadn't just heard them gossiping away at the back. Their tune changed quickly, and they greeted Jess's mom with a warm hello and praise on the center's last activity.

Jess rolled her eyes. These women would fall all over themselves to bake something or volunteer for community events, but with their next breath they would say Jess's running shorts were too tiny (she was inviting something with those, didn't she know?), or how Nora's Spanish could use some help (it must be tough with a single mother), or why didn't Lee speak it at all (so sad about her mother, though), and snide comments on Nora's and Ryan's sexuality (fuck them on that, truly).

On and on they went, like they were the protectors of

the Latino community and anyone that didn't fit their narrow definition was frowned upon. She wasn't even sure Jennifer Lopez made the cut.

They weren't all bad, though. For example Doña Ines was an angel sent from heaven. But the chismosas seemed to outweigh them all and left a bad taste in Jess's mouth.

Jess scrunched up her face. "Why are they like that?"

"Don't let it get to you. It's not worth it; they aren't worth it." Her mother helped her up and together they carried the garbage bin to the back of the building.

"Gracias por ayudarme."

"No problem." It wasn't her favorite way to spend a Saturday, but there was something about the way her mother looked at her after a long day at the center that warmed Jess's heart.

And Jess didn't mind helping as long as it was far away from the toxic people.

"I was thinking," her mother said as they entered her tiny office at the back. "When you are done with the mini library, we could look at what new books we could bring in? We have a bit of a budget, and we could use a few updates! What do you think?"

The smile on her mother's face was hard to resist. "Sounds good."

"Fantástico." Her mother clapped her hands together. She excused herself to attend a planning meeting and gave Jess free rein of her computer for book-finding purposes.

One hour later she had a list of fifty new books divided by age range, and she'd managed to do two more SAT workbook pages.

Her mother burst back in, dropping papers on her desk and slumping down on the chair across from Jess. "Bureaucracy is truly the enemy of progress, Mija."

"Long meeting?" Jess half stood, signaling the chair was hers if she wanted it, but her mother waved her down.

"They all are." Her mother stretched. "How did the research go?"

Jess turned the monitor to show her mother the list of books she recommended along with links from where to buy them. "You should also check out Capitol Hill Books or Fahrenheit for their used book selection, though people might complain about too many English books in the library again."

Her mother scoffed. "They complain about everything. Nothing is ever good enough, but I like that idea. Would you like to spearhead it?"

"Me?"

"I know, I'm sorry. You've already helped enough." Her mother stood, moving to file the papers she'd dumped on her desk. "We truly appreciate it, though, you know? Everyone at the meeting noticed."

"They did?" Jess warmed at the praise.

"They did. We don't get a lot of young people volunteering these days." Her mother smiled. "It reminds us what we are working toward."

Tucking her hair behind her ear, Jess returned her mother's smile. Despite the long hours and the run-in with the old ladies, today hadn't been so bad. One kid even gave Jess a hug after she finished organizing the tiny picture book library.

"Don't worry. I won't take away the next weekend, I promise. I know you have things to do."

True. It always seemed like she did these days, particularly now that she was cramming SAT prep into every free moment she could find. But then she came back to her mother's smile and the fact that people seemed to notice her good work, and she was actually making a difference. "It's okay. I don't mind. I even got a little SAT prep done while you were in your meeting."

"SATs!" her mother shouted. "I almost forgot. And feel free to say no, but everyone was so impressed with your work today and they know how smart you are. . . ."

Jess could see a request coming a mile away and knew there was no getting out of it.

"And they—we—were wondering if you'd consider helping out with some of the SAT tutoring these next few weeks?"

"I've never really done SAT tutoring before. . . ." Helping Nora with the test didn't count. Neither did being overly prepared for everything. "I haven't even taken the SATs yet!"

"Lo se," her mother continued. "Think of it as a compliment, Mija."

How often would she have to tutor? How many? Would it mess up her own SAT studying? She was already wringing her hands, trying to fit everything into her schedule.

"Think about it. I said I would ask and if you think it's too much, you know I have no problem turning it down."

"Okay," Jess said, knowing she'd have to say yes eventually. At least with a bit more time she could decide when she had time to volunteer.

"Hey. Feel like taking a trip to one of the used bookstores now to see what we can find?"

Jess was itching to look over her schedule and ease the doubts creeping in, but she nodded. They packed up and spent the rest of the day walking down bookstore aisles.

The next day Jess added ten new books to the library, half of which went to the kids' library. She didn't fight the smile that came to her lips as she watched the kids find their brand-new—slightly used—books.

RYAN

HIS GRANDMOTHER WAS psychic. Most of the supplies he needed replaced for his first class he found in the boxes of gifts she'd sent. He'd have to thank her later and find a way to casually mention she didn't have to buy the most expensive version . . . although suggestions were probably a bad idea. You never critique your grandmother's gifts, especially to her face.

He'd packed everything in his bag and so far he was doing a great job of not freaking out . . . until his car broke down halfway to the class.

Classic.

He texted the group:

HELP! SOS. Car broke down and need to get to class. Any suggestions?

Nora: Tow?

Lee: Lyft? Cab it?

Jess: Ugh. I'd come for you, but David has the car.

Ryan: Fuck.

He was ready to call it a message from the universe when a head popped through his window, startling Ryan so much he dropped his phone.

"Fancy meeting you here, on the side of the road, on this random street."

Blake leaned in on the open window. He was wearing a paint-splattered tee and his purple hair was braided down the middle, the sides much shaggier than the last time Ryan had seen him. "Car trouble?"

Ryan held up his hand. "Hold up, I need a second, my soul hadn't returned to my body yet."

"I'll wait." He opened the side door and sat in the passenger seat. "Nice car."

Their gray, seven-year-old Toyota was hardly impressive, but it was usually more reliable than this. "It's my dad's—it was this or the minivan."

"Oh, I love a good minivan. They're like the corgis of the car world."

Ryan laughed, his heart finally back to normal.

"So you need a boost?"

"That would be great—also, if you know how to do that, that would be even better."

He did not, and they ended up calling Ryan's dad, who

tried walking them through it until they realized they had no jumper cables. Ryan and Blake ended up pushing the car near the closest metered parking spot and leaving it for Ryan's dad before hopping in Blake's car.

"Sorry about the mess," Blake said as he took a curve a bit too fast, causing two empty coffee cups to roll around Ryan's feet. "I would make some excuse about being busy, but it would be a lie."

Ryan smiled but glanced anxiously at the clock.

"You'll be like ten minutes late, it's not a huge deal. You'll probably miss introductions, but I can fill you in. There's obviously going to be a Jenny, maybe a Matt. Totally a Robert, Robert is really into hot yoga." Blake pulled up to the designated parking area, and despite his laid-back attitude, rushed up the steps with Ryan. "Good luck," he called as he walked away to his own class.

"Thank you!" Ryan called back, steps away from his classroom. He entered and tried not to look as flustered as he felt.

"Can I help you?" A woman in cargo pants and a black tank top holding a clipboard turned toward him.

"I—" Everyone was looking at him. Awesome.

She looked down to her clipboard. "Ryan . . . um . . . Wang Mercado?" She tripped over his middle name as so many did.

"Yeah," Ryan replied. "That's me. I'm sorry I'm late, my car broke down."

She waved it away. "Literally happened to me yesterday." She motioned to the only empty seat left. "Get situated. I'm Candace, and we are just going around introducing ourselves."

Ryan hurried forward, trying to make as little noise as possible. He could still feel people looking at him. He shrugged it off as he took a glance around the room, noticing he was the youngest person by at least fifteen years. Everyone had out a sketchbook and a set of pens, so he did the same. He caught a few people's names but was still too frazzled to store them properly.

Candace turned to him. He waved, regretting it instantly.

"I'm Ryan," he said, scratching the back of his neck.

Candace nodded, clapping her hands, bringing the attention back to her. "Great!

"So you're here because you haven't painted in a while and are probably asking yourself, 'Am I still an artist?' The answer is YES, but I'm hoping that by the end of this class, you won't care what I have to think and know for yourself." She clapped again. "Let's start with some basics—some stretching, if you will. Get those muscles going again."

Candace placed a series of spheres on a pedestal. "Is there anything more annoying than trying to draw a perfect circle?" A few people laughed, even Ryan cracked a smile, though he wasn't sure if it was actually funny or he was just nervous and wanted to fit in. "In our first class I'm going to use this magnificent little timer to loosen those muscles and get you out of that 'Am I an artist?' spiral so many of us fall into. Let's tap into muscle memory, shall we? Here's how we're going to go. You have thirty seconds to draw the items you see. When I say 'time,' you flip the page and start again. I say 'time' . . . that's right, you flip the page and start again."

That seemed easy, so why was he gripping the pen so tightly he could break it? He took out his phone, looking over the texts he'd received that morning from Nora, Lee, and Jess. Twenty "you can do it" messages—why did it feel like they all needed them lately? Before putting it away he paused and typed out a message to Jason:

> Reclaiming artistic self about to start. Totally cool if I puke in class, right?

His finger hovered over the send button. The whole art thing was never Jason's thing, but he'd texted him about everything else. He'd even tried to plan a catch-up date while Jason was visiting for the weekend, but it turned out to be his parents' something-or-other. He hit send and stashed the phone away. With a deep breath and exhale, he took out his black pen. Around him there were people with varying degrees of fancy pens; the fancier the pen the more embarrassed the person seemed to be. He would be in good company when he brought in more of his grandmother's gifts. Ryan pulled the cap off, his hand shaking for a moment.

The blank page stared at him like a dare. Past-Ryan would fill pages and pages of doodles, but all Present-Ryan could think of was how he was about to ruin a perfectly good blank page.

"Nervous?" his teacher said—it took him a moment to realize she was talking to everyone. "Just breathe in. No need to shit your pants on day one."

Another nervous laugh.

"Okay. Go!"

His pen touched the paper—it was already in the wrong place—it should be higher to start with the bigger ball to accommodate the smaller ones. He stared at the arrangement, cataloging all he needed to do: shadows, framing, perspective.

"Time," she called.

The smudge was all Ryan had. He didn't look around at everyone else's work. It would all be better than a damn smudge. He dove in this time with the biggest of the four, sketching the circle. It was lopsided, and he wanted to rip the paper in half. As he added the third circle she called time.

Another blank page waiting to be filled with his lopsided scratches. He rolled his wrist and closed his eyes for just a moment. He heard her call time again, but he would not let it unfocus him. He let his wrist draw the circles as it wished; they did not overlap as much as they should have, but all four were on the paper. He added some shadows.

"Time."

Not perfect, but less wobbly. He only looked up once before starting each circle to check on perspective, letting the pen glide on the paper. If it faltered or wobbled as it curved he stopped noticing, or more accurately he didn't let it bother him.

"Time."

Sharper lines, the pen barely lifting from the paper. He played more with perspective now, cared less about how clean the work was. His hand did not shake, and he held the pen loose enough to let the wrist do all the work. Several times he forgot to look up and focused on the feel of pen against paper and the delicious sound it made as it glided across it. His eyes focused on the paper absorbing the ink, blooming as the circle came to life.

He wondered if he could switch pens to test each tip out on the page.

"Okay!" Her voice pulled him out of the trance. He looked up from the page, remembering where he was again. "Excellent work for your first day. I know it seems like we didn't do much, but take a look at that first try and the final one. Take a moment."

Ryan laughed at the smudge on his first page—if that didn't say anything about his approach to painting over the last year he didn't know what. Could you even see it if you weren't looking for it? Compared to his final pages, the smudge was nonexistent while the final page was someone whose body—maybe—was starting to listen to him; a passion that maybe hadn't abandoned him after all.

He tried to think back to the last time he'd been so absorbed with something that the passage of time was non-existent, and all he could think of was the afternoons with Jason.

"Before you leave I have an assignment for you: trees."

Okay . . .

"You heard me: trees. Seven of them. I want seven sketches of trees, in pen, just simple sketches. Can be seven of the same tree, different perspectives please, or seven different trees, whatever, you get it, okay? Great. See you Saturday."

They all shuffled off, a few sticking behind to chat. Ryan waited outside for his dad to pick him up, going over the sketches one more time. It'd felt good to get lost again on the page. Even to feel the frustration when he hadn't gotten something quite right. Why had he put this away?

But it was hard, wasn't it? To choose between the two: Jason and his art. To pull himself away from Jason's arms when it was so much easier to hold on. And his painting wasn't Jason's thing. Art in general wasn't Jason's thing. While Ryan could spend hours studying brushstrokes at the Denver Art Museum, Jason was never interested in coming along.

"I'll just come over when you're done," he'd say.

"But there's a new exhibit I want to show you. I actually think you might like it because—"

Jason shook his head. "You know I can't focus in museums for very long."

He'd never told him how much it hurt him.

Ryan's phone vibrated.

Jess: How did it go?

She'd texted outside the group chat that went back to the age of Methuselah. She was being cautious, in case Ryan didn't want to talk to everyone.

Ryan: Good.

Jess: Actually good or are you being facetious?

Ryan: Facetious? I love you so much.

Jess: ♥ Seriously, how did it go?

Ryan: Like . . . I don't know, I thought it would be beginnery

(is that even a word?) but . . . ugh, words. I'm trying to say it

felt fine, it didn't suck.

Which was as close as he could get to describing the feeling that the years he'd shoved it aside weren't as unforgivable as he thought.

There was a tap on his shoulder, and he looked up to see Blake.

"So?" he asked. "How'd it go?"

"I survived." Ryan looked back down as Blake sat next to him, his beat-up Chucks almost matching Ryan's for wear.

Blake's hands, paint-stained shirt, and jeans were covered in new specks of clay. "Sculpting—new to it, but I really like the feel of it, you know?"

Ryan reached over, picking off a flake of clay from Blake's clothes, realizing afterward he shouldn't have assumed the familiarity. "I've always wanted to try it," he said.

"Yeah—I think you'd like it." He smiled. "Now if I can just get the clay to look like the shit in my head."

"Said every artist ever."

"True. Feels like whenever I do it's an accident—there's a lesson in there somewhere, but I refuse to learn it." He smiled again, which was getting more and more charming. "Need a ride? We can maybe get some coffee on the way and talk about how much our art wants to kill us."

Ryan was surprised by how much he wanted to. Even just talking about art with someone who got it sounded nice. "Maybe next time? My dad is on his way to pick me up."

Blake nodded. "Sexy—see you next week for a totally platonic coffee date after class then?"

Ryan laughed. "Sure. It's a platonic date."

LEE

SO TURNS OUT the center hadn't been sucked down into the pits of hell after a freak sinkhole accident.

Bummer.

Lee was not a fan of the community center. True, neither were Jess, Nora, or Ryan, but it reminded Lee of a particularly vulnerable time that loved to kick its way to the surface whenever she visited.

But Jess couldn't get away and had begged Lee to meet her here for their first Spanish lesson, so here she was. Lee braced for whatever was to come, the memory of her first visit bubbling to the surface.

It had been less than a year after her mother's death, and Lee was an open wound.

Unease rose along her spine as she walked through the

entrance. It was colder than it should be, or maybe Lee was just nervous. She tugged her jacket around her like it could save her from everything inside.

"¡Mira quién es!" The old woman who usually greeted people came around her little station toward Lee. Lee took a step, trying to place her. Had she been one of the many to pepper her with questions? Had she asked Lee if she spoke Spanish only to look at her with disappointment when she'd said only a little?

Lee braced herself as the woman approached her then put a hand on her shoulder. Lee still couldn't place her, and by her smile the old woman knew it.

"¿No te acuerdas de mí?"

Which one were you? Which way was I not enough for you?

She shook her head. "Sorry, I mean, perdón."

"No te preocupes, Francheska."

"Lee," she corrected.

"Ines." The woman smiled, bringing her in for a hug so warm it made Lee wonder if she had met her before. Her warm brown eyes held no judgment that she could see, and she seemed genuinely happy to see Lee.

"It's," she said, pausing between each word, "good to see you."

Lee nodded and offered a bit of a smile before indicating there was somewhere she needed to be.

"Jessica esta con su madre en la oficina," Ines said,

giving Lee's shoulder a squeeze and returning to the front table. Was there even an official greeter position at the center, or did Ines just show up each day without asking? Lee was certain it was the second.

Inside, the center was less shabby than she remembered. The walls were repainted, the bookshelves filled with the new (but used) books Jess had bought, even the announcement board looked less of a mess. Lee knew, somehow, that this was all Jess.

They didn't deserve her.

Her father had meant well. The center was supposed to be a way to keep in touch with her mother's culture, instead each question in Spanish she couldn't answer fast enough was a fresh cut.

Speaking of Jess, she found her in the office as Ines said, but deep in conversation with her mother.

Not wanting to interrupt, she texted her to say she would wait for her by the mini library, which was also home to the super-comfy chairs. She picked the biggest one and sank into it. The chair engulfed her. She'd sat here on the first day, too—after the barrage of questions she'd retreated to this corner and sent her aunt a text.

Can I come stay with you? I'm not sure I can do this.

Her aunt's response was quick:

I have no doubt you can.

"Hey." David plopped down in the chair beside her, and she snapped out of the memory.

"Hey," she replied, attempting to straighten but not having much luck in the chair.

"Waiting for Jess?"

"Yeah—first lesson."

"That's today?" David had better luck with his chair and shifted to get a better view of Lee. It made Lee want to look away but smile at the same time. He'd cut his hair short, only leaving the slightest hint of his curls at the top.

"Yep."

"Cool."

"Is it?"

"Yeah." His dark-brown eyes followed her fingers as she tied her own loose curls back up in a messy knot. "Now you can curse properly."

"I'm not sure that's on the lesson plan," Lee said, wondering why everything about her was so interesting, "and those words, I already know."

"Don't let her fool you." He leaned in, the sleeves of his long sleeve shirt pushed up showing his tawny skin and dark hair that ran along his arms. "She curses like a sailor, especially recently."

"Really?" Trying to find anywhere else to look but his eyes, she noticed a message from Jess saying she would be there in ten minutes, twenty minutes ago. So unlike her.

"Here she comes."

Jess sat down, looking as deflated as the chair she sat on.

"Rough day?" Both Lee and David shifted their

attention to Jess, except for the few moments where Lee couldn't help but sneak looks. Each time something new drew her eye, like how his fingers kept busy, or the way his eyes also flicked back to her, catching her looking.

But when Jess finally spoke Lee's attention snapped back, this time not wavering. "Mom wants me to do all the kiddie story times over the summer."

Oh God. Lee might not be a regular at the center, but she knew from Jess's stories and the one time Nora came in for some catering event that kiddie story times were the seventh circle of hell. Maybe Jess's mom meant Mandarin story time at the TAA? Ryan said those were pretty fun . . . but probably not.

"Yikes," David said. "Didn't you just help with some SAT prep stuff? Did you say no?"

Jess glanced at Lee, who cringed just a bit. "No, I said yes."

Of course she would say yes. Not only was non-resolution Jessica always willing to help, but resolution Jessica seemed to be a beacon for new responsibilities. This was not what the resolution was about. Jess didn't need more responsibility, she needed less.

"That's the worst job. I would rather clean the toilets than be on story-time duty."

David was not helping.

"It just takes a little reshuffling," Jess said, though it felt like she was saying it more to herself than Lee. She tapped some things into her phone, then looked up at Lee. "I might have to adjust our lessons, pero"—she took a breath and smiled—"everything will be okay."

Lee really wanted to believe her, but she recognized that smile. She'd had that same smile on plenty of times. She was that same scared-and-out-of-her-depth when Ryan and Jess found her hiding from everyone at the center years ago and sealed their friendship.

Lee still remembered how tall Jess was even back then.

"You okay?" She'd crouched down beside her.

"Fine." Lee had smiled that smile that was so easy for her after years of practice, as her mom got sicker and helping hands became annoying hands.

"Don't let them get to you," Ryan had said, extending his hand. "They tried the same are-you-Latino-enough shit on us all the time until my mom ripped them to shreds." When she didn't take his hand he sat down next to her. "I'm Ryan, the half-Boricua, half-Taiwanese, one hundred percent gay boy you'll probably hear about eventually. You can imagine the field day they had with me. Jess saw you run in here, and we thought we should say hi."

"I'm Jessica," Jess had said, flanking Lee on the other side. "I don't have a cool introduction, but you can call me Jess."

"Somewhere in this place is a girl named Nora," Ryan continued. "And we are the coolest people here, who also don't give a fuck. Want to be friends?"

And they'd meant it. They'd met her one day, and they'd flanked around her the rest of the day, keeping the curious people with their questions at bay. She still remembered how Jess would turn the conversation on them. Anyone who came to ask Lee about her mom quickly found themselves talking about their dog or hadn't their son gotten into trouble recently? But that's who they were; that's who Jess was.

So, yeah—she recognized the smile on Jess now, and she'd be damned if she was the cause of it.

"Jess, you don't have to—"

"No. I want to, I promise," Jess tried again, but Lee could still see the strain, the hint of worry. She wondered if Jess even knew she might be spreading herself too thin? Lee had to figure out how to show her that the resolutions were meant to loosen her up, not wind her tighter.

"You have a lot going on," Lee tried again.

"I made a lesson plan already." She pulled out the pages to prove it—there were many.

"You did that for me?"

Jess smiled, a genuine one this time. "Of course."

Guilt mixed with happiness at the thought of all the work Jess had put into Lee's resolution. *I have no doubt you can*, her aunt had said. She had a feeling that Jess would agree.

"Gracias."

"Knock that one off the vocab list," David said,

149

reminding Jess he was still there. "How about I take over? I'd be happy to help." He plucked the lesson plan from Jess's shocked face and looked it over. "Detailed. As expected."

The shock faded fast, and Jess reached for the papers. David moved them out of her reach and turned to Lee with a quirk of his lips as his twin tried to snag the papers back. "You game?"

What was it about that smile? Why was she just noticing now?

"Okay." Lee surprised herself, and Jess, who stopped midreach.

"Really?" David didn't hide his amusement.

"But . . . ," Jess sputtered.

"Jess." Lee knew Jess would feel bad, but she also knew her friend would continue to take on responsibility with no regard for herself, and Lee simply wouldn't let that happen. True, there was the bonus of getting to nerd out a bit more with David—their party conversation had been pretty great—and his laid-back attitude would give her a chance to figure out how to show Jess what her resolutions were truly for. "Let this one go, okay? You aren't letting me down, I swear."

"I—" Jess took a breath, looking back down to her phone. Lee realized she was reviewing the epic calendar that held every moment of Jess's life. She exhaled and nodded. "Yeah. Okay."

"Awesome." David stuffed the paper in his bag and

stood. "I'll email you tonight and we can work out when to start."

With a hug Jess returned to the office and whatever task awaited her. Lee really needed to do something to help Jess with her resolutions. To show her how fun they could be. How fun she could be. To be the friend Jess was to her on the day they'd met. Could she do it?

I have no doubt you can.

JESS

JESS WAS DEEP into her history notes when Ryan sat next to her in the cafeteria, followed by Nora, Beth, and Lee. She did not look up, focusing on repeating dates in her mind, making them stick one more time. Finals week had snuck up on her fast, and with her work at the center plus prepping for the SATs, she didn't feel as prepared as she usually was. But it was fine. Stress was normal, wasn't it? Out of the corner of her eye she caught Ryan taking one of her baby carrots, then another, then finally her entire tray.

She rolled her eyes, the corners of her mouth tilting up, but still she needed to push through one final revision. If her grades slipped even a bit . . . no. She couldn't think of that. Everything would be fine.

"Jess." Ryan leaned in. "Earth to Jessica."

His hand slipped into view, blocking her notes. "Okay,

okay," she said, closing her eyes and repeating the key dates one more time.

You'll be fine, she repeated, though more and more she wondered if she was right. She didn't want to blame the resolution, but it did feel like she had less and less time to think. Think less, maybe that was the key.

"Jess?" Ryan tried again.

"Sorry." She finally looked up. "Finals week is just getting to me. Plus the SATs are seconds away and—"

"All I see you do is study, Jess." Ryan slid back her tray, and she munched on a baby carrot. "You'll be fine."

She nodded. She would be, wouldn't she?

"I saw you earlier in Miss Anderson's office," Lee said, popping open her soda can. "What homework did she give you?"

No one left Miss Anderson's office without homework. When her fingers started to reach for her notebook again, Jess shoved it into her bag, concentrating on eating the heck out of the baby carrots. "College stuff—mainly scholarships."

"Oh, which ones?" Beth asked.

"Not sure yet. Which is why we met, she wants me to have a game plan, a list of scholarships to apply to," Jess continued. "They'd slipped my mind with all the SAT stuff, so it was a good reminder."

She couldn't let anything else slip her mind. Especially not something like a scholarship.

Though her parents worked full-time, she knew it would

be hard on them to send both David and Jess to school at the same time. And she may have seen some second-mortgage paperwork tucked into her mother's purse the other day. Miss Anderson wanted Jess to make a list of at least ten scholarships to go through, but as Jess thought of those papers she wondered if that was enough.

"She means well." Jess shrugged.

"Oh," Nora exclaimed. Then she rummaged through her backpack. "I have something for you."

"Did you figure out your resolutions?" Jess said with a smile. She should've asked sooner, but it had also slipped her mind. But Nora would've told her if she had, she reassured herself. Don't add more things to worry about.

Nora stuck her tongue out and unfolded the bright-yellow paper. "No—for Ryan."

He perked up, reaching for it. "Nora loves me best, don't be jealous." He looked over the paper. "A gallery?"

"An exhibit, a gallery exhibit, I'm pretty sure I read it right. Thought it might be interesting." Nora took the paper back and placed it on the table where they could all read it. "It sounded pretty cool, it's an art exhibit all about different artists using old art movements and making them their own. You might"—she shrugged—"find it inspiring or something. They also have a virtual tour, so you don't have to go anywhere."

Ryan scanned the paper again. The exhibit was titled "The Sincerest Form of Flattery" and boasted some of the best up-and-coming artists in Colorado. Ryan nodded but didn't look overly excited about it. Did the second resolution still feel daunting even though he was almost done with his art class? "Does sound pretty cool. Thanks."

They all bounced to the next topic. Jess nodded and tried to follow along, but her mind took her back to the yellow paper in front of her. She watched Ryan as he swirled the ketchup around on his plate like he was working with a palette. Dark lines of carbon edged his fingernails, bringing a smile to Jess's face. She'd missed his paint-stained hands and the splotches of sneaky color that hid behind his ear because he would touch his neck without noticing.

Nora was the same but with sugar; at least once a month Nora came to school with some form of food caught in a strand of hair.

The carbon-stained fingers were a great sign.

Lee laughed, throwing her head back. Jess couldn't shake the fact that she'd let Lee down with the lessons no matter how many times she'd said it was fine. But it wasn't just that; she'd also been looking forward to hanging out with Lee.

It all came down to time again—it felt like they had so little of it.

She reached for the flyer, her eyes landed on the address and she plugged it into her phone, an idea immediately forming.

"Why not go in person?" Jess said.

Nora stopped first. "What?"

Jess held up the paper. "Why don't we just go? It's two, okay, maybe three hours to Salida. And wouldn't it be better if we saw it in person?"

They'd never done a road trip, and having that time together would be fun. Plus, it would be nice to think of something that wasn't the SATs or the test she had to take in a few minutes. At least that's what her heart told her.

"You might even meet some of the artists, Ryan." That didn't make Ryan as happy as she thought it would. "Or not."

"I don't know," Lee said. "It's pretty short notice. . . ."

"Oh, come on! It would be fun—Nora, you can be in charge of the music. Ryan and I can switch off driving, and Lee can snark from the back."

"I want to resent that division of labor, but it's pretty accurate," Lee said.

"We can also do a bus, it doesn't matter." Why was everyone so reluctant about it? Jess was usually the over-planner, and according to the resolutions the one that needed to "loosen up." "Don't you want to see the art up close?"

"Let me think about it," Ryan finally said.

"I'll check with my mom, but I'm not sure I can take the day off."

"We can do it Sunday," Jess said. "You guys are closed on Sundays."

"That could work," Nora agreed. "Though I heard

there's supposed to be another good party that weekend."

Jess rolled her eyes. "Who cares about crappy parties? The last one wasn't even that good."

"Hey!" Nora said with a pout. "I liked it."

They would not miss this road-trip opportunity for just another party. She could look forward to the road trip. Another party felt like the last thing she needed. "They aren't that hard to throw and there will be another one before you know it. Anyone can throw a party."

"Then you throw one," Ryan said with a devious smile. Catching Jess off guard.

"What?" Where was this going? This was about the gallery, not Jess. "I'm talking about the show. We should totally go."

"Yeah, I got that. I'll think about it." Ryan stuffed the flyer in his bag. "Getting back to the party thing, though."

"Uh, Ryan." Lee's eyes were wide, and she was trying to get Ryan's attention. "Maybe not the best time with finals and SATs."

"Not now, obviously," Ryan said, "but my comment still stands, Miss Anyone-Can-Throw-a-Party."

Ugh.

Did she have to? Technically, yes, she reminded herself.

She exhaled, which everyone took as a yes.

"Don't look so sullen." Ryan put his arm around her as the bell rang. "We aren't going to leave you to the wolves. Consider us your party planners."

"Really?" The thought of her friends helping her eased

the growing panic to a manageable worry.

"Of course!" Nora said, looping her arm around Beth's.

"You know," Beth said, "no one's claimed a Halloween party yet."

"Isn't Halloween kind of big?"

Jess was thinking more of a run-of-the-mill party that would be quickly forgotten should it go horribly wrong.

Ryan shrugged. "Not really. It's just slightly sluttier."

"Okay . . ." The worry was creeping back to a panic, but Jess wouldn't let it. "Halloween it is."

"It does give me enough time to think about a costume," Lee said.

"You're going to wear a costume?"

"I said think about it."

Jess: SAT hype thread. You can do this! You can do this! Make sure to get lots of sleep. Eat breakfast. Don't throw up breakfast. Wear comfortable clothes.

Lee: Is this for you or for us . . .

Ryan: Thanks, Mom.

Jess: For all of us! Including me.

Nora: Everything hurts, and I hate meringues.

Lee: What did those heavenly things ever do to you?

Nora: I think I've made several thousand of them over the course of the week. I hate them, and I want them to die.

Lee: Noooo! Give them to me. I'll need the sugar tomorrow.

Nora: I dream about them. They're in my dreams.

Ryan: Zombie meringues!

Nora: I don't want to dream of meringues. I want to dream of Beth if anything.

Ryan: Oh I see. * wiggles eyebrows *

Nora: Exactly.

Jess: No sugar! You'll crash after.

Nora: You know I carry a layer of sugar no matter how hard I try, Jess. It's part of me now. I am sugar.

Lee: So we should lick you if we feel like we need a boost?

Ryan: Well this conversation just got interesting. * puts down pencil *

Nora: I would need Beth's approval, but pretty much.

Lee: Sweet.

Jess: Were you just sketching!?!

Ryan: Did you know that Roxane Gay did a movie review of Magic Mike XXL? It's the best thing ever.

Lee: Is that on the test? I hope so.

Jess: WERE YOU JUST SKETCHING?

Ryan: It's a great review though . . .

Jess: RYAN.

Ryan: Síííííí. Dios mío. Like, chill. I got inspired by all the Magic Mike XXL gifs in the review and also, I wanted to avoid studying. So . . . YES I'M SKETCHING.

Lee: I can feel Jess's smile through the phone.

Jess: I AM smiling.

Ryan: Thanks, Mom.

Lee: Less effective the second time around.

Ryan: . . . thanks, Mom.

Lee: Rude.

Jess: I should be grilling you guys on vocabulary. Turn your test books to page 42.

Nora: Jessssss, I'm pretty sure we've learned all we are going to learn.

Ryan: It's pretty late. I remember you saying something about getting a good night's rest?

Jess: True! Everyone go to sleep.

Nora: Already in bed. Have been this entire time. Bed is life now.

Jess: SATs are life.

Lee: I refuse.

Ryan: Refuse what?

Lee: Everything.

Ryan: Sounds about right.

Nora: I can hear the meringues calling me now. Buenas noches.

Jess: OK, OK. Buenas noches. See you all tomorrow!

Lee: If you must.

THANK GOD IT'S SUMMER

JESS

THE SATS WERE over. They'd celebrated by eating way too much fried food and watching the original Star Wars trilogy in Lee's room, because she was the only one with a VHS player to watch the original theatrical version Lee insisted they celebrate with. Jess had fallen asleep somewhere between *Empire* and *Return of the Jedi,* and according to Ryan she mumbled vocabulary words in her sleep.

She thought she did well, but nowadays every thought came with a nagging postscript of "but are you sure?" It's not like she'd never had doubts, but why were they suddenly harder to power through?

Jess was in her pj's when the first pebble hit her window. She was up and opening the window when the second hit. The third hit her face.

"¿Qué carajo?" Jess rubbed at the spot on her forehead.

"Sorry!" Lee and Nora were huddled under her window. Lee had a few more pebbles in her hand. "Was already midthrow when you came out."

They were both in long pj bottoms (Lee's were little skulls, Nora's pineapples) and hoodies.

"Um, hey?" Jess leaned out a bit. "What's up?"

"Prison break!" Nora whisper-shouted, her eagerness making her bounce on her toes.

Prison break?

"What?" Jess leaned out a bit more in case she'd misheard.

"We are breaking you out!" Nora repeated.

"From my room?"

Lee tossed the last of the pebbles in the yard and patted Nora on the shoulder. "She's not grounded, so it's not really a prison break, Nora. We're kidnapping you, so come down . . . but, like, sneakily so your parents don't figure it out."

"Where are we going?"

"Just come down!" Lee shouted back then mumbled: "This kidnapping shit is hard."

It was almost midnight. What could they want? She slipped on her jacket and snagged her phone as she tiptoed downstairs.

David was on his phone, lounging on the couch with the TV on when she came down the stairs. He spotted her and his face scrunched up in confusion. "Hey . . . super-late-night run?"

"I'm being kidnapped, I think." How ridiculous that sounded, but David simply nodded. He always seemed so laid-back about everything. Why was it so hard for her to be the same?

"Interesting," he said, going back to the TV. "Have fun I guess. Say hello to Lee for me."

Outside in the dark Ryan's resurrected car waited on the curb. She ran up to it; even through the fogged-up windows she could see Nora and Lee in the back.

"What's going on?"

"Get in!" Nora shouted like they were in a heist movie.

Why was no one telling her what was going on? "Where are we—"

Ryan leaned over, unlocking the side door. "Jess, just say yes and get in."

So she did.

JESS'S HEART FELT like it would burst as she looked up at the stars above her. So many she could never count them. There was always something about them that could just brush everything else aside.

They laid out a giant blanket, settling in with milkshakes in one hand and a pile of french fries in front of them. Lee handed Jess a blanket in case the night got colder. "We figured that you might not be having a lot of fun with your resolution so far, and fun was the whole point. So we wanted to do something to show you that saying yes can be fun, and to start the summer off right."

Lee settled in beside her, milkshake in hand.

"It was all Lee's idea," Nora said, sucking on her milkshake straw.

"Really?" Jess looked over to Lee, who simply shrugged, hiding the smile from her face by immediately shoving a french fry in her mouth. It was no secret that Lee cared, despite the way she hid behind well-timed snarks and quips. Knowing she'd put all this together for Jess reminded her of why she'd wanted to do the resolutions in the first place. Her friends deserved the best year ever. Together.

"This was good—thank you."

Jess pointed out constellations as they sipped and munched, falling into a new conversation.

"I got a job," Ryan said, "for the summer."

"Really?" Jess had no idea Ryan was even looking—or had she not been paying attention? She brushed off the second of guilt and doubt.

"No big deal, it's just helping out after my classes, keeping the studios clean, helping Candace when she needs it. It doesn't pay anything."

"That's not a job, dude," Lee said.

Ryan scarfed down several fries. "It's more of a trade. Free classes for the work, that way I can keep taking the next session in the summer and maybe even in the fall if it goes well."

"That's really good," Jess said with a small smile. Her heart danced with happiness—at least someone's resolution was doing its job.

"Oh no." Lee pointed to Jess. "Her 'I'm proud of you' smile is out. Look out!"

Jess threw a fry. "I am. I can't help it."

"Well, I'm happy I won't be the only one working this summer." Nora swished her strawberry milkshake. "Summer is full-blown La Islita time."

"Don't let it take over the whole summer," Jess cautioned, but she knew Nora and her mother lived and breathed the shop during the summer.

"Has your dad gotten his hooks in you yet, Lee?"

"Pretty much," Lee said with a sigh. "Internships build character after all, even though I'm pretty sure I'll just be running documents up and down floors all day. Thankfully, I managed to get it down to three days a week, thanks to David."

"David?"

"The lessons. My dad is really happy about them, so he wants to make sure I have all the time I need." Lee smirked. "I may have fibbed about how many hours the lessons were."

Ryan laughed, tossing a french fry at Lee then taking out his phone. "Lean in."

They huddled for the photo, Lee sticking out her tongue at the last minute. As Jess watched Ryan post the photo, his fingers hovered over his phone before going to his messages.

"You still talking to Jason?"

"Yes." He tucked the phone away. "I know you don't approve."

"I don't disapprove."

"It just feels nice to talk to him again. It's almost like we never broke up."

"But you did."

"I remember." Ryan was silent. Jess worried she'd been too callous with her words. "Do you think . . . do you think if he saw the absolutely awesome self-assured painter I am, he'd be totally devastated he broke up with me?"

"Are you?" Jess said. "An absolutely awesome self-assured painter."

Ryan groaned.

"Well, maybe not yet. I am better, though. Happier, I think. But it would be nice if that the happiness actually got me somewhere."

"Happiness is a journey, not a destination," Nora cut in.

"Shouldn't you be eating hemp seeds while you say that?" Ryan teased. "You know that's not a soy milkshake, right?"

"Soy shake." Lee burst out laughing. "Oh my God, it sounds like 'I am shake,' right? Soy shake?"

Ryan pulled away Lee's own milkshake even as he laughed. "That's enough shake for you."

• • •

AS THE AIR grew colder, Ryan and Jess huddled together and stared at the stars dotting the sky above the mountains.

"I'll do the gallery show," Ryan said.

"You will?"

"Yeah."

"You don't seem happy about it."

"I just . . ." He stared up, maybe finding the courage among the stars. "These people made it, you know? They probably never gave up."

"You don't know that."

"Neither do you."

"That's true." She stared up at the stars, the vastness comforting. Jess wanted to say something more, to let Ryan know he wasn't alone. "You know, I'm scared too." She felt Ryan shift and turn to watch her. How quickly she wanted to turn back. Not to say anything. Her body felt angry for even offering. "Of letting people down."

"I don't think you can let me down."

She turned to him and smiled. Even now her mind started to list everything she needed to do the following day. How much time had she wasted eating french fries and drinking milkshakes? She shook that last thought away, refusing to let any negativity infect the night. She would make up the time somewhere.

Somehow.

Ryan brought his head closer, whispering, "You think I can do it? The resolution?"

"Yeah."

He looked up at the stars, and Jess hoped he imagined good things. Of galleries filled with his art. Of happiness. Of love.

Jess thought of the summer ahead. She pictured efficiency. She pictured herself tackling each responsibility like it was nothing more than a stone to be stepped on.

But then she stumbled. And the stones turned to mountains. Jess shut her eyes, driving the image away. "You think I can do it?"

She held her breath.

"Yeah."

They linked hands and squeezed.

RYAN

JESS AND BETH took turns driving his parents' minivan. If they were going to make this trip, their parents insisted on using a car that hadn't broken down recently. Ryan would've volunteered to drive, but he still wasn't sure about this whole gallery thing and they suspected he might just drive in circles for hours.

And there was the second failed attempt for a Jason hangout. Ryan had thought that they could swing by Boulder first and have a totally-not-awkward group coffee date during one of Jason's internship breaks, but once again Jason was too busy, and the timing didn't work out.

Internships, family events, summer courses . . . everything in Jason's life seemed designed to keep them apart. Now you're being dramatic, he thought.

Nora kicked his seat and he turned to look back at her,

catching Blake's eyes as well. After another failed platonic date he'd decided to kill two birds with one stone and invite Blake along. Nora was obsessed with his hair the moment they met, which now included a stripe of cobalt blue.

"Are we almost there?" Nora said.

"Is that why you kicked me?"

"Yes, plus I like kicking you." She stuck out her tongue.

"Well I don't know how long, let me ask navigation."

In turn Ryan kicked Jess. "Hey, Navigation, how much time left?"

"Twenty minutes," Jess said. "And no kicking."

"That was Nora."

"Nora's all the way in the back."

"Right, but she wanted me to kick you."

Jess rolled her eyes then went back to watching the little dot on her phone get closer to the other dot on her phone. Not that she needed to—the voice always popped up and told them what to do—but she'd been particularly focused on the task.

Ryan: You OK?

Jess: No texting while I'm navigating.

Ryan: OK, just . . . I know you didn't plan for Blake to come.

Jess: It's fine.

Ryan: I know you . . .

He could see Jess shift, her shoulders sagging as she texted back.

Jess: Yeah. OK, maybe I was thinking of more of a just the

four of us bonding time.

Ryan: We can still bond. I promise. He's a nice guy, I swear.

Jess: I believe you, and Beth's here anyway, so.

Jess turned in her seat a bit as the next text came.

Jess: You like him?

Ryan: Don't start. Just friends.

She smiled and turned around.

Jess: Just checking—now stop texting me.

Ryan had been to plenty of galleries before, walked around streets where people displayed their art, visited art museums, but today felt different. Before he'd see the pieces and think, *Maybe one day, if I'm brave enough, this might be me.* But now it would be him. If he followed through with his resolution, his art would hang on a wall for people to walk around, judge, point to. . . . What would they say? What would they think? Would they see the hesitation?

Jess bumped against him, looping her arm around his. "Ready?"

Probably not. "I think so."

She gave his arm a gentle squeeze, and they started to move, eventually breaking off into groups of three as they explored: Ryan, Jess, and Blake. Nora, Beth, and Lee.

The exhibit was amazing, and soon Ryan turned into an unofficial tour guide, pointing out the brilliance in each piece. Once or twice he caught Jess and Blake sharing a smile as he bounded from piece to piece. Each artist had started their work with an iconic piece of art as their inspiration, then brought their own style or medium to the work. One artist re-created incredibly detailed Renaissance paintings but replaced the figures with pop culture icons. Lee squealed when she saw the portrait of Princess Leia—General Organa—as the *Mona Lisa*.

As he walked from piece to piece he wondered how he would reinterpret the portraits. The image of his grandmother as the *Mona Lisa* came like a spark. He had promised a portrait, after all. She would love it, claiming it to be better than the original itself. It would be perfect.

When he imagined putting brush to canvas he faltered, feeling old insecurities rise up. Sketches and doodles of old trees and inanimate objects were fine, but a portrait? A portrait would reveal to the world what he knew in his heart: he wasn't good enough. He wasn't enough, period.

Blake's hand slipped into his, pulling him out of his own spiral and into the next room.

"Just wait," Blake said, pointing to the different sculptures hanging by the ceiling. As he led Ryan around them, they started to coalesce into a familiar figure.

"*The Scream*," Blake said with a megawatt smile. "I kind of want to bow down and worship this piece."

They went round and round the piece, viewing it from every angle. Ryan turned to study the latticework on the left side when he accidentally slammed up against Blake, their faces close for just a second. Their eyes locked, and when Blake's eyes flicked down to Ryan's lips, he leaned forward and closed the gap.

Holy shit was all Ryan could think as Blake returned his kiss, taking it from tentative to full-on heat. Hands slipped up shirts and they leaned on each other for balance. When Ryan's tongue gently pressed against Blake's lips, the resulting moan sent shivers up Ryan's back.

Ryan stepped away from the kiss with reluctance, his mind a confusing mess of want and worry. What did this mean? Why had he done that? He wasn't ready for another relationship. He wasn't even sure he even had anything left to offer in a relationship, and Blake didn't deserve that. He took a breath, his body screaming to close the gap once again, to feel that good again.

Ryan took a step back, keeping his heart steady. "I'm going to, uh, see what else is around. Want to come?"

Blake smiled, but Ryan could tell he was disappointed. He wished he was ready. He wished he knew what it would even mean to be ready. "I'll stick around here for a while."

Ryan walked out of the room, hoping he hadn't just messed up a friendship, when the next room took what remained of his breath away. There were no lights save for the ones coming from behind the stained-glass pieces: three giant works of art that took up each wall. In the middle of the room was a set of benches perfectly positioned to sit in awe, which is just what Ryan did.

As he sat there, Ryan began to understand what Jess saw when she looked up at the night sky. He understood how darkness could soothe and light inspire.

Whoever the artist was, she was a genius, transforming *The Starry Night*, *Guernica*, and *Water Lilies* into revelations of light. It reminded him of *Glacier Melting*, one of his favorite series by artist Marlene Tseng Yu. Like her series, each piece felt as if it were on fire as the light shone through it. If he could move his bed and center it in the middle of this room he'd die happy. He sat by *The Starry Night*, taking in every cut of the glass and how the metal seamlessly joined the colors when a couple walked in, moving around the room, taking in each piece.

As they moved Ryan could hear their conversation.

"Originality is dead, I guess," the man said.

"You don't like it?" his date replied.

"It's just a copy." The man waved his hand around. "The others had some form of interpretation, but this . . . I understand it was a lot of work, I just don't think it shows the artist's originality."

Ryan was so taken aback that he must have made some sort of sound because the couple shifted to him, realizing he was also in the room. He turned away, looking back at the piece in front of him.

Not original? What kind of stupid comment was that? The couple left, and Ryan sat, fuming. How could anyone think the piece was anything more than stunning? Yes it recreated something done, but how could anyone look at this fusion of glass and iron and not be awestruck? If anything, the piece drew you to the power of light in the original pieces.

The comment lodged in his brain, picking away at the

piece even as he stared at it. If this wasn't above judgment, how would he be? What's to stop anyone from ripping his work to shreds?

"There you are." Jess came around the corner as his mind reeled with thoughts of inadequacy. "You okay?"

"I don't know if I can do it."

"Do what?"

Ryan told her about the couple. "If something this beautiful can get comments like that . . . they would tear me apart, Jess. I don't—I don't think I can do it. Let other people—random people—decide something is not worth it. Fuck that."

He waited for Jess to say she believed in him, that he was being silly, but he wasn't expecting her to smile.

"Are you laughing at me?"

"I would never—not even if you told a joke."

He put his head in his hands.

"I don't know how many times I can tell you how amazing you are, for you to believe it." She leaned on his shoulder. "But I'm not going to stop—I'm going to keep saying it."

"Aren't you tired?"

"I'm relentless."

He relaxed. "You kind of are."

As they were about to exit, a woman about his mother's age came into the room, right up to *The Starry Night*, took a deep breath, and sighed. Not again, he thought, hurrying to leave when she caught his eye.

"What do you think?" she asked, pointing straight at him. "Be honest."

He squared his shoulders. "It's fucking gorgeous."

Then the woman laughed, turning back to the piece. Ryan wasn't sure what to say to that, when she said, "Fuck yeah it is. Took me almost a year to finish it." She scratched her head. "More than a year, come to think of it."

"You . . ." Ryan pointed to the piece then back to her, shock and embarrassment mingling on his face.

She smiled. "Thank you, by the way. This piece was an asshole, but it was worth it."

"It's . . . I mean, I love it." He fumbled over his words, struggling to find a way to tell her how amazing it was, how the play between light and color took it to another dimension.

She laughed again. "You better stop before I take you home with me. I need you for the times I can barely stand my work."

"You have those?" Ryan looked back at the intricacy of each piece. How could anyone hate work like this?

"Of course." She walked over to Ryan, coming up to his shoulder. "I almost threw the *Water Lilies* out twice, I was so angry at how the blues played together, pieces kept shattering in the wrong places, I kept burning my arm, it felt like I was cursed. You an artist?"

Was he? Ryan didn't know how to answer that. Who determined that?

"I paint." He shrugged. "Or at least, I'm trying to get back into painting."

She nodded, gently squeezing his shoulder. "I hate that question too. Don't let it mess with your head—validation and all that. It's a bitch."

Ryan couldn't help but laugh. He should sketch it: validation is a bitch.

"Can I ask you a question?"

"Shoot."

"How do you put your work out there? Isn't this scary?"

"Absolutely—and this isn't even the worst part. Now some critic is going to come in here and tell the world if this is worth it or not. And it's terrifying."

"So it doesn't go away?" He'd hoped it would with time.

"No—never—not for me at least, and I've been at this for twenty years." She waited for him, seeming to see he had another question brewing inside him.

"What if you aren't good enough?"

She motioned around her, implying the gallery. "For this?"

"For your art," Ryan whispered.

"Shit." She looked taken aback. "That's intense and not something I can answer for you. I imagine you have to look at where those feelings are coming from and ask yourself who is doing the judging. Because, I'll tell you this, a hundred percent of the time it's going to be you."

• • •

THE CAR RIDE home was quiet. They each zoned out to Nora's playlist as the sunset played with the sky. Ryan drove back with Blake by his side. Behind him Jess listened to Lee's glowing review of the General Organa portrait (of which she now owned a print) and Nora and Beth cuddled all the way in the back.

Though the kiss played over in his mind, it was the thought that he was judging himself that took up the most room. Of course painting wasn't the problem, he was. But how do you move past an obstacle you put in your own path? He'd had Jason and he'd lost that. He'd had painting and he'd put it aside, and now that he'd picked it up again it felt like something was still missing.

His phone buzzed in his pocket and he flicked it to voice mail without looking. His parents never liked him to talk and drive. When it rang again he took it out: his dad. The previous call had been from his mom.

"Jess?" He held the phone out. "Can you answer this while I'm driving? Just let them know we're, like, forty minutes away."

Jess took the phone.

"Ryan," Jess's voice was soft. "You should pull over."

"What?" He found Jess's eyes in the rearview mirror. "What's wrong?"

"It's about your grandmother."

NORA

NORA HID HER phone before her mother could see her on it again. She'd been texting all morning in between taking pans in and out of the oven. It was a miracle that she hadn't baked it into one of the batter trays. Ryan's grandmother had broken her hip and gone into surgery, and everyone was checking in on their text thread. Ryan had just checked in and said she was recovering in the hospital, in good spirits and praising the hospital's pain medication in particular.

Nora wondered if she should try to make a batch of his grandmother's favorite Taiwanese pineapple cakes but instead promised to send her polvorones when she had a moment to breathe, though it didn't feel like that would be anytime soon.

She placed the last batch of pastries on the tray and

covered it with foil. She would dust them with a sprinkling of powdered sugar once she got to the venue. If she did that now it would soak into the warm dough and she'd have to dust them all over again. She checked the clock and took off for a quick shower back at her apartment as Hector and Astrid loaded the van.

Nora would rather stay at the store, but as La Islita's future owner she needed to get used to being front and center during catering jobs.

"Who knows?" her mother said as they got home for the shower. "You might be running the place sooner than you think, and I can retire somewhere in Culebra."

Nora rolled her eyes. As if her mother would ever retire. "You'll be working there until you can no longer stir that giant caldero spoon."

"True, that's why I have you. You can stir, and I'll just supervise." Her mother laughed as she entered her room. "Salgo rapidito."

Nora closed the bathroom door and pulled off her dirty clothes, a dusting of flour littering the ground as she did. Her hair smelled like frying oil; it usually did on catering days when they all took turns dipping morsels of food into the oil. But it bothered her recently, how it followed her. No matter how many times she'd shampoo, the smell of oil clung to her.

Nora hopped in the shower and scrubbed everything away. Catering was good for business, and business was good. Good enough to keep Nora busy, and more tired than usual. She worried the summer would pass her by as she filled in orders and plated food. But what if it was more than just summer that passed her by?

She tied her hair up in a bun so tight it made her scalp hurt, but it looked professional. For a moment she fantasized taking her scissors and cutting off the bulk of her hair until a halo of wild curls adorned her head, too short to be pulled back. She imagined the curls bright pink and smiled. Pink hair felt like her—even though she knew her mom would hate it.

Her mother knocked on the door, reminding her of the time. She stored away the pink-haired Nora for another day.

LOOKING HAPPY WAS exhausting. But it only took one slip of your face for someone to call you surly or tell you to smile, so Nora made sure to always set her face in a pleasant way as she continued to reload the trays and walk people through each of the items on the table. She wasn't sure how many times she could list every single ingredient in a dish and made a mental note to tell her mother they should print out ingredient cards for the next event to avoid these sorts of questions.

"Excuse me," said someone to her left as Nora reloaded the tiny cups of tembleque on the dessert table.

"How can I help you?" Nora said instantly, wondering

what question it would be this time.

"I just want to say that this is fucking delicious," said the lady, who was maybe in her late twenties. She placed a hand over her mouth. "Sorry. Didn't mean to curse. What are you, like, fourteen?"

Nora sighed. "Seventeen."

"Well, Seventeen, these are amazing." She took a sugary bite of the pastelitos de guayaba, leaving a trail of powdered sugar along her top lip. "This is my third one. What do you put in them?"

Nora handed her a napkin for her lip. "A lot of sugar."

The woman nodded and finished off the pastry. "This might be rude, but could I steal the recipe? I would love to have my students try and make this."

"Your students?"

"I'm a pastry chef."

Nora perked up and for the first time took a real look at the woman. Her long black hair hung past her shoulders, and her eyes were bright green and kind.

"Where do you teach?" If it was here in Denver, maybe Nora could pop in for a class.

"Out in San Francisco."

"Oh." Too far then. "I've never been."

"It is by far the most expensive of the cities I've lived in," she said with a laugh. "But it's home for now. I don't stay in one place for long without getting restless. I'm Cassie, by the way."

"Nora," she said, shaking her hand. "Where else have you lived?"

Cassie grabbed another pastry before listing off locations: "New York, Vegas, and now San Fran."

So many amazing places. "That's a lot of cities."

"Yes, but it was worth it. I'm not sure where I would've been if I hadn't traveled around. Probably a lot more bored and boring."

Cassie kept going, musing over her summer in Paris, while Nora's mind buzzed with possibilities. What things would Nora learn if she went to Paris? New York? Even back to Puerto Rico? New ideas, that's for sure—ideas that stretched outside of La Islita's culinary reach.

"Do you bake?" Cassie asked, making Nora fidget a bit. If you'd never been to La Islita before, you'd think Nora was just an employee and not the brains behind the entire dessert menu.

Nora nodded, pointing to the pastries on Cassie's plate.

"Really?" Cassie was visibly impressed. "That is talent, girl. Can I hire you?"

Nora blushed. "Family business, sorry."

"Did you create this recipe yourself?"

"Have the burn scars to prove it."

"Okay." Cassie's grin couldn't be wider. "Are you sure I can't steal you?"

"I'm sure."

"That sucks," Cassie said. "How old are you again?"

"Seventeen."

"So you are what, a junior?"

"Going into my senior year."

"I better brush up on my skills before you get out in the world, then," Cassie said. "So I can be some sort of competition."

Nora's smile faltered. She wouldn't be out in the world. She'd be right here in Denver. Cassie pulled out a business card and wrote something on the back, handing it to Nora.

"You should look these places up. I learned some of my best skills at these programs, and I can only imagine what you could do with them."

Nora stuffed the card into her back pocket, and Cassie excused herself, returning to the engagement party. Nora went back to refilling trays and stacking empty pans in the back, all the while the card burned a hole in her back pocket.

I can only imagine what you could do.

l to wait until the summer and after the SATs t
live in, meeting at least twice a week to tackle Jess'
s: past tense, present tense, vocabulary, with a littl
David's own syllabi in the mix. Last week he gave Lee
of *Relato de un Náufrago* and asked her to read a
of chapters by today to discuss.

etting through," she replied. "It's not bad . . . but not
ither. I've been googling a lot when I get lost."

o shame in that." Her father nodded, tossing the tat-
copy of the book back on the bed. "I'll let you finish
he arrives. Oh, and Lee." He paused by the open
"Keep the door open, please."

Really?" Was he serious? This was David they were
g about. Jess's twin brother. Her mind flashed to his
for just a moment.

Really."

SPENT THE moments before David's arrival cleaning
r room. Her dad had almost caught the pros and cons
nd she couldn't let another incident like that happen.
opened her top drawer to stuff the notebook in but
ed for a moment, eyes locked on the album she'd hid-
away.

She'd ignored it all this time, not really understanding
. It would be easy to drop her notebook on top and
et about it again. But maybe she could be brave today,
nly for a second.

LEE

THE PROS AND cons list had not grown aside from the one note in each column since she'd started it: knowing. The rest of the page was mostly dotted with splashes of ink like Morse code from when she'd intended to write more but never did. She didn't try to draw out the paths again either. Because, really, was there more to it than that one word that held all her fear, worries, and hope? She moved it to the side, and opened the bookmarked browser windows she'd saved on local Huntington's support groups.

The fact that she had looked into them made her feel better about the stagnant list.

There was a knock on the door and her dad poked his head in.

"When is David coming over?" He made a motion

asking if he could come in, and she nodded.

"An hour." Lee closed her laptop. "You still going out?"

"About that . . . I know I said it was a friend thing." Her father sat by her desk, hand resting too close to the notebook with the opened page. Way to forget, Lee. Luckily his eyes stayed on her as he spoke, and Lee did the same. If she pretended it wasn't there maybe he'd never notice. "It is a friend thing and well, sort of, get together with a work colleague, Denise, I don't know if you remember, or if I've talked about her. She gave me that grilled cheese tip and the goat cheese salad recipe"—she noticed he kept fidgeting with his hands—"the one where you bread and fry the cheese so it is nice and warm over the salad."

"Dad, you're babbling." And not paying attention to the notebook, she noticed with relief. "Let's move to the bed before you break my desk."

He nodded, and they both shifted to the bed, but not before Lee closed the notebook just in case. Her dad took a deep breath before blurting it all out. "Well, Denise is very nice and well, I asked her out on a date, which I know I said was just a friend thing, but I wasn't sure how to tell you about it, and she is a friend, but today is less of a friend and more of a date thing, though I suppose it can be both."

Finished, he crossed his arms over his chest but then seemed to think better of it and placed them on his thighs.

"So you're going on a date?" She needed a moment to process now that she wasn't thinking about her father

seeing the contents of the open n

"Yes."

With Denise of the grilled che

"Does she know?"

Her dad took a deep breath for the question, any questions, b to answer them.

"Yes. Yes she does." He reache it. "I'm not going to forget your me

Lee concentrated on her father, ried of how she would react. It re given her and her mom. Of how m how much he deserved to be happy. no idea how to address the emotions of a future or happiness didn't mean to. "You should go on your date."

"Are you sure? I can cancel."

She mustered the best smile she c to do cartwheels over it, but I don't w

From the smile on his face Lee k right decision. Her father deserved thi be. "Okay, well . . ." His eye caught s moment Lee thought she'd left someth about the testing, but when she turned she relaxed. It was just the book Davi their first lesson.

"How's the reading?" He reached f

decide
really
syllabu
bit of I
a copy
couple

"
great

"
tered
before
door.

"
talki
smile

"

LEE
up h
list
She
pau
den

why
forg
if o

She sat at the base of her bed and opened it. Her breath caught, a smile spreading as her fingers touched the image of her mother, so young, so alive. She was standing, hands cupped around her belly, her smile warm and her cheeks full. Full of life.

"Lee?" Her breath caught at the voice. David stood in the doorway, shoulders shrugging in apology. "Your dad let me in."

She set the album aside, and he walked in.

"Family album?" he asked.

"Yeah. I mean sí." She corrected herself.

David smiled, eyes warm as he sat next to her. Their shoulders touched for a moment before he adjusted to give her space. Lee found herself wanting to close that space again. "Do you want to see?"

His eyes searched hers. "Are you sure?"

She thought for a moment before answering. "Might be easier to get through."

He nodded. "Then yes."

Lee opened the album on the photo of her mother holding her belly; the following was a photo of Lee's dad and her mom as snow fell around them.

"My mom loved Christmas in DC. She was obsessed with all the old movies with the magical Navidades with the snow. I always found it kind of overrated. Whenever it snowed everything just shut down, which was weird because it snowed every year, so you'd think they'd prepare."

"Do you miss DC?"

She used to think there were too many painful memories in DC, woven into every street: the route they took to the doctor's, the corner store for her favorite snacks. But each visit back to visit Auntie Rose was less and less painful.

When her mother died Lee and her father shot to the opposite ends of grief. Where Lee tried her best to let go, to forget, her father fought to remember. Where they told her to hold on, they told him to move on.

"Sometimes. I miss my family there."

They flipped the pages to birthdays and first memories. A small envelope held a clipping of Lee's hair, her mother's notes faithfully detailing each addition. First haircut. First ice cream.

Lee touched her own hair, bringing a strand to the photo, matching black for black. She pointed out the slow breakdown of her mom's penmanship. "She started this when she was diagnosed, see?" The penmanship was rocky, tilting up. "It became harder to hold a pen, or anything really. . . ."

Little Lee grew bolder and bolder on the pages, climbing trees, dressing up for Halloween with her mom and dad. As Lee grew bolder, her mother faded.

The penmanship by the photos changed to her father's and the photos themselves were now less of Lee and more of the three of them trick or treating, out to dinner, as many of them smiling and happy as her father could find.

The final photo was a sleeping Lee, curled next to her mother in the medical bed, hands linked. She didn't remember when it was taken, but there had been many moments like that.

David shifted next to her as she slid the album toward her desk. "Thank you for sharing that with me."

She wasn't sure what to say to that. "You're welcome" didn't feel quite right, so instead she twisted around and reached for the book, changing the subject.

"I like the book, by the way."

"Really?" He brightened.

"Some of it is confusing but yeah, kind of scary in parts." She shoved her leg under the other, then changed her mind and straightened it out again. All nerves.

"Right?" he said. His entire body was animated as he talked. "When he's floating out at sea talking about all the creatures that were passing below him."

"Terrifying." Lee shivered at the thought of being lost at sea, floating in the ocean as life passed underneath you unseen.

"Exactly. I loved it. Really just that section, everything else was fine, but the thought of not knowing what was swimming underneath you when you are all alone. The ocean is a scary place."

"Is that why it has all those cracks in the spine?"

He smiled, rubbing the back of his head. "Well, it was my dad's before it was mine. He had to read it in school."

"Oh—was it his favorite too?"

"You know, I asked him that once, and he didn't even remember he had the book at all. I just found it on his shelf when I was bored one day." He shrugged.

"Oh."

"Yeah, story bummer."

"Totally—I was expecting a story of father and son bonding."

"Not even close. I think it did more harm than good." He laughed, his eyes settled on her in a way that made her want to be close yet far away from him at the same time.

"So, I guess we should start with the lesson. . . ."

Before the silence stretched any longer.

"Right." David pulled out a bunch of papers from his backpack. "I figure we could do a little conjugating and maybe vocabulary, as scintillating as that sounds. And then I brought a movie."

"A movie?"

"Yeah." He handed Lee the DVD; it was a kid's movie. "This is a full-service tutoring program, plus it's a good way to listen to accents and cadence. Also it's a movie so it feels like you're slacking off when you're really learning."

She laughed, handing the DVD back. "Okay, let's start then."

David was a gentle teacher, which, as it turned out, was what she needed. Whenever her tongue tripped on a word, she panicked, a thousand condemnations coming to mind. She wasn't good enough. She could never do this. Each word felt like a test between what would let her down faster: her tongue or her brain.

But while her own mind criticized, David simply smiled and encouraged her.

"This is a good start," he said as they took a break and settled into the movie. They sat side by side and thoughts of her faulty tongue vanished when his knee touched hers and didn't move. It was hard to follow the movie when all she could think of was moving her leg and keeping it still at the same time. She tried focusing anywhere else and landed on the open drawer, one end of her notebook poking out. Not helpful.

"Everything okay?" David paused the movie, shifting to look at Lee. "You seem nervous."

"I'm fine," she said too quickly, her voice carrying more than she wanted. We're so used to the weight of emotions we don't notice we carry them everywhere. "It's kind of a long story."

He shrugged, rearranging himself so he could give her his full attention. "I like long stories—especially trilogies."

"It's not—" she said with a shaky laugh. "I guess it does feel like an epic. Just one I can't seem to talk about."

"Then don't say anything. You don't have to."

"And just sit here in silence?"

"I don't mind." He leaned in like he was whispering a secret, and she found herself unable to look away from his eyes. They were a deep warm brown under the longest lashes she'd ever seen. "Particularly in this company."

"Right." Lee could feel the flush traveling up her neck.

She stuffed her hands between her thighs, pressing them together until the blood slowed. She was afraid to look up, knowing that David's gaze hadn't shifted, and she liked it.

They sat in silence as Lee filtered through her emotions, telling her body to rein itself in. There was so much happening today: her dad, the album, the resolutions, and now her body was going haywire.

"I'm just wondering how to make a decision I'd rather ignore."

More than one decision if she was honest. More than one thing she was now trying to ignore. "What happens if you ignore it?"

She let out a breath. "Nothing and everything."

"Like Schrödinger's cat."

"What was that again?"

"The one about the box with the cat that could be dead or not dead at the same time because the box is closed so both possibilities are correct. . . . I think."

That was exactly it. She could test for HD and know, while if she didn't either future was still possible. She could kiss David and know what that felt like, or not and stamp down whatever was happening now.

Lee pulled at her hair, which reached down past her shoulders in one long French braid.

"I just keep confusing myself the more I think about it."

"I do that all the time." David reached up, taking her hand in his. "Sometimes it's easier to put things away until we are ready to deal with them."

"I don't know if I'm ready." She stared down at David's hands in hers, how they felt so anchored. "I don't know if I want to be ready."

"Is this about your mom?"

Yes and no, but Lee simply nodded.

He licked his lips. "I think you're amazing, and I think you can do whatever it is you need to do, and just because you didn't figure things out right away, who cares? It doesn't work that way and anyone who tells you differently never lost someone." He cleared his throat and dropped Lee's hand reluctantly. "Sorry—got carried away."

"I liked it." She clasped her hands together to stop them from reaching for his again. Why was she stopping herself when they'd felt so good?

"I just . . . don't apologize for taking the time you need. You don't . . . you don't need to—"

Lee watched David stumble through his own words, noticing the flush to his cheeks, the way he no longer met her eyes. She felt warm all over, and the feel of his body so close gave her goose bumps, melting every other trouble away. Why was she fighting this? Why was closing herself off so much easier when this felt so good? She'd wanted her dad to be happy, why couldn't she be too?

"I'm just saying, um . . ."

Her body was already leaning toward his. Her eyes following the curve of his lips and the way his hands inched closer to hers. Don't hide, she thought, feel, want, need. You can have this. "Can I kiss you?"

He exhaled. "Fuck yes."

They reached for each other at the same time. His lips were soft and welcoming. Lee felt his hand caress her face, cupping it as he pulled at her bottom lip; it sent shivers down her spine. Good decision. She did the same with his, wondering if he felt the same shivers. When she pulled away, he smiled against her lips, his fingers trailing down her neck.

"Right, that was . . ."

A very good decision. Her body echoed the sentiment.

"Not part of the lesson plan."

They laughed as Lee reached for him again.

So much for open doors.

RYAN

RYAN WAS BLUE today—not blue as in sad, blue as in calm, blue like the vast ocean. Blue that felt endless and lost; blue that bled into the sky and strained your eyes till you no longer saw the line dividing it; the blue of a long sigh, of a breath released.

"Okay, everyone." Candace clapped, getting everyone's attention. Ryan wondered what the prompt would be today. "We're doing portraits today. I know, exciting."

Across from him Blake, who was taking the same summer course, arched a brow, drawing a smile from Ryan. He'd been trying his best not to treat Blake differently after the museum, but every now and then he'd notice the curve of Blake's jaw or the flakes of clay that stuck to his skin. And his skin would flush and he'd forget what he was about to say. Then there were moments when remembering their kiss made Ryan think of Jason, which was infuriating and ridiculous.

There were a few moments where Ryan was sure Blake was going to bring up the kiss and ask what was going on between them, but he always made sure to keep their conversations to painting. Ryan was a mess that didn't know who he was or what he wanted. Blake didn't deserve that. But he didn't feel like talking about it yet.

"You're probably already thinking about doing one of your mom or that super-cute barista you've been meaning to ask out. Well, tough luck. We're doing self-portraits."

She might as well fail him now. A self-portrait? He hadn't attempted a self-portrait in years. The last one he'd done he'd hated within months of finishing it. Why was it so much easier to capture someone else on canvas? At least in a regular portrait assignment he could try and get his grandmother that second painting she'd wanted.

Or even . . . a portrait of Jason? They'd texted earlier today, catching him up on Ryan's grandmother. They'd talked until Ryan forgot they'd even broken up and Jason had to run to his internship. They made no plans to meet up—Ryan hadn't been strong enough to fail again.

He was imagining the palette he'd use for Jason's portrait when Candace broke into his thoughts again. "I know. I'm a monster. How could I assign a self-portrait? Isn't there a bowl of fruit or meadow somewhere that needs painting? I'm sure there is, but I want to see you. Not the you that I see every day, because to be honest, I don't know you. So I want you to take that good ol' blank canvas and show me yourself. And I don't just mean here's a face, I mean *you*. If you is your dog or your favorite shirt or, heck, a pretty meadow, then do that. But you better make me feel it. Use whatever you want. You've got the whole week for this one." She smiled. "So take your time."

Could he ask for a year's extension?

Candace came around, so he leaned in like he was studying the canvas instead of wishing for its untimely death. He pursed his lips, blowing out a breath. He ran a hand through his hair, long enough to tuck behind his ears now. Jason had loved his hair; he'd close his eyes and run his hands through it before pulling Ryan's mouth down to his.

He would draw Jason straight on like a classic portrait, eyes boring into him, so blue they hurt.

Another time, apparently. He filtered through the piles of oils, searching for inspiration in tones of blues, greens, titanium white, before realizing that he was picking out the colors of Jason's eyes.

Stop thinking about Jason. You are more than Jason.

In response his mind reminded him of the green just at the corner of Jason's eyes and the soft plush of his lips.

Who are you?

He looked down at his hands, specks of paint stuck to his skin. Last year around this time his arms had been clean, untouched by paint, too busy traveling up shirts and pulling Jason's body closer or holding his hand in the dark of a theater they'd snuck into.

This is unhelpful.

How would his grandmother see him?

Ryan smiled, remembering the framed portrait he'd made when he was just thirteen. It hung proudly in her living room, the perfect location to show it off. What would that Ryan paint? He'd do a straight-on portrait no doubt—a confident Ryan with a smile on his face. But that Ryan was gone.

Which Ryan was left?

"Okay, time's up for today," Candace announced. "See you all Thursday. You can leave your canvases here or take them home if you want, just please clean up your stations." Ryan stared at his blank canvas. He'd be back here tomorrow to help at the studio, so he could technically just leave the canvas here, but he decided against it. Maybe tonight he'd feel inspired and work on it at home.

THE COFFEE SHOP was packed, but Ryan and Blake managed to snag a wobbly table. "In a way the blank canvas IS me." Ryan turned the canvas around so he wouldn't have to look at it anymore. "So technically I have completed my assignment."

"Congratulations. I'm sure they'll hang it at MoMA." Blake sipped his iced coffee, a smile flashing on his face.

Ryan shot him a look. "We are no longer friends." He swirled his own iced coffee until he was certain all the caramel syrup was evenly distributed.

"How's yours coming along?"

Blake had left his piece in the classroom since he'd be going back tomorrow for another class on sculpting. He'd gotten so good over the spring and the teacher had encouraged him to continue into the summer. "I have some ideas, just trying to figure out if they're physically possible."

"What do you mean?"

Blake pulled out his phone. "I have this idea about using painting like a sculpture on the canvas." He slid Ryan his phone with a series of photos to slide through of other painters who used paint like clay.

"That looks amazing." Ryan slid the phone back. He couldn't help but feel a little jealous that Blake didn't seem to be struggling with his portrait.

"Why don't you make a list?"

"List?"

"Of things you like, things that are important to you, your family, your friends. It might be silly, but it could lead to something." He took another sip of his coffee. "You have to find your heart and paint it all over the canvas."

"Can you find your heart if it's broken?"

"Is it?" Blake said. "Make the list. Doesn't hurt to try."

FAMILY.

He wrote on the paper as he started his list. A safe place to start.

Ryan was his family. He was his mom and dad. He

was Katie. He was his grandmother. He was his Taiwanese and Puerto Rican heritage equally, regardless of any back-handed comments. He was his lu rou fan with a side of tostones. He was gay. He'd been in love.

He was still in love. . . .

He was broken.

He was a heart that still tugged to the past, tethered to a boy who didn't think about him like that anymore.

Or did he? Should he ask . . . ?

He went back to the list, trying to push away each thought of Jason that popped up even as they kept coming.

He was heartache.

He was empty.

He was insecure. A hand that still paused before it reached for pencil or brush; that still second-guessed and chided.

He was skin that missed Jason's touch and a mind that quickly obliged with memories of him.

Who are you without him?

He was a boy who did not know.

"What are you doing?"

Katie bounced in, oblivious to the goings-on in Ryan's mind. As she hopped over a pile of dirty laundry, her long braid swung back and forth in an exaggerated way.

"Knock."

"Door was open." She pointed to the list. "What does that say?"

"Just a list. Did you do your language homework?"

"Yes." She rolled her eyes. "A list of what?"

"Me?" When she scrunched her face he tried explaining further. "I have to draw a portrait of myself and I'm not sure where to start, so Blake told me to make a list of who I thought I was."

"Did it work?"

"Not yet."

"You can draw me instead if you want?" Ama taught her well. Katie swung her braid to the front, tugging at the strands. She was already so tall for her age, just like Ryan had been.

"It's kind of an assignment so I can't get out of it."

"Okay . . . ," she grumbled. "Want to draw a dinosaur?"

"What?"

"Let me show you."

She bounced out of the room coming back with a dinosaur coloring book. The kind you bought in line at the grocery store or pharmacy. It came with a three pack of waxy crayons that glided cheaply over the paper. Katie also brought her favorite box of crayons as well. "See, you connect the dots to make a dinosaur and then you color."

"I see. That's pretty good."

"It has puzzles too, in the back. Do you want to color?"

"I'm . . ."

"You said the list isn't working, so maybe you need a

break. My teacher said breaks are good when you are having a hard day."

He was having a hard day. Katie pushed the box of crayons on his lap placing the coloring book between them. "You can rip out the pages, see? So we can color at the same time. You want to do a T. rex or the bronto . . . brontosaurus?"

Ryan smiled, putting the list away. Maybe a break was just what he needed, or a different assignment. "Which one do you want?"

"The T. rex. I want to make him purple."

He carefully ripped the page and handed it to Katie. "That leaves longneck for me."

They traded crayons, Ryan sticking to shades of green for his while Katie giggled, coloring hers shades of purple and orange. All the while he thought about the list and the question: Who are you?

JESS

HOW LONG COULD Jess watch the fan above her head, twisting in her sheets, rearranging herself until her body finally listened?

It wasn't listening to her much lately. Jess shifted to her left, placing a pillow between her legs to lessen the ache she felt. No, ache was the wrong word. She knew ache, ache could be alleviated. Ache was familiar; this was new. This was skin that disliked the feel of fabric against itself that tightened sheets around her body. It was bones and muscles that felt restless even after a long run, like they could not get enough even as her heart begged her to stop.

Restless, yes, they were restless. She pressed her thighs into the pillow and shifted to her right, pulling her hair away from her neck, though it was already soaked. Every part of her wanted to run, even with how tired she was. Her legs pulsed, speaking of the paths they could go, the things she could forget if she just moved and never stopped moving. Jess closed her eyes. She read if you kept your eyes closed and body still for ten minutes you could fall asleep. She tried to keep her body still, and it hurt; her skin itched, and she could hear a mosquito buzzing by her ear. She flinched and started again. She just needed ten good minutes, just ten good minutes.

Her bones felt dull, like lead sinking into the bed. Not the sinking as you fell into sleep, not like that at all. Jess wrestled out of her sheets, pushing them to the bottom of her bed. She pulled her knees to her chest, feeling the muscles in her thighs stretch. She couldn't run to appease them, but maybe this would help. She lifted one leg toward the ceiling, and flexed, then the other. The dullness was still there. Out of her bed she paced around the room, clearing space for the yoga mat that Nora gifted her. She placed the dozens of college books, library books, and notebooks in loose piles, taking a moment to note that her room had never been this messy before. The piles made it feel like hers again.

She unrolled the mat and sat cross-legged, and stared out to her room, breathing in and out like Nora taught her, her body taking her from pose to pose until she was flat on her back and the pain in her bones was soft enough to ignore. She wished Nora was there guiding her through, her voice a calm focal point as she corrected Jess's form, then stepped back like a proud mama. Jess sat up and checked the clock: 1:05 a.m. Maybe someone would be awake right now. She reached for her phone on her nightstand, then set it back. She didn't want to wake anyone if they weren't already up.

She brought her laptop to her bed and logged into her chat. No Lee or Nora, but Ryan was idle so there was a possibility. She sent a message, testing the waters, and waited. No response. She drifted from site to site, not sure what she was looking for.

2:00 a.m.

This would bite her in the ass in the morning. She pulled her book from her nightstand, flicking on her lamp. Jess read until her eyes hurt and the words made no sense no matter how many times she read them. Plunged back into darkness, the burn in her eyes eased, and she pulled the sheets over her body again.

3:15 a.m.

Jess pressed her face into her pillow and pushed at the bed's backboard, relishing the sound of the wood bending to her strength. There was an itch on her back, could she ignore it? How long would it take for that itch to make her body scream? Jess made her hands go limp, trying for the magical ten minutes again. Please, please, please.

3:49 a.m.

There was no burn in her eyes. The darkness only helped

them feel refreshed. Great. She stared at the changing light outside her window—the sun not yet up but the occasional passing cars painted light across her walls. She bolted from her bed, attacking the itch on her back first, then the piles on her floor. Rolling the yoga mat, she flipped on a lamp and organized the piles.

She opened up her calendar schedule, staring at the color-coded masterpiece. Practice. Volunteering. Local college visits. All in there. Even the possible college course her mom was throwing around was in there—she'd be thankful to have those credits checked off once she was in college, after all.

The longer she stared at each task the more her head swam. People had a summer break, right? Some people at least. She'd even scheduled in hangout time now because everyone was so busy or tired or grumpy that they were barely seeing each other lately.

Weren't the resolutions supposed to be bringing them closer?

Further into the calendar was a bright-yellow spot. The party.

She couldn't think about that now, but she marked a date in her calendar to start prepping for it. That done she started adjusting dates, the center had gone from two days a week to four—Jess was so helpful after all, could she find some time to come and help? Yes, yes, of course she could. At the beginning helping had felt good; she loved seeing her contributions come to life, but now there was so much. Her mind spun again. There were so many more notes in her calendar now: start thinking about this. Don't forget to do that.

Figure out books for community center, she wrote in her calendar. It was getting harder and harder to find books because half of them had to be bilingual or fully in Spanish. Jess had cheated a bit by reading the same bilingual book at the end of each class to close out the read along, but parents would eventually notice.

She needed more time to do some research, which, contrary to what people thought, wasn't what every teen wanted to do over the summer, even Jess. The class was scheduled for one hour but was more like three between the setup (who doesn't love props? Turns out: Jess) and waiting for parents to drop off and pick up their kids, because for some reason parents equated story time with free babysitting.

When Jess had told her mom how tired she was after one week of story time, she'd smiled and pointed to Jess and David, saying, "Try it every day."

"Touché, Mami," Jess had replied, and pushed through it. She'd been doing that a lot lately, pushing through the day, not allowing herself to feel overwhelmed even as her heart quickened and she needed more and more moments alone, sometimes in a utility closet where she had to pretend she needed something when someone found her. No time to feel or breathe. Maybe she could schedule that in too?

College, she thought, peering at the stack of books by her desk. She was supposed to share them with David after she'd taken a look, but she kept pushing them farther and farther away like they were at the edge of a cliff. She wrote: "Finish list, set aside dates to visit top five. . . ." Her parents wanted her to apply to their alma maters, so make that top seven. Yay, resolutions.

She remembered another thing and cursed, the words echoing in her room: "look into more scholarships," underlining it twice.

She'd meant to do it weeks ago—what was wrong with her? Jess wanted to fling the laptop across the room, her throat suddenly burning—this wasn't like her, to forget something like that. Hadn't her mom reminded her? She let out a breath and set an alarm on the event, declaring the research her priority for the week.

She glared at the dumb college books, her leg shooting out for a kick, watching them tumble to the floor. Then she picked them up again. She had a headache nestled between her eyes, and she rubbed the spot with her fingers, feeling the oil on her skin. Disgusted, she washed her face, scrubbing until her skin was raw.

4:30 a.m.

Her running schedule looked overwhelming, but it actually kept her sane. She broke down the hours in a day: hours to sleep. Hours to eat. How long do I take to shower?

Time at the center, time studying, researching colleges, maybe she could give herself another day off? How many hours of sleep did she need? If she went by tonight, not many; her heart was speeding up by the second.

Finally she circled back to the party. It didn't have to be super complicated, just drinks, snacks, loud music. . . . How bad could that be? She added a preparation schedule into the calendar in bright blocks of yellow when another thing popped into her head: the AP classes. She'd signed up for three. Why would anyone do that in their senior year? Oh yeah, Miss Anderson had thought she should pump up her course schedule the first semester, and Jess had said yes. And then came the class elections, how could she forget that? Push it aside, she told herself, push it aside, that's months away.

The light started to bother her eyes, she'd never had a migraine, but maybe this was one.

"Focus, focus."

She listed what she thought she needed for the party, making a mental note to show Ryan, Lee, and Nora. Later she hit the button that showed her a three-month period displaying rainbow colors. She pinched her nose as little whispers started.

You are drowning in a sea of your own making.

The colors started to bleed together.

I can do this, Jess told herself. She felt the tears welling up and blew her nose on the hem of her shirt as she sat up straight. Good luck, her thoughts echoed. "I don't need luck. I don't need luck." She closed her eyes, goose bumps sprouting all over her skin as her mind ran over the tasks she'd prioritized for the week, finding that the repetition made her heart pick up the pace.

5:30 a.m.

She left her room and settled on the couch, wrapping a blanket around her body. She watched commercials for magical knives that cut through bricks and food vacuum sealers that saved you thousands until her father came down the stairs, a little less of a zombie than his daughter.

"Up early." He yawned, heading to the kitchen and filling up his travel cup with coffee made the night before. He took a sip, making a face before sealing the lid.

"Couldn't sleep?"

"Yeah."

"Wish I had your stamina."

"On call?"

"Yep. I know, I know, how did I get so lucky?" He grabbed his house keys and gave Jess a peck on the head. "See you later. Te amo, Mija."

"Love you."

Jess pulled the blanket closer, returning to the vacuums and knives until her mind stopped yelling and her body gave up.

Her eyes were closing when she heard the alarm in her room go off, alerting her that it was time to run.

NORA

NORA WAS ON a beach in Puerto Rico at sunset. Palm trees dotted the shoreline and the wind tangled in her hair. She knew it was a dream, since moments ago she'd been kissing Beth in her bed and now they were both walking along the shore of a beach with sky-blue waters.

She'd been to Puerto Rico twice, both times before La Islita demanded so much more of their time. Nora could barely remember the visits, though when her mother spoke about them she did so with a certainty that those memories should last Nora a lifetime.

Nora could almost taste the salt in the air as she opened her eyes. She couldn't bring herself to move, which was usually the case when she was in Beth's bed, but her parents would be home soon.

"Do you have to put your clothes back on?" she asked Beth, who was walking around her room, picking up everything Nora had just moments ago taken off.

"As much as it pains me, yes." Beth grinned as she tossed Nora her clothes and watched as she pulled them on. "Do you have any idea how unbelievably sexy your hips are in those jeans?"

"What, these old things?" Nora motioned to her thighs that wiggled as she pulled up her jeans. "You are the only person on earth who loves this muffin top."

Beth smiled, tugging the loop in Nora's jeans until they were close enough to kiss. "I love everything about you." With a quick kiss Beth pulled away. "Now get dressed before my parents get home—I really don't want the talk again."

"But the last one was so awkward, how could you not want it again?"

Beth giggled as Nora's phone buzzed. Beth reached over to check it. "Your mom."

She tossed it over. Nora read the message and frowned.

"What's up?" Beth asked.

"I'm needed back. So much for some time off. It was a beautiful thought while it lasted."

Her hands shook just a bit as she shoved her phone in her bag and quickly put on the rest of her clothes. She felt the gentle brush of fingers on her waist and turned to Beth.

"You want me to come with you?" she asked. "I could help."

Yes—a hundred times yes. Just looking at Beth made her feel better sometimes, but if she was needed back so soon it meant the shop was swamped and Nora needed to go into overdrive to get through the day. The less she had to think about, the better.

"No. It's okay. I'll text you later."

"Promise?"

"Yeah, promise."

Beth kissed her like she could give her whatever strength she needed, and Nora soaked it all up, grateful for every ounce.

LA ISLITA WAS packed, with a line running out the door.

"¡Finalmente!" her mother said when she came through the mass of people. She tossed Nora an apron and shifted out of the way so she could run the front of the house.

"What's going on?"

Her mother was all energy and high spirits. "Apparently this website said we were hot shit and well . . ." She motioned to the line.

"Which website?"

But her mother had already disappeared, leaving Nora to deal with the line. She boxed order after order of quesitos, masa real, and meringues; ladled cup after cup of asopao until her wrists hurt. It wasn't long till they were out of a few items and customers had to wait or pick something else if they wanted to leave with anything. Nora, Hector, and her mother traded off front of house duty as each was needed back in the kitchen. Pastries were flying off the shelf so fast Nora was serving them hot out of the oven. By the late afternoon she'd added one more guayaba paste burn to her arm as she tried to arrange them neatly on the tray.

It was still three hours to closing when someone gently tapped her on the shoulder.

"Excuse me."

"Yes? What would you like to order?" Nora asked. Pen, paper, and smile at the ready.

"I already ordered."

"Oh." Nora's mind was usually a steel vault and could remember each customer's order, but as she stared at the guy's face she completely blanked. "I'm sorry. We are just a bit slow right now with the rush. What did you order?"

"I ordered the flan de coco, latte, and the medianoche, but I'm fine waiting. I actually wanted to ask you something else," he said with a smile. "I write for the local newspaper and was doing a piece on local restaurants and particularly the people behind them. Wondering if the owner was here and had a moment for a quick chat? Or we can set something up for another time."

"Can you wait just one moment?"

"Of course!"

Nora dashed to the back to find her mother who then ran to the bathroom to fix her hair, change her apron, and meet the reporter. They stepped outside to talk, and Nora pulled a batch of baby flans from the oven.

The crowds slowed down to a manageable pace, and Nora no longer had to hand out pastry boxes with a "careful, it's hot" warning at the end. She put a fresh batch of besitos de coco on the display shelf when her mother returned.

"Nora, fix your hair," her mother said. Which was not an unusual thing for her to say. "They want to take our picture and interview you."

"Me? Why me?"

"Because you are part of La Islita."

"So is Hector. Why isn't he fixing his hair?"

"Ay, no seas chistosa." Her mother started to pull the tie off her hair and fix Nora's curls. "Go and change your apron, answer a few questions, then they'll take our picture."

Once she was presentable Nora stepped out to meet the reporter on the bench just outside the shop.

"My name is Cristian, by the way." He stood, extending a hand as Nora sat next to him. "I should've introduced myself earlier."

"Nora," she replied.

"Thank you so much for taking the time to speak with me." Cristian took out his phone, turning on the recording app as he spoke. "I'll be super quick, so I don't take more of your time, and just dive into my questions. Is that okay?"

"Sounds fine."

"How long have you been working here?"

"La Islita has been open for ten years, so . . . ten years."

"So you grew up working here?"

"Pretty much." She smiled. "I do my homework behind the counter when it gets quiet."

"Doesn't look like it ever gets quiet." Cristian eyed the line.

"This is a bit unusual for us, but it's great." It wasn't. She wanted the old pace back even though it meant less customers, less money for La Islita. But that was wrong, right? She should want more days like this . . . shouldn't she?

"Your mom told me you handle the desserts here. That's kind of a big job for someone so young, does it ever get daunting?"

"Sometimes," she said with a smile. "Depends on school, but I love to bake. It's what keeps me calm."

"Where do you pull your inspiration from?"

"Well, we are all about classic Puerto Rican flavors," Nora said, channeling her mother. "We want you to feel like you are eating at your abuela's house when you come here, so we stick to desserts that remind us of home, like flan and tres leches."

"Have you ever wanted to try something new?"

A million times.

"Sometimes," she said with a smile that would hopefully brush away any further questions, "but those experiments only make it to my friends."

"Well, I'm totally jealous." He tapped something into

his phone. Nora shifted in her seat, looking behind her to where her mother stood behind the counter. Maybe she should've skipped that question altogether. "So, you grew up working here, and it seems like you also have your postgraduation plans figured out with college and La Islita." Nora nodded, of course her mother would've said something. "It might be safe to say that this shop is your whole life?"

"Um . . ." Every part of Nora wanted to say no just then. No, this was not her whole life.

"Sorry, that was a leap, of course you have school and friends, so it's not your whole life. I'm just a little amazed by your dedication and your love for this place and want to make sure I capture it correctly." When Nora nodded again, he continued, picking his next words better. "Have you ever thought of doing anything different?"

No, she was about to say, but instead what came was: "Yes."

Wait, don't say that out loud.

"I mean, no." She tried to laugh it off, to find something funny to defuse the moment with. "Depends on how tired I am."

When Cristian laughed she exhaled. "Right."

"But no, not really," she continued. "Couldn't even imagine what that would be like."

You could try.

"Final question, if you could recommend one dessert

from La Islita that people should simply not miss which would it be?"

"My mom would say it's our budin, but it's actually our flan. People forget how good flan can be, and ours reminds you."

AFTER NORA WENT back to work, the interview was still on her mind. Had she ever thought of a future outside La Islita? What would that even be like? No matter how hard she tried her thoughts came back to these walls, to her mother, to that damn counter.

Maná serenaded her through the speakers.

Her mother's favorite music to think to; she found it inspiring. Maybe it would inspire Nora now. As the beat picked up she pictured herself on the beach again with Beth. That could be a future, couldn't it?

No. As much as she loved the image, it was not a future. She could travel, just like Cassie. She closed her eyes, imagining herself in Paris or New York, learning new techniques and discovering new ingredients. The image lasted only seconds until Paris became Denver and the walls around her became La Islita again.

Cristian was right. It was her life. It was all she knew.

She felt her mother's arms around her, as her head rested on Nora's shoulder.

"Hoy fue un buen día," her mother said.

Nora nodded. Her mother tugged at Nora's hair,

pulling at a particularly annoying tangle, then ran her fingers through and sighed.

"You didn't tell me how the interview went?"

"It was good."

I have no life, but yeah, good.

"Bueno, I can't wait to see what it will bring. Can you imagine?"

Yes, she could. Days at La Islita, that she could imagine, that her mind needed no help with, but anything else? Apparently that was too much to ask.

THAT NIGHT, WHEN Nora closed her eyes and pictured herself back on the beach, she wondered if she even knew what the Puerto Rican sun actually felt like. Would she ever? Did she want to go to culinary school? Would they even accept her? She tried to imagine herself in an apron in a classroom, but it simply wouldn't stick. Nothing stuck. Nothing stuck but the damn bell from the front door, and an oven that took two tries to turn on. Did she truly want a life outside La Islita if she couldn't even think of what she wanted to do?

In the other room her mother yelled.

"We got another wedding!"

And they would have another and another and another. Her future was written, but did it have to be? NO, her mind screamed, but what? What would that future be if not La Islita?

Frustrated, she headed to the bathroom to splash some water on her face, fixating on her reflection.

Where are you going? Where do you want to go?

Blank. Nothing. It was like reaching into the darkness and finding nothing there. She pulled her hair down, letting the curls cascade around her face.

What do you want? Is there anything you want? ANYTHING?

She wanted Beth. She had Beth. She wanted her friends. She had her friends. She skipped over the La Islita question, as it wouldn't be helpful. What else?

She ran her hands through her hair and stopped, examining a strand.

I could have this. Her mother would be angry, but . . .

Sí. I can have this.

THE NEXT DAY they gathered in Ryan's room, huddled around Nora like they were about to commit a crime.

"Are you sure?" Ryan asked, mixing the bowl of hair bleach.

Beth hovered behind her, offering a thumbs-up while Jess and Lee watched from outside the bathroom.

After she'd made the decision she thought she would wake up and change her mind; backing out like she'd done so many times before this. But she hadn't. Though the morning brought no solution to her thoughts on La Islita, it was resolute about this decision.

She'd always wanted this, so why not? It was the clearest image in her head, and she wouldn't let it go again.

Maybe, just maybe, this new pink-haired Nora would bring with her a new future.

"Do it," she said, her voice firm.

LEE

LEE LIKED SPENDING time with David. She liked how easy
it was to talk to him. She liked the way he looked at her
when he thought she wasn't looking. That he leaned forward whenever she talked, and he texted her nerdy things
at night just because. That he lent her his favorite book
even though she guarded her editions like a bank.

After the first kiss, and the second, and the third, they'd
gone from meeting twice a week to three times a week.
For the lessons of course. And they were going well. Lee
remembered more than she'd given herself credit for, and
even though her brain would sometimes blank on a word
only to find it minutes later, it bothered her less and less.
And then there was David . . .

Each session started out well as they dutifully went

over vocabulary and whatever book they were reading, but soon they devolved into long conversations about comic book storylines and anything that came to mind until her knees bumped against his or his gaze focused on her and her breath caught. Then their tongues practiced different things, and her skin flushed, her hands slipping through his hair until a text or the sounds of keys on a lock shocked them apart.

It was so easy with David. When they were together nothing else got through, her body was so busy pulling and touching and reaching that she had no time to think about resolutions or test results. It was too busy living.

Lee felt flushed when she thought of the time her father almost caught them: she'd lunged for her shirt all the way across the room, while David reached for the nearest pillow and opened the book they were supposed to be reading. She couldn't even remember the name of it, but Lee remembered the way her legs twined with his and how he'd lifted her on her desk, her legs straddling his waist.

"Oh my God!" she said to herself. She really needed to get a grip—she could barely read a sentence without thinking about David. She closed the book she was reading (*Cien Años de Soledad*) and tossed it on her nightstand. "Something bad happen?" Her father popped into her room, his presence like an ice-cold bath compared to the thoughts she was having before.

"Huh?"

"Heard you say, 'Oh my God.'" He pointed toward the book.

"Oh—no, it's dragging. I was just . . ." Remembering the boy I was making out with just days ago . . . in my bed. "Spacing out, I guess."

"Hmm." When he sat on her bed all thoughts of David evaporated. "How are the lessons going?"

"Bien." Lee tried to keep her mind clean, but her mind felt wicked, flashing images of David's hands traveling up her thighs until she could feel them again. Later, she told herself. "I think the book thing is working, instead of going over syntax and stuff. Feels less . . ."

"Boring?"

"Academic, I guess? Like I'm not trying to pass a test or anything, just remember what my brain forgot, or shut out . . ."

Her mind quieted, following instructions. She leaned her head against his shoulder.

"Did I say I was proud of you already?" he said.

"Yes." She groaned. "Don't make it worse."

"I can get mushy if I want to." He squeezed her hand. "Hey, you know what?"

"What?"

"It's been a while since you and I had some hangout time together. How about I order us some pizza and we watch one of those movies you like?"

Lee perked up. Her dad hated her taste in movies, which

revolved mostly around horror, science fiction, and fantasy. "Really?"

"Really."

She narrowed her eyes. "You going to make it through a whole movie?"

He laughed, nodding. "Just keep the blood to a minimum, please. I'll handle the grub—meet you on the couch in ten minutes?"

Lee sifted through her movies, looking for the ones with the least gore in them, until she found one her father just might be able to watch. Prepping the film, she plopped down on the couch and waited for her dad, a smile creeping on her face. It had been so long since they'd done this, she'd almost forgotten how good it felt to spend time with her dad with no expectations. Back when her mom was still alive, they'd have movie nights like this, just the three of them.

Her phone buzzed; it was David:

Solo diciendo hola.

She felt a sudden lightening of her heart. She texted back:

Hola.

When her father settled in beside her she couldn't keep the smile off her face, making him smile as well.

"Good?" It felt like less of a question and more of a statement. Or maybe both. As the movie started she waited for the sadness, for the memories to come back and hurt, but they didn't. Though she missed the time spent with her mother curled on the couch watching her favorite films, the memories didn't sting. As she curled against her dad she knew they weren't forgetting her, they were honoring her.

"Good," she said, and it felt true.

RYAN

LEE FIDGETED. NORA giggled. Jess was quiet, eyes drifting far above Ryan. They'd all sat unofficially for portraits before in one way or another, usually while hanging out, then been told to stand still while Ryan's hand flew over the paper. Ryan had drawn Lee in the past, carbon outlining the curve of her lips or the look in her eyes. But she'd never sat for Ryan on purpose until now.

"Is this okay?"

She wiggled her fingers at him.

"Stop moving," Ryan chastised. "The sketch will be blurry."

Lee rolled her eyes, a move Ryan wondered if he could capture on the page. He added another curl, and another, until the Lee on the page was an echo of the one that stood in front of him.

Good, he thought.

The spring and summer classes had blown the cobwebs from his bones, and though there was still a hesitation, still moments when sections of paper were rubbed raw with doubt, today had been a good day.

Enough to make Ryan forget about the self-portrait that still plagued him. And not just him. There were so many fellow students who hadn't finished the assignment that Candace gave them "as long as they needed" to finish.

He wouldn't think about that now. He didn't need the doubt. Instead he focused on the task that Candace called "Mix and Match." Three portraits, each requiring a new approach chosen to match the subject.

Lee would be watercolors, which he hadn't told Lee. He could not explain why but there was something about watercolor that felt right for her, a combination of gentle and striking that embodied his vision of her.

He took in every angle he could until the weight of her hair and lift of her lips came naturally. His hand felt at home, gliding over the pages, watching another Lee come to life, almost like he'd never put down the pencil in the first place.

"Is it ready?" Lee asked, trying to sneak a glimpse of the portrait.

He flipped the sketchbook to face her. "Take a look."

Lee smiled. Good. "What now?"

"Now you both disappear and I paint." He rubbed the

graphite off on his jeans . . . or into his jeans. "I need to yell at this thing on my own."

"We can see it once it's done, though?"

"Obviously." Or he'd burn it . . . either/or.

Nora popped up from Ryan's bed where she was reading. "God, you are such a demanding muse," Nora said to Lee before turning to Ryan. "Don't worry, I'll be nicer when you paint me, and of course my mom will want to frame it."

"I'm honored." Not thinking about the possibility that it would be up on the walls of La Islita where people could see it and shit.

"When do I get to pose again?"

"Later." He waved them away. "Okay, muses, time to leave me to my demons, or whatever dramatic shit people say."

"Demons is pretty good." Lee helped Nora up. "Let us know if you need a break, I can bring you a coffee."

"Un cafecito." Nora nodded.

"Some joe." Lee's lip quirked.

Back to Nora. "Java."

He had to stop them before they kept going.

"Okay." Ryan pushed Lee out of his room.

HE SPREAD OUT the sketches until he could look at each one head-on. Lee looked at him from each sketch, a delicate balance playing across her face. Ryan wondered if she knew how much he could see in her eyes: her compassion, her worry, and something new, close to happiness, but more like satisfaction. It teased at her lips.

Ryan settled his watercolors, sending a silent thank-you to his grandmother for the colors that shone from their containers. Stepping away from the paints, he lay on his bed, strumming his fingers on his stomach when his phone buzzed. It was Jason.

> Jason: How is your grandmother doing?

His heart did a little shimmy.

> Ryan: Better. She's pushing herself a bit too hard and talking about planning her next trip.
>
> Jason: Nothing can slow her down! She's incredible.
>
> Ryan: Pretty much. Wish I was like that.
>
> Jason: Me too. Let me know if you need anything, OK? I know I'm Mr. Summer Internships and can't be relied on for anything, but I'm here.
>
> Ryan: Thanks!

Ryan wasn't sure what else to say. He typed and deleted his message so many times he wondered what Jason was thinking on the other side. His grandmother would never be this confused. She'd dive right in and say just what she wanted with no hesitations.

But there were so many things. He'd wanted to ask Jason for a friend-date the last two weeks but had never been able to form the words. He also wanted to send Jason some of his work and maybe even invite him to the current plague of Ryan's existence: a gallery show.

A damn gallery show. He'd even kept it from the girls, specifically Jess. Earlier that week Candace had announced there was a gallery showing open to students in the winter. There weren't many slots available, so anyone interested—she'd said that part straight to Ryan—should sign up immediately. She'd followed it up with a group email.

Blake had signed up and then continued to text Ryan about it every day since the announcement. Still he danced around it, sitting on the thing for a week, convincing himself that there were no spots left, so what did it matter?

In a move that was part procrastination, part self-hate, Ryan checked Jason's feed. There were two new photos.

Two.

Ryan swiped through them. The photos were annoying, the faces too happy, too fake. This was the college life that would be too hard on a relationship? Whatever he hoped he would find in the photos, whatever justification he needed, Ryan couldn't see it.

He should text him that: Why?

Until the answer satisfied him.

Why?

Until it made any sense.

Instead Ryan went back to the sketches, to the eyes staring at him in unison.

He filled several cups with water, wetting the paint: black, brown, white, blue, green, then red, so many choices to work with. He started with the dark brown of Lee's skin, layering until the paper soaked in the paint, echoing the rich umber. He made her cheekbones sharp, popping out of the paper, and added red to her lips.

Her tight curls took in shades of black and strokes of blue, defining the tiny curls that haloed her face. Lee had worn her hair loose today. He added a hint of green to her brown eyes, like the echo of a lush forest and a wash of yellow all around her.

Ryan stepped back. "Not bad."

It wasn't a lie, and his heart flushed with a pride he hadn't felt in a long while. But not only that, he looked down at the other Lees waiting for the brush, and all he wanted to do was dive in. He tackled them one by one, mixing new colors and combinations, excited to watch the colors interact. Ryan left one sketch unpainted and set the others to dry. His fingers ached, and the jars of water resembled mud puddles after a rainy day.

Tired but satisfied he opened up his laptop and read the email one more time.

His heart sped at the thought of the exhibit, of people seeing and judging his work. But he could always pull out—give some sorry excuse. He shook his head, not ready yet, and dove toward his paints, organizing his supplies in a way that would make Jess proud.

Ryan ironed out the next portraits: he would use pastels for Nora, to capture the eternal fae nature in her smile, the feel of sunshine that radiated from Nora at her best. He formed the image in his head, pushing away the growing fear that the exhibit was a horrible idea and he'd never finish that damn self-portrait and held on to the emotions the current portraits brought forth.

What else?

Her smile would be the focus, then you'd notice her eyes, and the way her short pink hair curled against her cheeks like a silent-movie star. A style that fitted Nora's no-fuss attitude. His fingers itched to start right then.

Where had this itch been these last few months?

Keep going.

Jess would be acrylic, bold colors that required a quick hand on canvas. Would he paint her as a blur? Flashing across the canvas, long tawny legs claiming the path in front of her. Ryan hesitated. Something about the oils called out to him, something in Jess's nature called for the patience of oils over acrylic.

Yes, he thought, oils are better.

He thought of painting her face, brown eyes looking straight at you, but his mind rejected it. There was something about Jess lately, making him think you shouldn't be able to see her eyes, not fully. That something hid behind them. He made a mental note to think more about it later.

He was smiling, he realized. Actually smiling. His hand ached from working all day, but it was a good ache. One that would reach for the brush again if he let himself. A hopeful ache.

His second resolution rang in his head: show your work.

For the first time in a very long time, he felt like maybe he could do that.

Seizing the feeling, he opened up his computer and replied to Candace's gallery-show email, asking if there was still space. Her answer came almost instantly:

Yes. Took you long enough.

He felt a rush of anxiety but tamped it down. He could do this; he could believe in himself as much as others did— it was only fair, right? Ryan sent a quick text to Blake and the girls. Blake responded with a photo of giant bear giving a thumbs-up, making Ryan laugh and the anxiety disappear just a bit more. By the time it was officially in Jess's calendar, his grandmother had also sent a series of odd emojis announcing that she would be there, hip or no hip and to make sure he invited the entire Denver Taiwanese community or she would.

There was one person left. One message left to send. Would he ride this wave of confidence and send it?

And if he did, if Ryan invited him to the show, would he even come? Not only had Jason never cared about Ryan's art before, but the summer was riddled with failed date attempts. Still, he needed to talk to Jason, to sort out his heart. He needed to see him in person.

He sent the image of the flyer with the text:

Absolutely terrified, but excited! Want to come?

Ryan waited for a century for the reply, though actually it was more like a minute.

Jason: That's great! Not sure if I can make it, but I'll let you know.

Ryan's heart faltered for a moment before recovering.

Ryan: Sounds good. Would love to see you but no worries if you can't!

His art was not tied to Jason. No matter how hard his damn heart tried to convince him that it was.

JESS

WHERE WAS HER notebook? She'd put it down for one minute and now it was gone. Half of her scholarship research was in that thing. All around Jess little kids ran amok as they waited for their parents to arrive. Only a few minutes ago they'd been semi-angels while Jess read to them, but as soon as she closed that book it was anarchy.

Early in the summer Jess had tried to calm them down after they got like this, but eventually she learned that it was best to let them run until their little legs couldn't carry them anymore.

"¡Elena, dije que no muerdas a Miguel!" Jess shouted as the little girl tried to take another bite out of her friend. What was it with kids and biting?

She spotted her notebook among the chaos and rushed

to pry it from a little boy's hands before he colored over her meticulous scholarships notes even more.

He smiled up at Jess, not caring about the hours she'd spent jotting down specifics and due dates.

Breathe.

How many times had she told herself that today?

She hid the notebook behind the mini library and waited as patiently as she could for each of the parents to come retrieve their children. It helped to stay active, to pick up stray crayons and wrappers from half-eaten granola bars, even though every time Jess picked up one thing the kids dropped five new things on the floor.

But she couldn't sit. Sitting made her anxiety travel up her spine like an itch. It made her squirm in her seat and her hands fidget until they found something to do.

It was an hour later on the dot when the last child was picked up. He left kicking and screaming, declaring he never got to do anything fun EVER.

Jess waved goodbye, already tucking away the toys he'd been playing with just moments ago.

Finally.

She just needed to wipe everything down with the strongest disinfectant known to man and she was free until she had to set up for the weekly domino game they'd recently introduced.

But first things first, she snagged her notebook, locked herself in her mother's office, and turned off the lights. She felt her way to the chair and placed her head on the table, relishing the quiet.

Then deep breaths until she no longer felt the need to run out of the center and keep running until her legs gave out.

Though her body could use another ten minutes in the dark, her mind reminded her of everything still waiting to be done. Fumbling for the switch, she flipped the lights back on and found her laptop.

Between the time Jess had put down her notebook and when she'd found it later, five pages of scholarship notes were colored over. Some were still visible, but one particularly ambitious drawing had ruined a page to the point that it was impossible to figure out what was once on it.

She thought of turning the light off again so she wouldn't be able to see all the wasted work. She should've just jotted things down on her laptop from the beginning, but the notebook was a lot lighter to keep on her as she was running around the center.

This is all your fault.

She'd have to redo most of whatever was on that page.

Placing her hand on her face she took three deep breaths, reminding herself that she could worry later and just get things done now. She stretched out and tackled the pages she could still read. Opening her laptop, she wrote down scholarship requirements and deadlines, pausing to double- and triple-check them online. Once confirmed she added them to her calendar, blocking out times to write her essays and ask for letters of recommendation.

Rolling her shoulders, she started a list of teachers and people at the center she could ask for recommendations and made notes as to which scholarship each letter would be better for.

Jess ignored the gnawing in her stomach as she added task after task to her punch list. Each time she wrote one deadline down she thought of ten more things to add to the list; every thought a never-ending string of reminders.

Think smarter.

She would save time by writing one central essay and adjusting for each scholarship.

Good.

The ruined research page was a mess of black and brown crayon, but she was able to suss out what had been on it from a previous scholarship list she'd made. Now she only had to look up deadlines and requirements all over again.

"Jessica!" She heard her mother at the door. "¡Abre la puerta!"

Saving her work, she quickly opened the door. "Sorry. I was hiding."

"Did you get all your work done?" Her mother came in, dropping a folder on her desk.

All the work? Not even close. She still had to research the scholarships from that ruined page. Once those deadlines were in her schedule, she had to start writing the essays. A thought that made her just a bit queasy. What would she say? Between all her work at the center, research, and track, she could barely keep one thought in her head for more than a panicked minute before they spiraled into a thousand other thoughts.

"Almost!" she replied.

"Do you mind helping me set up early?" her mother asked. "You are free to disappear once we are all set up."

"Really?" Her mom always asked her to stay for domino night to help clean up after.

"Really. I'll ask someone else. You've helped enough today, and I can tell you're tired."

Jess stood up straight. She felt tired, but she thought she was hiding it better than that. "I do?"

Her mother nodded, placing a hand on Jess's cheek. "This place has a way of making even the strongest person tired, Mija."

"I could use more time to look into scholarships." Like a hundred more hours in a week.

"Then let's get going!" They left the office. "The faster we set up, the sooner you are released."

They carted out the folding tables and chairs, spacing them out on the main room of the center. Each table got four chairs and a set of dominos. When that was done they set up a table for drinks and snacks brought in by the players.

"In record time!" her mother declared, turning on the salsa music over the speakers. "You are free to go."

Images of the productive night ahead swam in her head. She would get so much done. But once she reached her room, it didn't take more than a few minutes for her body to give up on her and for her eyes to close.

Jess passed out, sleeping through the whole night for the first time in two weeks and right through her alarm for work at the center.

NORA

THE BLINDFOLD WAS a little itchy, but Beth assured her they would be there soon. She kept her hands folded on her lap even though all they wanted to do was tug at the little pink spirals that haloed her face. Each time she thought of the decision to dye her hair pink there was a rush of energy and pride.

She could feel it all the way down to her heart that she'd made the right decision. The certainty was what kept her going despite her mother's silent-treatment tactic that was now on its second week. Nora could still see how her eyes widened and her shoulders squared when Nora revealed her hair.

But still, something had clicked into place with the change, and no silent treatment would deter it.

"Where are we going again?" she tried one more time, but Beth had been very good about keeping the secret.

"I'm not going to slip up," Beth said. She had picked Nora up just ten minutes before for their anniversary date, blindfolded her, and refused to tell Nora where they were going.

"Come on," she lowered the timbre of her voice. "I can keep a secret."

"Cute. But we are actually here. Stay in the car for a second." She heard the slam of the door before she could reply. Almost a minute ticked by before her own door opened. "Sorry, had to make sure the valet didn't give it all away."

Beth held her hand and helped her out of the car so she didn't bump her head as she exited.

"I keep thinking I'm going to hit someone." Nora kept one hand out even though she trusted Beth to guide her forward.

"I'll keep you safe," Beth said. Nora heard a door open and the hum of many voices just out of reach. "Here we are."

"And where would that be?"

Beth untied the blindfold. Her gorgeous smile was the first thing Nora saw before following Beth's finger, which pointed to the sign right above them.

"Holy shit."

How on earth had she managed this?

"EL CALDERO? Oh my God. You—" Nora squealed,

immediately placing her hands over her mouth. "Are you serious?"

Beth nodded. "Happy anniversary!"

"How did you even?"

El Caldero was the hottest new restaurant in Denver, and it was notoriously hard to get a table, not to mention pricey.

"I have my ways," Beth said.

"Which are?" If anyone would have restaurant connections it would be Nora, so how did Beth even manage this?

"Constantly checking, calling, emailing for a table until there was a cancelation and voilà!" Beth bounded up to the door, holding it open for Nora. "Our evening awaits."

NORA WAS IN awe. The tablecloths, the fancy wooden chandeliers, the damn forks—everything was amazing. And the food hadn't even arrived yet.

"You are hopping out of your seat," Beth said across their table.

"This is just—" She couldn't contain her smile. "So amazing. You are amazing. I can't believe you did this. I love you, you know that?"

Beth reached across the table and kissed her. "I love you too."

Their meals arrived, and she shimmied in her seat with each new bite of food. Fresh avocados drizzled with sweet balsamic glaze, garlic roasted chicken with a side of mushrooms Nora had never seen in her life—everything melted in her mouth.

"Saved room for dessert?" the waiter asked.

They ordered three: crème caramel, Eton mess (which Beth insisted they try after seeing it on a British TV show), and a scoop of their homemade chocolate ice cream.

The crème caramel melted in her mouth, and she stopped herself before she pulled the plate away from Beth to snag the silky dessert for herself. The play on textures from the Eton mess had Nora bubbling with new ideas for how to re-create it for La Islita with different flavors and fruit. She ignored the little voice reminding her it wasn't a traditional dessert and dove into the ice cream's chocolate bliss.

"This is heaven," Nora said, certain of it. "I have three plates of dessert in front of me and the most beautiful girl in the world."

She felt Beth's foot under the table, firm against hers.

"Ditto," Beth replied.

"This night is perfect. Thank you," Nora said.

"There's more," Beth said with a wicked grin, her eyes traveling somewhere behind Nora.

When Nora turned the waiter stood right behind her with an arm outstretched.

"Come with me, the chef is ready for you."

The chef is what? Nora swung back to face Beth. "What?"

Beth was already up and waiting for Nora, a little dance in her step. "Part two of your gift. And I have to say, I kind of outdid myself with this one."

The waiter led them past the tables and through the double doors that led to the kitchen, all the while Nora's heart kicked up in speed. Stepping through the double doors was like entering a new world. She'd been in a kitchen for most of her life, but this was a KITCHEN. It was more than twice the size of La Islita—front and back of store— and packed with busy cooks putting out dish after dish in this beautiful synchronized choreography of sharp knives and fresh herbs.

They stuck close to the walls as they were led through to the back, the scent of caramelized sugar awaiting them.

"Beth?"

Beth squeezed her arm. "Just wait."

They approached a woman placing the final touches on a giant chocolate cake that looked like each slice would weigh at least a pound. When she saw them she smiled and rushed forward.

"Which one of you is Nora?" the woman said.

"Me?" Nora said.

Before she knew it she was hugged by a woman twice her size. "I'm Yan. That must mean you are Beth!"

Then Yan and Beth hugged. "Do you have any idea how many times this one emailed me about you?"

"No." Knowing Beth, a lot.

"She even sent over that article they did on your restaurant recently."

Nora's eyes widened even as Beth smiled. "Oh God."

Yan laughed, motioning them forward. "Let me give you a tour."

As they walked in, Beth leaned close to Nora. "I thought it would be cool for you to meet her—she's the head baker here."

Though she was slightly embarrassed that Yan had seen the article, the fact that Beth had put all this together made Nora's heart swell with love. "You are amazing."

"'Tis true."

Yan walked them through the kitchen, showing Nora how she and her team whipped up dessert after dessert. "I mean, I don't have to tell you. You know what it is to be covered in sugar all day."

Nora could fly out of El Caldero right now with how happy she was. Yan continued to prepare each dessert as orders came in, but still made time to commiserate with Nora about the daily grind of restaurant life and small tips and shortcuts that Nora could try. Eventually Nora talked about the notebooks filled with recipes where she jotted down ideas and experiments.

Yan approved, revealing she had her own notebooks. When Yan asked what they'd thought about their desserts, Nora raved, going on about the textures and how well the flavors played together.

"I even thought of doing it a little different," Nora confessed. "Particularly the Eton mess. Try some Caribbean flavors."

Delighted, Yan listened to Nora's ideas. "That sounds delicious. I'll make sure and stop by La Islita to try it out."

Nora's heart skipped a beat. Yan wouldn't be able to stop by La Islita to give it a try, as that dessert would never make the menu . . . but maybe Nora could bring it by one day and see what she thought?

Not as good, her heart replied. If she was truly the head of La Islita's dessert menu, shouldn't she have a say in what went on it and how it changed?

"How did you—" Nora asked. "End up here?"

"Oh"—Yan leaned against the counter—"that's a long journey, but the short version is I was a banker, hated my job, but loved baking, so I decided to switch careers. I moved to California to study at the Culinary Institute and haven't looked back since."

Culinary school. That's the second time Nora had met someone who went to culinary school.

"Did you like culinary school?"

"It's like love and hate together." Yan laughed. "It was tough, but I learned so much. I absolutely became a better pastry chef because of it."

The thought wormed its way into her mind—maybe that was something she should look into? An entire place dedicated to learning and experimenting and discovering new things.

That is what I need. Her heart wrapped itself around the idea, holding firm.

At the end Yan gave both Nora and Beth a giant hug goodbye, a fourth dessert, Yan's personal email address, and a promise she would visit La Islita soon.

Nora left with her arm wrapped around Beth, still walking on air and with a new idea to look into.

LEE

THE SUMMER FELT breathless. Time flew by in a flurry of tangled limbs and heated moments. Of hands brushing back hair and late-night messaging. Of small moments that filled out the rest of the day, though they lasted only minutes.

It felt good. She felt strong.

Like she'd forgotten there was more to her body than the possibility of a future betrayal.

But she still hadn't told Jess about David. She told David they would do it at some point, but it never felt like Jess had any time—which was true, Jess seemed to have more to do in the summer than she did during the school year, but that wasn't the whole truth.

If Lee thought hard enough, she would see it was all

connected: whenever she was with David she forgot about the possible future, the way her body could be weak and vulnerable, and what might lie beneath the surface. It made her forget about the test. If Jess knew about the relationship, she would see that. She would see that Lee was hiding, because she was right, Lee did need a push. It was so easy to slip back into the shadows, to ignore, to walk back down the path rather than move through the fork in the road.

And David . . . would he see it too?

DAVID HAD FOUND Lee some graphic novels in Spanish, and she was finishing the final one when her dad sat across from her.

He cleared his throat. "I wanted to talk to you about something."

She sat up, putting the novel on the floor. Her mind was already cataloging the many horrible things that could be wrong; she started with the least likely one.

"You break up with Denise or something?"

"What? No, no, everything is fine. She's a lovely lady."

Lee smirked at her father's wording.

"Too old-fashioned?" he said.

"Very."

"Well, there's nothing much to report. We have a nice time together and—"

"Please don't say anything gross."

"Francheska Lee." His tone became more amused,

which was good; it meant whatever he had to say was not truly that bad. He must be being cautious.

"I'm just saying, there's such a thing as too many details."

"I wasn't planning on it." He pulled something from his pocket—a DVD disc in a plastic cover. "Don't know if you remember that old camera I lugged around everywhere we went."

"Oh God." How could she forget; it was like a third arm. She'd hated it, she was pretty sure it had captured some of her worst moments. "It lives?"

"Barely, but, well, you know me, had to take a look. I found some old memories and had them transferred to a DVD. I thought it might help." He handed it to Lee, who turned it over in her hand.

"Help?"

"I was dropping some laundry off and I noticed your notebook on your desk. It had a pro and con list. I didn't mean to pry, I swear. . . ." His shrug was apologetic, even though it was Lee's fault for not hiding the notebook again.

"Dad . . ."

"Let me just, let me just get it out." He took a breath. "Your mother and I never really discussed you being tested. She would start the conversation, but I—I couldn't handle it, I couldn't handle thinking what was taking her away from me could take you too, but . . ."

Lee didn't know if she wanted to hear this, but her

mind was working too slowly to stop it.

"We argued about it a lot—when we could still argue, that is.

"We shouldn't have wasted so much energy fighting, but your mom wouldn't let it go. Whenever I thought we'd swept it under the rug she'd bring it back up again, until she couldn't anymore. I never wanted to listen. I regret that." He squeezed her hand, thankful she still sat by his side. "I really do."

"Okay."

"I don't know if you remember when she was diagnosed."

She didn't, she was just three when it happened. But the diagnosis had echoed for many years after that, to the hollow of her mother's eyes, to the quiet times she'd shut herself away in her room for days. To the moments everything seemed fine, but for a pause, a quick jerk of an arm, or a tumble down the stairs, and her mom's eyes would well up and she would leave the room. Lee never told her she could hear her crying through the door.

"Not specifically, a lot of it is a jumble."

"Time will do that."

Time. She wished she could go back and tell herself to remember everything. Not to get frustrated when her mom knocked something over or angry at friends and family who didn't know what to say when they visited. Not to waste time on jealousy over a different life, because she loved her mother more than anything in the world.

"The time leading up to the diagnosis was stressful. You were a fussy child," he said, giving Lee a soft smile, "and our first, so we made up a lot of excuses in our minds. If we thought about it long enough we could find a logical reason behind everything. Her irritability was just a bad day, dropping things was just clumsiness from being over-tired. . . ." Lee squeezed her dad's hand and shifted closer. "There was no history we could point to—we didn't know your mom's estranged father had died from HD as well. We wasted time, we wasted time, but we didn't know until there was just the truth and the truth had no solution."

She stared at her father's hands, remembering how they helped her mom out of bed and pulled her up on the sofa after she'd slid down. How her own mother's hands danced through the air as if to a song only she could hear. It was called *chorea*, and her mother had no control over it.

But they were a team. Lee and her father would trade meal duty, Lee feeding her mom breakfast while her father handled lunch and dinner, until they could no longer do it alone and hired a nurse.

Paula Maria Perez-Carter died of pneumonia after ten years with the disease. Her immune system was so compromised, that's all it took.

"We caught it so late," he said.

Caught was the wrong word; catching it early wouldn't have done shit. "What would that matter?"

"I, well, we'd have had more time to prepare, maybe."

"I don't think you can prepare for something like that. I think knowing would've just made it sadder sooner."

He looked up at her, eyes sad. "Is that what you think?"

"Yes."

He nodded. Lee knew it wasn't the answer he'd wanted, but it was all she had. "So that's on your con list?"

She nodded.

"It's a big one," he said. "Knowing and the burden that comes with it."

Her body felt so tired, her throat ached with unshed sobs. She waited for more from her father, but when he didn't speak she asked, "Do you want me to take it?"

"Would you believe me if I said I have no idea?"

"Yes." She closed her eyes, leaning into him. "Because that's how I feel all the time. I'm both all the time. I want to know, and I don't. I want to forget, but my mind flicks back to it like an itch."

Every time she felt irritated or she dropped a glass or she stubbed her toe, she had a moment of panic. Every teenage mood swing was a symptom, a clumsy moment a confirmation of the life that awaited her. Maybe she should just get tested and finally get an answer, but who really wanted an end date?

"I don't want to know how little time I have. I don't want an expiration date just yet." Tears finally rolled down her cheeks, and when she met her father's eyes they echoed hers.

"I wish I could make the decision for you. I really do."

He pulled her close, wrapping his giant arms around her. Lee disappeared into her father's hug. "But I know Paula would want me to tell you this. Even in her saddest moments your mother always found a way to hold on to the positive. Do you remember the way she used to laugh about, well, nearly everything?"

Yes. Her laughter would echo all over the house, casting away any gloom.

"It astounded me," her father continued. "And don't get me wrong, she struggled. You know she struggled, but she fought for every ounce of her happiness, no matter how hard that disease tried to rip it from her."

It's why we celebrate her birthday, Lee reminded herself. Each year of her life was a blessing, and after her death they would continue to celebrate it.

"And because she's not here to tell you, I'm going to." He held her closer as Lee took a shuddering breath. "Find the light, baby. It's hard, I know, but you already know the darkness—you've researched it and, more important, you've seen it firsthand. Now look at the other side of taking that test. You can't let this thing take over—you can't let it have every damn bit of you."

He released her with reluctance, wiping the tears off his eyes as he made his way out the door.

"What if I do have it?" she said. He stopped and turned.

"I'm going to spend the rest of my life taking care of my daughter, no matter what."

When he left, Lee couldn't stand the echo of sadness in the room—the silence heightened the slow desperation that grew with each heartbeat. Find the happiness. She didn't know how to find that in the test, not yet, but she knew where to find it now. Grabbing her jacket and phone, she headed out of the apartment.

LEE HEARD THE thunder off in the distance, looking up at clouds that had blanketed the sky, eliminating the sun. Of course she hadn't brought an umbrella. It was too late to go back now, plus she needed to burn the uncertainty out of her mind for the moment. She turned as the first drops of rain fell, and pulling out her phone, she sent a quick text and kept walking, her feet onboard with her desired destination.

The sloppy drops soaked into her shirt, dripping down her back and cooling the heat in her skin. She concentrated on the sound of her shoes slapping on the sidewalk as she turned down the familiar road.

Lee knew she was crying and turned her head up toward the sky, letting the rain sting and mix with her tears. She hated that her mind could easily bring up the worst but struggled to find a happy memory. Her feet ached when she arrived; she couldn't tell the difference between herself and the rain. She knocked, the door opening instantly.

"I got your message," was all David got out before Lee stepped in and kissed him, feeling her body lean in, demanding more.

"What's wrong?" He gathered her in his arms as her lips found his again.

Lee took his hand and led him to his bedroom, tiny pools of water forming behind her.

"Lee . . ." David dropped her hand and hovered by the doorway.

She held out her hand, waiting. With only a moment of hesitation he followed her in and closed the door.

Maybe it wasn't fair to David to use his lips to push away the hurt. To let the feel of his hands on her hips eviscerate the thoughts of her future, a future so full of uncertainties and so out of control. But she needed it. When their skin touched, she felt alive, she felt possible.

David's shirt was wet from holding on to Lee so closely; it clung to his chest as she pulled it off. Hers landed with a plop on the floor, releasing her from a chill she hadn't noticed until now.

David's chest against hers was so warm she clung to him as his lips trailed down her neck. They tumbled toward the bed, hands tripping over zippers. She unclipped her bra and let it slide to the floor, taking deep breaths as David's eyes traveled up her body to meet hers.

"Are you sure?"

She tucked a strand of hair behind his ear. "I'm sure."

His lips engulfed hers as his hands slipped down her underwear, flirting with the heat in her body until it reached to the sky, breaking into a thousand stars to reassemble down on earth. David kissed down her neck, bringing her back to the bed and his arms. She teased his lips as she pulled down his jeans, feeling his heartbeat with every trail of her kisses. She didn't mind the awkwardness of naked body against naked body, of that gasp of a new sensation, and she focused on the touch of his hands and the look in his eyes as he broke into a million stars and gazed at her like the sun.

JESS

JESS WAS USUALLY early even when she tried to be late, but these last few weeks no matter how hard she tried, something always got in the way. She either slept through her alarms, got pulled into helping someone at the center, or got so involved in researching scholarships and deadlines that she lost track of time. Today was the first time in a while she'd managed to be early to anything.

Grateful for her time alone before Beth arrived for their run, she watched the sun rise above the massive trees that had populated the area for hundreds of years. Jess loved running here; there was something about the rattle of leaves as the sun pushed through the night that quieted everything. A little piece of magic. She was counting on the magic to quiet her mind once again, which started to push back whenever she tried to stomp down the worries.

Just as she found a new way to settle down, her mind pumped the worries back up again, mocking her. How would she survive senior year if she couldn't get through the summer? Two weeks left. Practically a ticking clock of incomplete tasks and looming deadlines.

Her body ached to start running, to silence the echoes in her head. She looked down at her watch; only five minutes had passed, but it felt more like thirty. Beth should be here by now. She tied and retied her laces, stretching by a nearby bench. She focused on the feel of her muscles pulling and bending, her skin flexing until it felt like it could tear. Jess dropped down into a downward-facing dog position and let her body loosen even more. Her muscles felt so much better after a few moves. She lifted her right leg up to the sky, then the left, when she heard the crunch of gravel behind her. Beth waved from the driver's side.

"Hey! I'm not super late, am I?"

"No." Jess twisted her torso to the left, hearing something pop, which pleased her. Then she twisted to the right. "I was early."

Jess parked herself on the bench, waiting for Beth to stretch, glad that no matter how late she'd recently been, Beth was always happy to adjust and switch up their running dates. Sometimes Jess wondered if Nora even knew how lucky she was to have her. She had to be the sweetest girl in the entire school. Then again, she was lucky to have Nora.

Beth tightened her long, blond hair in a ponytail. Jess's own dark-brown hair was contained at the top of her head in a giant bun, the streaks of blond highlights Nora had convinced her to get shooting up toward the sky, a halo of flyaways surrounding her head. Her hair was flat and wavy this morning, which was pretty good for her hair, even if the strands all headed in different directions.

Jess leaned her head back and cleared her mind, pushing away the passing of time and deadlines that always lingered at the corners of her mind. The sun streaked across the sky, illuminating details previously hidden in shadow. She focused on the dense of green in the distance, her mind wandering. The farther away they were, the more the trees looked like paintings on a canvas.

"Can you believe summer is almost over?" Beth said.

She could. She hadn't been able to forget it.

"Passed by so fast." Jess crunched the gravel below her feet, pressing it farther and farther into the earth, and hopefully her anxiety along with it.

"How fucked-up is it that we'll be seniors in a month? That is RIDICULOUS."

Jess nodded. She didn't want to think about everything that followed the party. Senior year, college applications, running for Student Council president . . . the first bead of sweat trickled down her spine.

"You okay?" Beth plopped down beside her, eager smile at the ready to tackle all of life's problems. "You're a bit quiet today."

She wondered if Beth had the same worries, if she felt the same pressure building with each passing day. She and Beth were usually tied for most things, so she imagined she would be, but it never felt like Beth let anything get to her. "Just a lot on my mind."

"I bet. Are you registered for any AP classes this year?"

"Yeah." The thought of them made her queasy. "Three."

"Ugh. So annoying, isn't it? I signed up for just two, and I already feel like a failure. Senior year should be fun, and all I can think about is how to make myself sound like I could be the next president of the United States on a scholarship essay." Beth rambled on, oblivious to Jess's mood. "Like you have to kill yourself with extracurricular activities just so someone thinks you're good enough to go to college and not be crushed by debt for the rest of your life. Sorry—clearly my essays are going well. How about you?"

"Same."

She'd started two scholarship essays already, scrapping and revising each time she read them, the due dates looming over her head each time she started anew.

"It's like a full-time job or something," Beth said. Jess wanted to ask which ones—if they were applying for the same ones, Jess might have less of a chance. She and Beth were just a few points away from each other academically, but Beth was better ranked as a runner. "I have no idea how you do it with all the work you do. Nora says she barely sees you now."

She barely saw anyone, and when she did her anxiety

screamed at her that she should be doing more productive things.

Her right leg was shaking—how long had it been shaking?

"Let's start. I need to blow off some stress."

Beth nodded.

Jess shook off the thoughts before they could continue to tumble. They both placed their earbuds in and dashed off, her legs singing as they picked up the pace. This, Jess thought, was what I needed. The feel of her legs as she bounded down the path, her muscles heating, the sound of her feet against the gravel, melting everything else away. She tuned the world to the beat of her own heart, the inhale of her lungs. Go, go, go. She felt Beth steady next to her, keeping pace, she hadn't broken away yet—she didn't need to. The steady burn and push was enough for her now.

The music changed beats, unfamiliar, faster—she hadn't remembered putting this on her phone. Checking the name, she found it came from the party playlist draft Nora started. It was your typical upbeat song, generic enough to become a runaway pop hit. How had she even ended up on it? She flipped back to her running playlist, eager to get back to her usual rhythm, but the party song was still stuck in her head. She didn't want to think of the damn party she had to throw in October because she opened her stupid mouth. Because her resolutions weren't going the way her friends wanted them to. It wasn't her fault no one had asked her to do anything fun. And why hadn't they? Was Jess not a fun person? People thought she should run for president, run complex programs at the center, but not . . .

But not what, Jess? You can't even think of any fun things to do! That should be a clue, shouldn't it?

She had the party. That party was a fun idea if it didn't come along at the worst time. She should've said no, no to everything. No to running for president, no to every damn program at the center, no to the party, even though it was the one thing that fit the true purpose of her resolution.

Damn, her heartbeat felt wrong, faster than it should be. And that song was snug in her head, making itself at home: *go, go, go, Jess.*

"I'm going to speed up, okay?" Beth yelled.

"Cool." Jess waved her off as Beth sped away, feeling a sting of jealousy. Did Beth feel like her mind was running away with thoughts most of the time? Had Beth's summer been filled with late nights freaking out over campaign strategies and losing her friends?

It only took a moment before the jumble of thoughts overpowered her. Everything was pumping—the music, her legs, her heart, a constant drumming that should've drowned out everything in her head but didn't. Louder and louder the thoughts became until a shouting match erupted.

You'll just have to work harder, you can work harder, you can work until your muscles ache and your brain fuzzes, you've done it before, what's the big deal? So what if you fail? Because you probably will. You're so close to it, don't you see? Failure is inevitable, why would you think you could do anything else?

Burn, burn, burn. Her muscles ached, she was breathing hard, her lungs struggling to keep up, she could feel her body slowing down.

God—you can't even run anymore! Isn't that supposed to be your thing? What else are you good for?

The ground wobbled, jutting out toward her at odd angles, and if she didn't slow down she would meet it face-first. She veered off the path, almost slamming into several trees as she did finally slow down enough to collapse in a small clearing. She closed her eyes tightly and tried to slow her breath as the swirl of thoughts circled around her, in and out with the deep drumming of her heart.

Worthless. *Beat.* Loser. *Beat.* Failure.

They circled round and round like a drain. She dragged gulps and gulps of breath from her body until she felt ragged, a sob retching free. She shook, a faint part of herself whispering: It's just the cold—you aren't broken. Even though she was certain it was a lie.

Her hand flexed; she felt the cool grass below.

Her heart would not quiet, her breath still labored on like her feet were still pounding away. Her body was betraying her, another gulp rushing up, a sob ready to break out again. In her mind, she listed out everything she needed to do for the party that was months away, unable to stop herself. Who knew her love of lists would backfire?

"Jess?" she heard Beth call out. Please don't find me this way.

She wanted out of her skin, so sticky and covered in sweat.

But how could she? She needed to buy the cups and make food. Did you serve food at a party? The first blade of grass tickled her fingers. Had she even asked her parents? The ground was colder than she expected. Did she even check if there was any summer homework for her AP classes? The dirt pushed between her fingernails, a sting of pain as it cut through her nail bed. How could she not check? Of course there would be homework. Christ, Jess, there's always stuff to do. She closed her eyes, pushing farther down, moving dirt and wiggling her fingers through when the ground would not give. When she could not push anymore she dug, pulling up clumps of packed dirt, loosening it with her hands before jutting them back in, her palms now covered in loose earth, cold earth, that felt like a cool glass of water in the desert. Shivers traveled up her arms, and she just sat, her breath settling to a bearable volume. She left her hands in the dirt, on occasion feeling a wiggle or two beneath her fingers.

It had never been this bad before. It felt like a virus, infecting anything in its path. She pulled her hands out of the ground, the summer day wrapping around them, and brushed the dirt off on her shorts. Looking at the black line under each fingernail she took one breath after another, closing the door on the multiplying thoughts, blocking them for another day, another moment with more time.

"Hey! What happened?" Beth came up to her, her gaze landing on Jess's hands.

"Just lost my balance." Jess plastered on the brightest smile she could as she held on to the feeling of the dirt below her fingers. "I'm fine."

NORA

NORA WAS MADE of sugar. There was sugar in her hair, down her lungs, and if she didn't take off her gloves before scratching her face there would be sugar in her eyes . . . again. But on the plus side, the baby flans looked adorable in their tiny aluminum cups as she packed them up for tomorrow. God bless desserts that could be made in advance.

After a quick dusting to remove any clinging sugar, she released Hector from the front of the house duties, to which he replied, "Gracias a Dios," before disappearing in the back. Hector despised working in the front of the house, but Nora needed the time to finish off her work and maybe even daydream a little.

Since her chance meeting with Cassie and her continued

conversation with Yan, Nora was spending most of her evenings looking up possible culinary schools. She researched programs, alumni, classes, and even took virtual trips of the campus until she could close her eyes and imagine herself walking down the streets on the way to a class or sipping café at the corner bistro as she strategized how to take her gelato to the next level.

What at first was a fanciful thought became an actual "why not?" that carried Nora through long days at La Islita.

After wiping down the counter she took out one of her old recipe notebooks, looking through each of them searching for something for La Islita's fall dessert menu.

Fall.

The fact that the summer had flown by in a flurry of coffee grinds and mountains of sugar should've saddened her more. Instead Nora wished time would move quicker, counting down the days until the program brochures she'd requested from the culinary schools arrived. And then, she'd told herself, she'd sit down and talk to her mother about her new ideas. She had finally stopped ignoring Nora and had even sweetly run her hands through Nora's bright-pink hair one time. Nora swore she saw the corners of her mouth tilt up in a smile, though it was gone in a second.

But it was enough to see that her mother could change, that the little dreams that now danced along in Nora's mind weren't foolish at all.

She flipped a page, landing on a recipe she'd jotted down but never tried: mallorcas. Bread always made Nora nervous; it was fickle and did what it wanted, which was always the opposite of what Nora needed. But today was different. When she saw the recipe she didn't see the challenges behind it, only the possibilities. Current Nora (even with her new pink hair) had a hard time with bread, but the Nora who went to the Culinary Institute in California or studied bread making in Paris? That Nora would be up for the challenge.

She toyed with the edges of her notebook when her mother rushed in.

"Baby!" Her mom ran toward her, grabbing both her hands; there were tears in her eyes.

"Did someone die?" Nora asked.

"¿Qué?" Her mother stopped, and Nora pointed to her tears, making her mother laugh. "No, no. I'm just so happy. Ven."

She pulled Nora to the back, yelling at Hector to take over in the front. He gave Nora a pleading look, but all she could do was shrug as she was taken back to the closet-size office they used for calls and any private business stuff.

"Mi amor, you are not going to believe it." Her mother was bursting out of her skin, still holding Nora's hand.

"What happened? What's wrong?" Nora's body felt alert now, waiting.

Whatever it was, her mother couldn't get to it fast enough. "Niña, we got it! We got it!"

"Got what? What are you talking about?"

Her mother pulled her into a hug, but her body rebelled, and she tugged at her mother until she could look her in the eye. "Mami, what is happening?"

Her mother took a deep breath. "We got the place! We got Rogelio's!" Her mother devolved into a series of whoops and jumps, not noticing that Nora's face did not hold the same merriment.

Nora's mind struggled for words. What did she mean, they got Rogelio's? She didn't know they put an offer on it in the first place. Hadn't they discussed this?

"But we can't afford it."

"I've been doing some work," her mother said. "Talking to other businesses and doing research."

"What does that mean?"

What did any of this mean?

"I knew they wouldn't take my offer seriously unless, like you said, we had the budget. So I got us a loan and made a proposal."

Nora's head was swimming. Was she dreaming? She must be dreaming.

"Ay, nena, you would've been so proud of me. I talked about our place in the community and how we were a cultural asset and they needed to preserve the spirit of the neighborhood." Her mother started to do a little dance as she told her story. "Then I channeled you and showed them the numbers. What we make, how the expansion will bring more revenue. It was like art, mi amor."

She felt shaky, like she needed to sit, but there was only one chair in the room and it was tucked behind her mother. "So you did it . . ."

"I know I should've told you, but I wanted it to be a surprise!" She giggled. "And just in case it didn't work out too."

"Right." She didn't know what to say. Her mind vacillated between shock and disbelief.

"¡Bueno, di algo!" her mother said.

But what could she say? That she didn't think this would ever happen? That she hoped it wouldn't? That for the last several weeks she'd been making plans outside of her life at La Islita? That she'd foolishly given herself hope, and she should've known better?

"I . . ." She could see happiness bursting from every pore of her mother's body; the kind of happiness that blinded everything else, even the slump in Nora's shoulders or the fact that she had yet to react in any way. What could she say? "This is a lot" was all that came out, not that it mattered.

Her mother's smile grew as she placed her hand on Nora's cheek. "I know, it's so much to think about! But we can do it; I know we can. It feels like my heart is going to burst, I still can't believe it!" Her eyes watered again. "This is it. This is what I wanted to leave for you, nena. I can't believe it's finally going to happen."

Her mother hugged her tight. Nora could feel her mother's dreams in that hug. If only she could feel her own.

SENIOR YEAR

JESS

EVERYTHING NEEDED TO get done right now. At least that's what her brain was telling Jess as it recited every single thing on her to-do list.

Essays.

Study for class.

Figure out campaign.

Scholarships.

Early admittance.

Practice.

Volunteering.

The party.

Find a way to help Nora.

She'd added the last one after trying to speak with Nora the day before, to try and convince her she should stand up to her mother. But Nora had refused and was slipping back to her old routine like her dreams never existed. Jess didn't know what to do. She didn't want to think of her friends as part of her to-do list, but lately that damn list was the only thing keeping Jess afloat, even if it never seemed to get any shorter.

Maybe if she had any energy she'd be able to think of something, anything, to help Nora out. Instead she sent another text asking if she wanted to talk later today and ran to class just as the bell rang.

In the middle of AP Lit class her phone reminded her she needed to work on the first scholarship essay due that week and her early admittance essay. She knew neither was what it needed to be, but time was running out to make changes. The thought of sending out a less than perfect essay made her stomach turn.

On the way to Biology she passed by Liz, who was already plastering the hallway walls with campaign posters. Shit. She needed to get on that. Where was it on her calendar? Had she scheduled it in yet? Jess had no idea what to use for a slogan (did she really need one?) and had totally forgotten to ask Ryan for help with the design of the poster. Put it on the list.

She started to make a note on her phone before deciding to just text Ryan that instant. With that done she followed it up with a text to the group:

Jess: Do you guys think I need a campaign slogan? Can't I

just say "Vote for Jess" and keep it simple?

Ryan: Hmm . . . it would help me think of designs (which I'm totally going to help you with) if you had a slogan. Plus they are fun!

Yes. And Jess could be fun, right?

Nora: "Vote for Jess, she's the best!" Too cheesy?

Lee: Even for you. I'll think of some puns during free period.

We'll figure it out.

The bell rang, and Jess ran to her next class, where every date, important figure, and lesson passed her by as she obsessively scribbled everything she had left to do on the margins on her notebook like listing them out would make things less stressful. It did not.

Respira.

She met with Miss Anderson during her lunch hour to go over her scholarship and college lists. Having been at this "college thing" for years, Miss Anderson gave her some insight into what some scholarship committees were looking for. She advised a total reframing of Jess's essay on running, which Miss Anderson promised to read if Jess could get it to her by the end of the week.

Move that one up the list.

As she typed in some essay brainstorming thoughts on her phone, another reminder went off: Follow up again with Mr. Caine for his recommendation.

Ugh.

It would be great if adults were even a little bit

dependable, she thought as she raced down the hallway before the next bell rang.

Her stomach rumbled as she entered the library, reminding her she hadn't eaten all day. There was a strict no-food-or-drink policy in the library, so she could either step outside and grab something from the vending machine or ignore the gnawing in her stomach and embrace the sweet silence of the library.

She chose the library, walking deep into the stacks and away from any other student in there. In the first quiet moment she had to herself all day, she still struggled to settle her heart and stop her mind from reminding her of the tasks yet to do.

Just take a breath, the day is almost over.

The library was colder than usual, or was she running hot after dashing through the halls earlier?

Respira.

Her body would not listen.

Her mind would not listen.

Both fought back more and more every day. When she needed to focus, her body wanted to run. When she wanted to run, her mind screamed about deadlines and time wasted.

Respira.

She should be calm in the library, relaxed, but the longer she sat here the less she could breathe.

It took almost the whole period to pull herself back in

until she could think again, breathe again.

And as she let out one long breath her phone dinged with another reminder.

She closed her eyes and cried.

RYAN

HIS GRANDMOTHER HAD put on her best blouse for the portrait. They sat in her backyard surrounded by plants she insisted were not overgrown, just atmospheric.

"They let them grow down walls in Italy!" she said, motioning to the tiny forest all around her.

Ryan shook his head but had to admit it was the perfect setting for her second portrait.

"You know you have to stay still for this," he said, focusing on the way the light filtered through the many leaves, making a pattern across her body.

"Dāng rán zhī dào. I'm not an amateur," she responded, tilting her chin up just a bit, indicating she was ready for Ryan to start.

He wasted no time picking up his pencil, outlining the

frame of her body, now once again strong and confident thanks to her new artificial hip. Behind him he could hear his parents and Katie running around the house, playing hide-and-seek. As time passed even Katie's squeals of joy grew fainter as he was more and more focused on the portrait.

His hand flew across the canvas, each pass capturing the warmth in her eyes, then the determined chin of a woman who'd arrived in the United States at the age of six, finishing with the smile of a grandmother who'd called him to celebrate the day Taiwan legalized same-sex marriage.

Satisfied with the sketch, he started to pick up the paints he would need, squeezing out dollops on a square plank he used for a palette. He layered the colors, bringing out the pink in her cheeks, the brown in her eyes, and the bright coral of her signature lipstick.

When he exhausted the paint on the palette and the natural light outside shifted, it was time to call it a day.

He looked from one face to the other, smiling. "I think that's good for today, we can keep going tomorrow."

"Good." She nodded, watching Ryan as he cleaned up the area.

Ryan wondered if she was waiting for him to finish, but she seemed to be content simply watching him put away his paints and set aside the portrait.

"You didn't give up," she finally said. "I'm glad."

She motioned for Ryan to pull up a chair and he did,

sitting close enough for her to grab his hand.

"You could've just put away this part of you forever and walked away. But you didn't, and I'm proud of you," she said, making Ryan blush. "I know it wasn't easy either— not with a broken heart."

She laughed a bit when Ryan looked away. "I know, who wants to talk about a broken heart with his grand-mother? But my heart has been broken more than once. I remember feeling like there was nothing left of me but the broken pieces he'd left behind. I remember hoping that his heart was as broken as mine."

Ryan had consoled himself with the same thought once or twice. "Did that help?"

"A little, but eventually that also went away," she said. "I see so much of myself in you, you know?"

He wished he was as strong as she was. "Maybe I should paint you as my self-portrait then."

"Self-portrait?"

"I have to do this self-portrait for class." The blank can-vas stood in a corner of his room, waiting for him. When everybody else had handed in theirs at the end of the sum-mer, Ryan had begged Candace for more time, any time. His begging, winning smile, and the fact that he was taking Candace's fall course was enough to win him an exten-sion. Now not only would he have to finish the portrait, but it would be the centerpiece of the fall gallery show. "But every time I try and picture myself, I just blank. Everything good I've felt over the last couple of months just collapses and it's like I've never held a brush before. I don't know what to do, I don't know who I am. How am I supposed to do a self-portrait if I don't know who I am?"

"You don't need to find yourself, you are yourself," she declared with a squeeze of his hand.

What does that mean?

"When something breaks what do you do?" she continued.

"I throw it away?"

"You put it back together."

"What if it's too broken to ever be the same?"

"Ah," she said, her eyes catching the light. "It won't be the same. You are not the same. Maybe that's why you are having trouble. You keep trying to rebuild, to find that version of you somewhere whose heart never broke, but he no longer exists. And you don't have to be the same to love the things you loved. To be loved again."

They sat in silence as her words sank in. Could he do that? Could he embrace the broken pieces instead of hide them?

"I don't know how to do that."

"I can't tell you what to do. I can tell you that you are stronger than you think you are."

"What did you do, when your heart broke?"

"I went right out and fell in love again." She shook her head, amused by her own story. "With your grandfather, and he broke my heart too."

"He did?" Ryan had never heard this story.

"He did, but then it was mended once again, and once again something new formed. You might not be able to see it, but there are years of scars here," she said, pointing to her heart. "Now, I don't know about you, but all this posing has me famished. How about a snack? I can make us some niu rou mian—it's good for the soul."

Ryan nodded—no one passed up his grandmother's beef noodle soup. He helped her up, and together they walked back into the house. She squeezed his hand. "Give yourself room to breathe. To make mistakes. Eventually you will see that you were always there, you just couldn't recognize yourself yet."

LEE

IT WAS A miracle no one had found them. They weren't even being that quiet, but fifteen minutes into their library make-out session they remained blissfully undetected.

David shifted, hand traveling up her thighs to her waist as he kissed her neck. She laced her hand through his hair and tugged his face up to her lips again.

"We should probably study," she said in between breaths. "This is a library after all."

He squeezed her waist and moved his hand until he found the skin underneath her T-shirt. "That sounds boring."

He dipped his head down and captured her lips once again, taking his time, his hand at home on her lower back.

Through the haze of lips and tongues Lee heard the

squeak of the library cart, and it cut straight through the rush of her beating heart. It hurt to put a hand on David's chest and push him away, but if she hadn't they would have been caught and on their way to the principal's office like so many other students.

"Close call," David said. The way he looked at her made her flush, and she moved away from their hiding place.

"Too close," she said, returning to the stack of books they'd left on the table at the start of the period.

David joined her, sitting next to her on the table, his leg pressing up against hers. She pressed hers back, relishing in the spark it brought.

He kept his eyes on her until she broke away. "Stop that. How are we supposed to study if you won't look away?"

"Maybe I'm studying you," he said.

"Oh yeah? And what have you discovered?" She held her breath, wondering what he would say, what he saw.

"That you're as amazing as I always thought you were."

Lee rolled her eyes but still smiled. "That's not going to work again."

He sighed dramatically before stealing a quick kiss. It was hard to pull herself away from him, to try and focus on something else when all she wanted to do was go back to the kissing nook.

But they would most definitely get caught. Lee smiled to herself, imagining the moment, then paused. Why was she smiling? Getting caught should not be a smiling moment.

Would it be that bad?

She was clearly still high off the make-out fumes and wasn't thinking straight. Getting caught wouldn't be a great way to tell Jess, or her father, but still the thought of people knowing about her and David was not as worrisome as it was before.

"I'm done with this one. Do want to take a look?" She snapped out of her thoughts and reached for the book David had finished.

America's Best Colleges.

"Jess threw it at me a few weeks ago," he said. "Almost broke my door."

"I doubt that."

"Made a wicked bang though."

She leafed through the book, skimming over the many lists. "God, this is overwhelming."

"There might be a list of best schools for film studies though," he said. "You should check the index."

Lee turned to David. "Film studies?"

"Yeah," he said with a smile. "Apparently you can study films in college. It's almost like they made it just for you."

It did sound like that. Lee loved movies, but she never thought that was something she could take past weekend marathons.

"I'm surprised you haven't heard about it before, it's pretty common."

She would have heard about it if college was something

she thought about more. She'd never admitted it out loud, but sometimes college seemed like a waste of time—of her life—since she didn't love school. And since the future felt so uncertain, why spend four more years in school?

"I don't really think about college a lot."

David shifted his body toward her. "Does that mean you aren't going to apply?"

She would apply—of course she would. Her father would send in each application himself if she dared whisper anything near the possibility of not getting a college education.

"I was just going to do local colleges." UC Denver was a perfectly good college, with perfectly good courses. What those courses were, Lee had no idea, but she would find something and just get it over with. "Nothing fancy."

"Do you like these schools, or are you just applying to have somewhere to apply to?" Lee narrowed her eyes, and David backed off. "I'm just asking. I'm on your side, I promise."

He placed his hand on top of hers before tugging the book back and turning to the index. His finger trailed along the page until he found what he was looking for, flipping to the desired page and shoving it toward Lee again.

It was a section all about film studies. Lee read over the names, recognizing a few as universities some of her favorite directors had attended.

Meanwhile David pulled out his laptop and opened up a search window. "Give me a school on the list," he said.

What was he doing? When Lee didn't respond, he nudged her leg. She sighed and read off the list. "Boston University."

Moments later they were in Boston University's Film & Television program. David shifted the laptop so Lee could read off the screen. "Look, this is pretty cool. They have a class all on David Cronenberg. And screenwriting and directing courses! Maybe you can make your own movies?"

Lee had more than once remarked when watching some horror movies that she could do a better job in her sleep. But she never considered it as an actual, realistic future.

She reached for the laptop just as David pushed it toward her. Lee scrolled down the offered courses, imagining a world where she could take Introduction to Screenwriting or the History of Global Cinema.

What else was out there?

"Can we try another one?"

David reached for the book, reading off the list. "Ithaca College."

That one was slightly less focused on the study of film and more on the technical side of things. They moved to another program, and when Lee found a course dedicated to the horror genre it felt like something lit up inside her.

"Can I send myself an email?" she asked David.

They spent the rest of the period looking through film programs. Lee jotted them all down in one long email to herself—noting which courses offered classes on genre film like sci-fi and horror. Those went to the top of her list.

She sent the list to herself, feeling a fierce need to protect this option, this possibility.

Mami would want this for me.

Find the positive, her father had said. Was she doing that now with the list? Allowing herself something she hadn't before . . .

Her mother would fight for this. Want this for Lee.

But more than that.

Lee might just want this for herself.

NORA

HER ALARM WOULD go off in ten minutes. Nora stared at her ceiling, waiting for the eventual wail from her phone. She'd been up early each morning, unable to keep away the dreams that had months before filled her with hope for the future. Now when Nora dreamed of walking down the streets of Paris and learning the art of the French macaron, she woke up to the somber reality that it would never happen.

The alarm went off. Nora felt the scream crawl up her throat until she reached for the nearest pillow and buried her face in it.

It was best to let it all out before school, before La Islita. Not that her mother would notice—she'd been running around in a whirlwind of plans since the news broke—which turned out well for Nora. It meant she didn't have to hide behind a smile as much.

Why was it so hard now? Why couldn't she slip back to the way she was before? She'd always been fine with a life at La Islita, why couldn't she be fine again?

Even as she tried to shut down the thoughts of what could've been, they continued to sneak in.

School was a flurry of classes and attempts at a brave face. All around her classmates talked college and majors, the grand dreams that awaited them as soon as the year was over. When asked about her own plans, Nora recited the future her mother had planned: working part-time at La Islita and taking business courses on the side. Finally taking over the store when the time called for it.

But no matter what she said, her mind continued to whisper: What if? What if? What if?

The whispers got stronger when she saw her reflection and the tangle of pink curls that begged for new adventures and bright futures. Where would that Nora be if it wasn't for the expansion? She'd curl her fingers through her hair wondering if she'd let this new Nora down somehow.

Jess was particularly invested in checking in on her each day.

Jess: Hey! How is it going?

Not great. Today whenever Nora's mind drifted it carried her to the warm sunny streets of California and the Culinary Institute campus. She really had studied those photos well.

Nora: Feel like running away?

Jess: Yes. When do we leave?

Nora stared at her phone and imagined buying a one-way ticket.

Jess: Seriously, I can leave tomorrow. You in?

Nora: Where would we go?

Jess: Anywhere. Let's do it!

Her heart answered for her: New York, California, Paris. The places she'd narrowed down for schools. Now just reminders of what a fool she was.

Jess: Nora?

Nora: Never mind. Talk later, OK?

It was her own fault she'd let herself dream. There was always just one path for her, and she would just need to remember that no matter what it took. No matter what it took from her.

RYAN

THE WEEKEND BEFORE the Halloween party they met for a day of pizza and movie marathons—they all needed it. Well, Ryan, Jess, and Nora needed it. Nora was doing her best to pretend La Islita's expansion wasn't crushing her soul. Even though they'd repeatedly told her she didn't have to put on a brave face with them and they would back her up with her mom if she needed it, she acted like she'd tossed out the dreams of culinary school and no longer cared. Jess was a frazzle of nerves, which made them admit that Jess's resolution wasn't going as planned. After the party they needed to find a way to bring it back to the original idea: fun.

Somehow.

Lee . . . well, Lee was actually fine. She was thinking of

doing film studies and smiling a lot more than usual, which made Ryan just a tad suspicious, but he was too preoccupied with trying to follow his grandmother's advice and uncover this new Ryan inside of him. And then figure out how to paint a portrait of him.

"Do you think Tim Burton knows there are other actors in the world?" Lee was hogging all the popcorn and making the most horrible faces at the screen.

"We can just change the channel." Ryan reached over Nora for a handful of buttery goodness.

"I'm waiting for *The Nightmare Before Christmas* to come on. It's the perfect combo of my two favorite holidays."

"That's not for like another hour. We can find something else to watch in the meantime."

Lee thought it over and decided to suffer through it. "Meh—déjalo, I'll just make fun of it."

"I thought you liked *Sweeney Todd*," Nora said.

"Sure, I like the story." Lee made another face at the screen, sticking out her tongue. "But this adaptation? Nope. It's so constrained."

"I'm pretty sure Burton used like eighty gallons of fake blood for his movie," Nora said.

"It has nothing to do with the blood, it's like there's so much passion and anger in the songs and everyone here is just like *blah* pretty singing *blah* don't I look so goth and shit, like whatever, make me FEEL it."

"Can you please pass the popcorn?" Ryan reached again as Lee held it farther and farther away.

"Why is this playlist five hours long now?" Jess peered at Nora's laptop screen. Nora hopped over, scooting Jess from the chair until they both had one butt cheek on it.

"Because it's a party."

"I know, but five hours?" Jess scratched her palm, Ryan wondered if the idea of it lasting that long was making her itch. The closer they got to the party, the more frazzled Jess seemed. "That feels excessive."

"It will be over before you know it, and you'll be able to check it off the List of Doom."

"It's not the List of Doom," Jess said, looking a bit hurt, though maybe she was just tired. "I just don't remember ever being at a party for that long."

"You haven't." Ryan tossed kernels at Jess until she smiled. "We usually leave after two hours, but people come at different times. Just relax. Everything will be fine."

"I still can't believe my parents said yes."

"Es . . ." Lee thought for a moment, testing out the Spanish for a second. It made them all super proud the more secure she felt in it. ". . . tu culpa?" Ryan nodded, and Lee smiled. "If you'd rebelled more they wouldn't trust so much."

"That's true." Nora curled up to Jess. "You have no one to blame but your awesome self."

There was a knock at Ryan's door as Sweeney Todd

split a man's neck open and a fountain of bright-red blood spurted out.

Katie stood transfixed by the shower of red.

"KatKat, don't look at the screen," Ryan shouted. "You'll get nightmares."

"I know that's fake. I'm not a child," Katie said, hands on hips.

He smiled at his sister. "I mean, you are . . . so . . ."

She stuck out her tongue. "Want to play? I built a fort to invade, then tea but it's really apple juice, then coloring, then a dance party."

"Sounds like a good time," Lee replied. "¿Quizás más tarde, okay?"

Katie squealed, running out of the room. It would be her bedtime in a half hour anyway.

Jess joined them on the floor, checking off things on her phone. "Okay, so playlist done, chips, cups . . ."

Ryan pulled the phone away from her. "Okay, you need a break, you are fine. You don't have to plan a five-course meal for this shit, it's a party, not a family event."

"But—"

"We understand the impulse, we've all been to a fair share of events with at least one buffet table." They all nodded. "But this is basic: drinks, low lighting, music, like a half a chip for everyone, THAT'S IT. Remember the bonfire?"

"Vaguely."

"I think I had one drink and a whisper of a chip—no one cares as long as there's loud music, beer, and low lighting."

"I told my parents no beer, though . . ."

"Jess, they aren't dumb, they know there will be beer."

"This is making me feel worse."

"I'll stop talking then."

"This movie does not get better." Lee finally caved and changed the channel. "Have you heard back from Jason?"

Ugh.

"Not after the initial invite reaction."

"So do you think he'll come?"

Probably not. It would be just another in the string of invites that Jason was either too busy to make or his life got in the way of. "Maybe."

A SENIOR YEAR miracle arrived the next day.

A message from Jason:

Shit—I'm so sorry about not messaging sooner. I'm a flake.

Ryan wanted to wait to respond, but only held out for ten minutes. Soon they fell into the back and forth of rapid texting. He'd almost had the courage to bring up the show again when:

You should come up this weekend! My friends are having
a party, and I'd love to see you. It's not that far of a ride.
What do you say? Will you let me show you off before the
big show makes you famous?

Holy shit.

He read the text again and again. He'd love to see him?

This weekend was Jess's party and he couldn't miss it, not after he made Jess throw it. What kind of a shit friend was he? His phone buzzed with a new message.

Jason: I hope I didn't scare you off.

Ryan: No. Not at all.

Jason: Really meant it. It would be great to see you.

Ryan: Me too. I've been hoping we could really catch up for a while now.

About the breakup. About himself. He thought back to what his grandmother said, that maybe he needed closure. Talking to Jason about why they broke up would be a start.

Jason: Yeah, me too. So will you come? I can send you the party details.

He should say no and suggest another day, but what if this was his last chance? What if this was exactly what he needed?

Jason: Helllooo?

Ryan: Can you give me a bit to figure it out? Had something that day but maybe I can do your party first and then head over there.

After all, closure didn't need to take all night, did it? And he could still be back in time for Jess's party. Most of it anyway.

Jason: Totally! I promise not to keep you long. ☺

He paced around the room—Jess would kill him, but he could make it up to her, of course. This was it; it had to be it. He would get all the answers he needed and then that would be it.

He started to text Jess, then thought better of it and called.

"Hey," Jess answered. "Is everything okay?"

"You are going to hate me." Ryan laid it all out and waited.

"Are you serious?" Her voice was quiet, sad more than pissed.

"Jess, please."

"The party was all your idea, and now you're going to bail on me?"

"Don't think of it as bailing," he argued. "I'm not flaking or anything, I just really need to do this."

Silence.

"I know you're angry."

She sighed but didn't reply.

"But you've got this, and I'll be back before you know it. I promise."

"I just . . ." He could hear the doubt in her voice.

"Jess . . . I need to see him in person. Between my classes, his internships, and apparently everything ever, we could only chat a little and now there's this opportunity to talk, to really talk, and, Jess, you know how life gets. What if this is it? And you guys were right."

"We are?"

He took a deep breath. "I have to move on, but it feels like I keep pulling myself back. And I know it has to do with Jason, and maybe if I can talk to him face-to-face, maybe . . . I don't know. Something will happen."

"Do you still love him?"

"I don't think so." Every part of him knew he was lying. Deep down he still had feelings for Jason, and a part of him wondered selfishly if this meeting would lead to other things.

"I don't know if I believe you."

He wouldn't believe him either.

"There's not really a first love manual, Jess, so I'm just trying to figure stuff out, and I think—I think the answer means going to see him and figuring it out."

"So you're going."

He realized that he'd never intended to ask permission. "Yes."

"Okay." Her voice was soft, defeated.

"Don't hate me."

"You know I can't hate you."

"I don't know, you're pretty good at everything."

"Doesn't really feel that way lately." Jess's voice was so quiet he could hardly hear it through the phone.

Neither of them spoke for a moment.

"Jess . . ."

"Yeah?"

"Thanks."

"Yeah, yeah." Her voice brightened. "Go get 'em, I guess. Good luck."

"Ditto."

His heart fluttered as they hung up. This was happening, this was really happening.

Ryan: All set. I will see you Saturday.

Jason: Can't wait! Sending you details now.

The empty canvas still sat across his room waiting for Ryan. Maybe after the weekend he would finally find himself. Now all he had to do was wait for the weekend to get here already.

JESS

THE WEEKEND NEEDED to be over already. Jess slashed another bag of ice into the bucket, contemplating throwing it over her head to drown out the repetitive thoughts calling her a huge failure.

She still couldn't believe it. How had she missed it? It was one of the big scholarships too—one that would've made it a lot easier for her parents to send two siblings to college at the same time—and Jess had missed the deadline.

Somehow, even through all of her obsessing and careful planning, all it took was one packed day to ruin everything. One day of school, Student Council meetings, track, and the center that resulted in Jess collapsing in bed, ignoring the flash of her phone signaling another reminder going off. One had gone off earlier that she'd forgotten to check between running from practice to the center, but she assured herself she would do it just as she got home. And she did, only to shoot up out of bed in a panic. *LAST DAY to mail the Unidos Scholarship.* She almost threw up the second she read it.

After weeks and weeks of reworking the essay and pushing it until the final moment, she'd missed it.

Now no matter how loud or fun Nora's playlist was, it couldn't drown out the disappointment in her head. In fact, the thrum of the beat was making her headache even worse. On top of that there was no room to breathe—the entire senior class was here—thanks in part to the mini panic attack she'd had while putting the guest list together and wondering who to invite and who to snub and eventually imagining what those who weren't invited would say about her. It was just easier to invite everyone in the class, but then of course she'd gotten questions about friends in other grades, causing another mini attack and well, in the end Jess had just said yes to everyone. Well, at least that's in keeping with my resolution, Jess thought grimly.

Now it was Halloween, and her house was packed with vampires, uninspired football "costumes," and anything that could be bought at the dollar store the day before. Costumes were not mandatory because if Jess had to add figuring that out into her schedule, she would, in fact, have hurt someone. Every other moment someone pushed up against her with a muffled "sorry" as she tried to navigate her house.

There would still be other scholarships, fifteen in fact, but who's to say she wouldn't miss those as well? She was already pushing herself as far as she could to get everything done, but what if that wasn't good enough? In a panic she pulled out her phone, once again checking that she hadn't missed sending in the early decision application to Brown. No not yet, but it was coming up soon.

I should be working on that and not hosting a stupid party.

The headache had started at the back of her head and had now traveled all the way to the bridge of her nose and neck. Her body was stiff and on alert as the world around her existed at too high a volume. Waste of time. Maybe she should run away, hide in her room while the whole thing just continued on without her. Maybe then she could get some work done. Looking around at the crowds of people gathered, she knew no one would give a shit if she disappeared.

Okay, maybe not no one. Her body relaxed for a second as she felt Nora slip her hands around her waist, placing a glitter-covered cheek just below her shoulder.

"How are you doing?"

She tried to laugh but wasn't sure that's what it sounded like. "Like the night is still young, and that's not a good thing."

Nora came around, her brown roots coming back in, making the bright pink stand out more. She'd worn a dark-pink short dress and wings to match her hair; Lee said she'd come straight out of the *Jem* comic book. "Just try to have fun. I know you're still thinking about the scholarship, but it will be okay, I promise." She wished she had Nora's confidence in her. "I locked all the bedroom doors so no one can go make out in them, and I gave David the key."

"Thank you." The last thing she needed was gross stains in her parents' bedroom, though, looking around, she wasn't so sure the rest of the house would fare any better.

Nora touched the tip of her nose when Jess kept avoiding eye contact. "You're already counting down the hours, aren't you?"

She nodded, taking a deep breath and counting to ten as she released it. "Helps me stay calm. Don't judge me."

"Never."

"How are you doing?" Jess needed to shift focus fast before her mind tumbled down alleys she didn't want it to. "Have you talked to your mom yet?"

Nora scrunched up her face and shook her head. "No, she's like in fantasyland and eventually I'll just come join her. I am so tired of dealing with it, and I guess tired of not dealing with it. Life sucks."

"Don't give up," Jess said—maybe to herself as much as Nora.

Nora placed her hands on Jess's shoulders. "¿Sabes qué?

Not tonight. Tonight I'm going to dance the crap out of this playlist with my girls." She pulled Jess's hand. "I can think about my future another day. How about you?"

"This is a great playlist . . ." Jess couldn't help but smile, even as she recognized Nora's favorite avoidance tactic. Like running was for Jess, Nora flushed her worries away with dance, though as she led them over to the dance floor, she wondered if that's really what she needed.

Nora found Beth immediately and her face transformed, a light taking over. Nora grabbed Jess's hand tighter, pulling her along with her. Jess was not as transformed, but she followed her friend to the dance floor, passing Lee, who was talking to David, and she grabbed her hand as well. Lee followed, rolling her eyes but not as annoyed as she let on. The feel of her friends' hands in hers made her stronger—like maybe the future she worried about was just a paranoid thought. The missed scholarship did not define her as much as her panic would like her to think. She was more than that. She had to be.

Nora pulled out her phone, turning to Jess and Lee. "Okay, this one's for Ryan. Show him what he is missing." Lee pulled Jess in, and the three turned to the camera on the phone. Jess hoped her smile would be enough to hide everything she really felt.

When she stepped off the dance floor, the world cracked just a bit, thoughts rushing in to remind her that the scholarship was the first of many mistakes. There was no room to breathe—how long was long enough to be considered a party? Would calling it off now be okay? Would it tick a box so she could move on to the ever-growing list of things to do?

"Hey, Madam President!" Liz came running toward her, arms open to hug Jess.

"Hey," Jess said, trying her best to smile. "Vice President."

"I told you you were a shoo-in."

"Yeah, I kind of ran unopposed though." Jess should've been happy for her win. Student Council president looked great on her transcript, according to Miss Anderson, and she might qualify for some leadership scholarships. Except for the one that you missed. Remember that one?

"I think with both of us," Liz continued, "this might actually be a year where we get shit done, you know? Like, actually make a difference."

"Right." Was it wrong to hope for the exact opposite? Jess didn't have time to make a difference; she didn't have time to do anything. Why had no one else run for president?

Because they are all smarter than you.

Her head swam with the echoes of her worries, and all her body could think of doing was grabbing empty cups and cleaning every dirty space around her. She excused herself and headed to the kitchen.

Her body was wound up so tightly she felt as if her

spine would snap the next time someone tried to talk to her. But it would serve her right, wouldn't it? You made your bed, her mind whispered. All around her people smiled and looked away. Were they talking about her, did they see how fake her smile was now? Could they tell she'd already failed a quiz her first week into senior year? That the thought of being Student Council president made her feel nauseated?

Someone grabbed her ass, and she couldn't turn to see who without smacking into a set of angel wings. A burst of laughter came from the right, shocking her nerves. Some-one she didn't know rolled his eyes at her as she passed. In dark corners people flushed against each other, giggling back into the throng. Smug, so smug.

"Fucking move, asshole." Another nameless face yelled at her, and all she wanted to do was push them away, scream at them to leave.

Everything just needed to be silent so she could think— no, so she could not think. The beer tasted bitter down her throat—why do people even drink this? The next cup was a little less bitter and her brain dulled just a little, and the voice became just a buzz that she could silence, so she poured herself another, and she leaned against a wall to wait till she could close the curtain on this chapter.

RYAN

RYAN WAS SWEATING in spite of the cool fall evening. But of course he was, nothing would be more embarrassing than arriving at Jason's party with two giant pit stains. Okay, maybe a few things would be, but still. He tugged at his shirt, fanning his body.

"Just be cool," he told himself. Nothing to worry about, except finally having that conversation with your ex that you've hinged everything on. Totally cool.

The door opened.

"Do I know you?" He was shorter than Ryan, which wasn't saying a lot, with buff muscles pressing against his T-shirt, a tattoo along his neck that was hard to see in this light.

"Uh—" Ryan was definitely sweating now. "I'm

Jason's . . ." Ex? Boyfriend? "Friend. Are you Jacob?"

"Nope—just the guy closest to the door." He stepped to the side to let Ryan pass. "Saw Jason by the kitchen all the way in the back."

"Thanks."

Ryan headed in, slipping around groups of people that acted like there wasn't someone trying to shimmy past them. When he found Jason, his heart gave a wicked beat. We talked about this—no fluttering, no emotion whatsoever, just a clean existential-crisis conversation, that's it.

Jason had yet to see him. He was holding a drink in one hand, his head tilting back, a monster laugh taking over the room. The guy next to Jason spotted him first, nudging Jason, who leaned in. Oh God, he wasn't ready. Not yet, he needed a good ten or fifteen minutes to pump himself up for the conversation. A quick shift and he could hide behind the group next to him.

Too late.

"Hey!" Jason shouted, waving him over. Ryan made his way through, stopping just short of him and his friend.

"Hey," Ryan replied, not knowing if he should lean in for a hug or not.

"Okay, this is weird." Jason laughed, stepping forward to engulf Ryan. God, he missed his smell—Jason always smelled like he'd just stepped out of the shower and a hint of cologne he didn't wear. His stomach flipped. "Fuck, it's so good to see you."

"Same." He hadn't seen Jason in forever, but standing with him now was almost like he'd always been there.

Jason turned to his friend. "This is Dylan, he's in my psych class—his boyfriend is throwing the party."

"Nice to meet you," Ryan said.

Dylan nodded, then looked him over. "So you're the painter ex."

Was that all he was? "Uh, yeah," he replied, not sure what else to say and suddenly wondering who else knew him as Jason's painter ex.

"Be nice!" Jason chided. Ryan hadn't realized he was being insulted.

"I am," Dylan replied. "I love painters and art. It's all about emotion and shit. I wish Jacob was a painter, but he's studying statistics, which to be honest no matter how many times he explains it to me, I just have no idea what he's talking about."

Jason laughed, so Ryan did as well, even though his body still ached for a quieter place. Hopefully they could find one before they talked. Ryan would absolutely not have that conversation in this crowd, or any crowd for that matter.

The dreaded awkward pause of people who barely knew each other passed over them. Ryan cleared his throat. "So, um, what do you study?"

Dylan finished off whatever was in his cup. "I am the clichéd undeclared freshman who will probably amount to nothing. Remember me when you're a famous painter with all your fancy gallery shows."

"Right."

Ryan would be happy to get through one gallery show.

"Oh." Jason put down his cup and looped his arm around Ryan's. "I'm a horrible not-host. I should introduce you to people, I've been talking you up all night."

"You have?" Something sparked in Ryan's belly as Jason tugged him toward group after group of people. Would tonight bring more than just the closure Ryan needed? Would it be the start of something new between them?

RYAN NURSED HIS drink as Jason took him around the party, introducing him to so many people his head spun. Each time it played out the same, he'd introduce Ryan—the ex—then drive into another conversation, making it almost impossible to join in. It wasn't Jason's fault. Ryan was the odd man out after all, and he wasn't as good at talking about himself as everyone else was.

Plus, he had no idea how much of an asshole Professor Davidson was and how ridiculous the latest assignment from . . . someone he'd already forgotten. Then there were the inside jokes and lives that Ryan knew nothing about. He didn't want to be that person who stopped a conversation just so he could get the backstory to what everyone was talking about. Staying quiet was easier, waiting for his moment was easier.

Figuring out when that moment was, though, when Jason barely took a breath all evening, that was a bit harder.

His phone buzzed with a photo of the ladies. He texted back:

Beautiful!!

Had this been a good idea? He thought he could come in and just talk with Jason, like there weren't a whole bunch of people here. Like, please ignore your friends so I can talk to you alone.

He should've insisted on another time.

Jason had left him to snag more drinks and had yet to come back. From where Ryan could see, he was stuck with someone in the kitchen. He's not stuck with someone in the kitchen; he's stuck with you.

"How's it going?" Neck Tattoo sat next to him, a rank-smelling drink in his hand.

"Uh—"

"Curtis." He pointed to himself, his drink splashing on his jeans.

"Ryan. And, um, not bad I guess."

"You look like you're having a ton of fun."

"I'm not really a party person." Well, at least not without Nora, Jess, and Lee. They made everything better. So far this was not a good idea. He wondered how foolish he would look trying to signal Jason from here.

"Jason talks a lot," Curtis said, following Ryan's line of sight.

"He was always better at it than I am." No matter what, Jason could always make himself at home in any situation. He probably didn't skip a beat when they broke up. Meanwhile here was Ryan, a bundle of questions and self-doubt just trying to figure out one thing about himself.

They really needed to talk. Ryan turned to Curtis, who had zoned out watching the people around him. "Is there somewhere here to have a quiet conversation?"

"Parties are where I go to get lost and drunk. Not really an intimate-situation type of environment."

"I guess not." Time to pack up and try another day?

"Actually, there's a terrace out back, might be useful," Curtis said. "I can't guarantee it's empty, but it's probably much less crowded than anywhere else in this place."

A terrace could work. Didn't people have intimate conversations on terraces all the time? Ryan had seen at least five movies with terrace scenes, and couples always ended up having meaningful conversations on them. A terrace could totally work.

NORA

NORA WAS MUSIC. She was the beat. She was hips that swayed and hands that tangled through hair. She was the lowlights that gave permission to the night. She was the sweat that soaked into her clothes and the tongue that darted out onto Beth's lips, coaxing them open to warm, welcoming love. She was all of this, and she was not her problems.

"Nora," her mother had cooed just yesterday, opening a blueprint on the kitchen table. "Mira. What do you think?"

Everything was moving too fast, plans drawn, contractors contacted. Her mother looped her into every decision until Nora's life was new tile choices and kitchen remodels.

No. She would not remember the future that loomed so close, the days in a brand-new store shouting orders and putting in new purchase orders. She was not the branded shirt that itched against her skin or the automatic responses and "have a nice day" always at the tip of her tongue.

"You know, I heard there's some fancy environmentally friendly paint we could use," her mother had offered.

"That sounds great." Nora had nodded and smiled because she knew that's what her mother needed.

"And look," her mom's finger traced the walls of the new kitchen, "this will be your area. You'll have an oven all to yourself and a new display case."

She was the sugar, and the eggs, and the heat that bound and delighted, but she was that for herself and no one else. And she would not let it sink the night, she would not let it curl inside her, taking it from her. She was music. She was love. She was beat. And she would not think of the future that was to come. It was not welcome, so she banished it with a sway, and a twirl, and a hand on the hip of a beautiful girl. A girl who smiled just for her. And that was all she needed, all she wanted tonight for dance after dance until it hurt, and then even the pain would drive it away.

"Do you want to take a break?" Beth spoke in her ear.

"Not yet," she begged. "One more song."

And one more and one more until it didn't matter whether or not they were tired, it would be worse to stop. To stop and remember.

LEE

LEE WANTED TO make out, but it was hard to do with all the people around her. A part of her itched to do it anyway, and she wondered at what point her thoughts on PDA had shifted. Things had started to shift inside her; when once retreating and hiding behind a well-placed joke was second nature, now something else had emerged. She couldn't quite put her finger on it.

"Solving a mystery?" David appeared next to her as if she'd conjured him, two drinks in his hand.

"Huh?"

"Your face looks like you're trying to figure out which of our classmates is a notorious serial killer."

"I guess I was deep in thought."

He hovered next to her, shoulder lightly touching,

reminding her of moments before, hidden in the corners at school, sneaking into the janitor's closet, moments where he felt like hers and her body held no medical history and only the present.

"Now you're smiling."

"I am not." She tested her face, realizing she had in fact been smiling. "Okay, maybe I was."

Was that so bad? A part of her wanted to smile again, to embrace the moment regardless of anyone who would see. Even Jess.

What is this?

More than his skin against hers, more than keeping her mind from wandering into the darkest thoughts. Was this what Nora felt when she was with Beth?

"We can leave, escape if you want." His voice held the promise of lips against lips and more.

Despite whatever had changed, Lee would not pass up a steamy hidden encounter if there was a possibility of one, but she wouldn't leave Jess alone, she'd promised. Just moments ago she'd removed a cleaning sponge from Jess's hand and sent her out onto the dance floor again to forget the worries that came so quickly to mind.

"I can't, Jess is one hour away from driving everyone out of here."

"Yeah." He nodded. "Maybe we should?"

"I tried—she said she was fine, but . . ."

"But?" David was so deliciously close.

"I don't know if I believe her. She puts on a brave face way too often." Lee hoped Jess wasn't suffering through it because of the resolutions. The point was to get her to loosen up, have fun, say yes to spontaneity. Maybe they should give Jess an out for the rest of the year? Yeah, right. Like she'd accept that as anything but a failure.

"Okay—you're the boss."

"Right." Lee scanned the crowd, spotting Jess talking to another classmate. No sponge in sight. That was good at least.

"So how long do you think before we should call it?"

"No more than an hour. Jess will want to clean up, and we can still hang after."

And maybe show her once again how fun the resolutions could be.

David nodded, placing a hand on the small of her back. "So we have an hour."

Lee elbowed him, unable to keep a grin off her face. "I said I couldn't leave, and I'm not making out in public, you know this."

He didn't look so sure of that anymore, and neither was Lee. "You're lucky I really like you, otherwise I would be hurt you're keeping me a secret."

Lee turned to him, her brown eyes locked with his. "Are you?"

"Hurt?"

She nodded.

"No," he said. "But I don't want to be a secret forever.

I would like to make it official."

"Official?"

He smiled, keeping his eyes leveled. "I want to call you my girlfriend."

"You do?" She felt a thrill up her spine, a warmth in her belly, every part of her already on board with this plan and inching her way toward him.

"I do."

So did she.

"We'll tell her. I know we have to . . . and I want to."

She wanted to shout it—a ridiculous thought, and one she would not do—but it was true. She wanted to close the gap between them and feel his lips on hers. And she wanted to sit and talk and hold hands and just be.

"Good," he said, touching his cup to hers as if they'd just made a toast. "Plus, I just happen to be the bearer of the keys to all the rooms in the house." His eyes lingered on her lips, making them quirk on the sides. "We can go take advantage of the hour we have before I have to pretend I don't want to kiss you every time I see you."

She felt his hands play with the skin on her back, fingers trailing the waist of her jeans.

"You're making it hard to think." Lee's thoughts clouded with memories of secret kisses and hurried touches on the way home.

"Sorry," David said, but not sorry at all. "My room is just a hallway away."

"How do we sneak in there without people seeing?"

"You overestimate how much people care. You sneak in first, then I'll follow." He slipped the key into Lee's hand. "Hurry up, we only have one hour, remember?"

He blended into a group, finding someone to talk to while the keys jangled in her hand. She pressed the smile down, her body singing with the possibilities.

David was right; no one was paying any attention, too involved in their own conversations or make-out sessions. Instead of going straight into David's room, she went into Jess's—figuring it was less conspicuous if someone did see. Jess's and David's rooms were connected through a shared bathroom you wouldn't know about unless you'd been in the house and heard the twins fight about privacy.

She crossed the bathroom into David's room, fighting the urge to turn on the light. Instead she left the bathroom light on, which was enough to go by. She lay on his bed, blushing at the memories it brought up.

In the quiet she listened to her heartbeat, feeling the cold of the bedsheets against her skin, marveling at herself, at what had happened the last few minutes.

I want to keep this. Whatever this is.

Happiness?

Hope?

Whatever it is, it's mine.

"Am I late?"

"Late?" A startled Lee almost jumped off the bed.

David stood in the bathroom doorway, a silhouette.

"My talking to randos worked too well." He half-closed the bathroom door, letting only a small amount of light in. "The hour isn't over yet, right?"

"Not yet."

"Good." He jumped on the bed; they both froze as the creak traveled across the room.

Lee slapped him on the shoulder. "Seriously, you have to be quiet."

He smiled, a wicked little grin. "I can't promise anything."

David placed his hand on her cheek, tracing her lips. It was almost too much and not enough.

I get to keep this.

"Enough of that." Lee tugged at David's shirt till his lips were a breath away. He closed the gap, hands wrapping around her waist as Lee's lips demanded more and more. She slipped her hands up his shirt as he cupped her butt. The darkness inviting so much, they reveled in it.

RYAN

SOME KNOWLEDGE OF astrology would be useful right now. It would at least help pass the time on the terrace while he waited for Jason. Instead he made the sky above him a canvas, painting it with a wide brush the size of his hand, navy blue and black, no gray of clouds tonight. A toothbrush loaded with white to make a cluster of stars, a thinner one for the brightest ones. It gave him an idea: he'd paint the night sky for Katie's ceiling. She hadn't asked, but every pirate needed a sky to sail by. He'd use fluorescent paint so she could fall asleep to the soft glow.

At least his painting had slowly fallen back into place, as long as he ignored the empty canvas where his portrait would live, but that was something else. That was deeper and, after tonight, hopefully nonexistent.

Where was Jason?

He peeked back in—no sign of him anywhere. Just relax, he thought, and sat on one of the rickety chairs in the terrace. He'd already been at this party far too long, he should be back to Jess's by now.

Jason wasn't answering his texts either.

"You know what?" he said out loud, startling the two smokers next to him. "Sorry."

Time to find Jason and figure this out.

Of course, Jason was surrounded by people. He showed no concern that Ryan was waiting for him outside.

His body coiled, angry. Maybe he had grandiose ideas and his expectations were a little high, but this? Why was he even here?

He moved toward Jason, intending to pull him aside and demand a conversation, when Jason's face split into the biggest grin he'd ever seen, arms wrapping around someone tall and blond. He'd never seen that smile before, not when he was with Ryan. He would've wondered what it meant if Jason hadn't kissed the blond guy, stopping only to laugh before they kissed again.

Shit. Jason is in love.

His smile gave it away. Jason's body leaned toward this new guy—made to fit each other. There were no awkward lulls in conversation or pauses. They were completely at ease with each other, and it tore Ryan's heart out.

Of course. Of course he's in love.

It was Ryan who was the broken one. Ryan whose pieces no longer fit together. Who was made of awkward conversations and long pauses. Whose hands would never hold another's like that again.

Then they were walking toward him, hand in hand, slow-mo. His brain needed to catch up with the present.

"Ryan," Jason was saying, "this is my boyfriend, Michael."

Michael with the blue eyes that mirrored Jason's. Michael who looked familiar, like he'd seen him in a photo, one of the many faces that surrounded Jason in his shots. "Nice to meet you," Michael said. Ryan's own hand extended before he could stop it.

"I've got to go" was all he got out as he broke through, shirt plastered to his chest.

Ryan turned at the sound of his name. Jason came down the hall, visibly confused and swinging into anger. "What was that?" he demanded. "I introduce you to my boyfriend and you just bail like that?"

Really? Did he not see why Ryan would be thrown?

"Yes." That was all that came, all he could manage.

"Why?" Jason's face crumbled a bit.

"I—" His voice cracked. "Was it so easy to put us away?"

"I didn't—" Jason sighed, moving closer to Ryan. "I didn't put you away, we still talk."

Ryan shook his head. "That's not what I mean, and you know it."

They were silent for longer than Ryan thought possible.

"Why did we break up?"

"Ryan—" Jason started to say but then stopped, finding the nearest wall and collapsing by it. "You know why."

"Actually I don't," Ryan said. "I really don't because you keep talking to me like it never happened, and Boulder is, like, just thirty minutes away, so I don't buy this long-distance relationship bullshit. So just tell me."

"Why does it matter?"

"Can you just try?"

"Why?"

Ryan sat by the wall opposite Jason, needing to look him in the eye as they talked. "Because . . ." My heart still feels broken. "I just . . ." Have no idea who I am anymore. "Was it me? Was it my fault?"

When Jason didn't answer right away, Ryan almost stood up and left right then. "Yes. And mine." Jason placed his head between his knees. "I don't know how you fall out of love, Ryan. I don't know how it happens."

"But you fell out of love with me?"

Good thing his heart was already broken, because this would surely break it.

"I did," Jason said. "I tried to . . ."

He knew what he meant. They'd tried to fix it before their second breakup, but it hadn't worked.

"It wasn't about you."

How could you fall out of love with someone and have

333

it not be about them? That made no sense. Jason must have seen that in Ryan's face because he added, "It's not a reflection of you. It wasn't."

"Feels like it is."

"If I didn't like you, I wouldn't still want to be friends with you."

"Yeah." Ryan thought back to all the texts and confused feelings. "That might not have been the best approach."

"What do you mean?"

"I mean maybe we should've given each other some space." He should've given himself some space. "It's my fault, really. I kept coming back to you, like a habit. No, more than a habit. If I'm honest with myself I thought there might be something still there, even after everything. It was like this little speck of hope covered in a coating of denial."

Jason stood, moving over to where Ryan was. Not the best move, considering they were just talking about giving each other space, but Ryan didn't have it in him to say anything. "I'm sorry."

"For?"

"I should've given you space." His hand drifted to Ryan's before pulling back. "But I liked having you there. And it felt like we could be friends, and I didn't want to lose you."

"That's not really fair." Jason couldn't break Ryan's heart and then expect him to hang out and chat without any repercussions to Ryan's heart.

A burst of sound shocked them as a group of people exited to the left. Ryan waited until the hallway was quiet once again before continuing.

"Was it easy to fall in love again?"

Jason took a breath. "I'm not sorry I found someone."

"That's not what I asked."

It was obvious from the earlier scene that Jason wasn't one bit sorry about his feelings toward Michael.

"No," Jason said, waiting for Ryan to meet his eyes before saying, "I did love you. I did. We were right together when we were right together. But then we weren't anymore. Breaking up was the right thing to do, but it wasn't easy. I missed talking to you and the way you made me feel. I worried I would never feel that way again."

Ryan felt something loosen within him, a worry released. At least he wasn't as easy to forget as he thought. "But then you did."

"I did."

"How? How did you move past it?"

How did he put everything back together?

"I—"

Ryan didn't wait, feeling the words fall out. "It feels like all of me was tied up with you and then I broke and the pieces don't fit together anymore."

Because they aren't the same. Hadn't his grandmother said that? That it was impossible to piece everything back together like they'd never broken. He was broken. Pieces of him shattered and changed. So why try to fit them the same way?

Jason hadn't said anything—just as well. The more they talked, the more Ryan realized he wouldn't get what he needed from this. Jason wasn't the key to figuring this out. He wasn't the key to Ryan.

Ryan stood, then helped Jason up. They did not hug or promise to talk. Jason didn't say he was sorry, nor did he need to.

Back in his car, he rested his head against the steering wheel, feeling strangely blank. He'd hoped for answers, ones that would lead him where he needed to go. Instead all he got was what he'd been avoiding all along: he needed to find himself. No one else. No magic words from Jason. Him.

Maybe when he got to Jess's he could hide in her room until the party was over. Jess would understand. She would stand by the door to guard him. He started up the car when his phone blew up. The screen blinded him in the dark.

A message from Lee:

There's been an accident. We're in the ER.

JESS

JESS WAS CLOSE to calling it. Nora was lost on the dance floor, Lee was in hiding, and the walls were too close for her liking. She nursed another cup of water after the beer invited another wicked headache in to stay and pull up a chair. What did everyone around her see, did they see the cracks? Was she not as careful as she thought?

She'd been good after Lee had caught her with the sponge. Jess had found someone to talk to, to smile and nod to when they needed it. Why was it so hard? Jess was usually a talker, but lately it was hard to concentrate—every empty second her mind would fill with reminders. She picked them well, knowing they would dominate the conversation with minimal input. And when the conversation died down she found another, checking her phone in between, counting down the minutes in her head, doing the math.

More than an hour till she could throw everyone out, then how long to clean? Two hours? After that she had a paper to write, and she'd promised the center she'd help schedule out fall courses to make them more efficient. And of course she should triple-check (or was it quadruple-check?) whichever deadline was next. She could not afford another mistake.

Why was nothing in her brain silent, like, ever? She could feel the itch starting down her back as she balanced from foot to foot. The concentration needed to keep from falling over often helped keep the thoughts away when the slow breathing and counting didn't work. Maybe it was time to research a few more techniques tomorrow?

Someone was smiling at Jess, someone she was supposed to be talking with, but she wasn't paying attention. They waited for her response, and all she could do was smile and excuse herself to get something to drink.

She recognized the signs of another panic attack fast: heartbeat, flushed skin, need for isolation, a domino of thought after thought after thought. Quiet, she needed quiet, if only for one moment to settle.

Cutting through the bodies with a smile plastered on her face, she reached the door to her room, realizing too late that David had the key. She tried the door just in case and gave a silent thank-you that Nora had forgotten to lock it.

The silence swallowed her up like water on a cool day. She'd left the bathroom light on, good, easier to find her bed and sink into it and the mountain of pillows she'd left on it. Her heart was a drumbeat that took no heed of the band or tempos. It beat until it was all she could hear; it took all her strength to rein it in.

She shut her eyes, remembering the chill of the earth under her fingers, dipping her hands under the pillows trying to mimic the feeling. Imagining the fabric under her palms was the dirt underneath her, till the beats slowed and she was alone in her room with just the distant sound of a song seeping through her door, but that she could handle.

She twisted, curling around a pillow, pressing it to her abdomen, feeling the material beneath her hand dissecting everything she felt and giving her mind nowhere to wander. She closed her eyes, her body stretching out, relaxing, when she heard a sound.

A breath taken, not hers.

She heard it again before it slipped away, a gasp both sharp and soft, cutting through the darkness. The gasp was in her room and all around her, then it was gone. Where did it come from? Or was it just a couple lingering in the halls, the sound traveling too far? But there it was again, this time sticking in her ears for what it was: an intrusion.

Seriously?

The sound came again, closer. She sagged. Someone was

in her brother's room. This was not what she needed and the reason she'd asked Nora to lock the doors. It made her body ache once again, tears welling up. This night would be the end of her. Nothing was going right—why couldn't anything just go right for once?

Jess could've stayed there, closed the bathroom door and let them have their fun, but her anger carried her up and to the connecting bathroom. The sounds were louder as she entered David's room, and Jess should've made a noise, should've warned them, if she'd been thinking clearly.

The light hit them like a stage light, highlighting every position, every missing article of clothing, like a scene in a play that Jess had not studied her lines for.

Jess's entire body flushed with confusion, keeping her frozen in place while hands rushed to find tossed shirts and offer explanations, but all she could hear was the sound of the bass in the hallway, her own heart beating, and eventually her mind screaming at her to leave.

So she ran.

Even as Lee called out and she bumped against anyone in her way, she ran. Somewhere along the way she found her car keys and kept going.

It was so much easier to breathe outside. She could stay here and wait until the volume in her head settled down. But David would follow, and Lee would follow, and Jess didn't want to talk, she just needed quiet, any quiet.

The keys in her hand offered a solution. She would

drive to a park or the mall and just sit and wait for everything to make sense.

That might take forever.

Then forever it would be.

You should just keep driving and don't stop. Doesn't that sound better than everything that's waiting for you here?

She started the car; her mind flashed to tangled limbs and bare skin.

Everyone's going to be talking about this tomorrow. Did everyone know but you? I bet they did—I bet Ryan and Nora knew all about Lee and David and just didn't tell you. Maybe they didn't think you could take it; you can barely keep yourself together, after all.

Nora hopped in the passenger seat as Jess was getting ready to pull out of the driveway. "What's wrong?"

Pulling out she saw Lee and David, now fully clothed, come out the door, looking for her. She should stop and talk, that would be the sensible thing to do, but already her body rebelled against her.

"Let's go back. Whatever it is we can talk about it," Nora coaxed from the passenger side. She could hear the caution in her voice. "It's late, you had some beers. This isn't safe." Jess nodded—it wasn't safe, of course it wasn't safe, and she didn't seem to care, why didn't she care? She gripped the wheel tighter; her body didn't feel like hers anymore.

"Jess," Nora tried again. "Stop the car, please, stop the car."

She felt Nora's hand on her shoulder, one squeeze, then another, each time saying: "Come back, Jess, come back." Nora's voice curled itself around her, guiding her out of the muck until she was almost herself again. They weren't far from the house, and Jess drove the car to the nearest space and stopped.

"Okay—good." Nora smiled, turning toward Jess, who would not look at her. "Are you okay?"

Jess's hands shook as she gripped the steering wheel, knuckles bled of their color. Her heartbeat was slowing down, but it still felt like she was jumping out of her skin. A part of her still wanted to lie, to say "fine" and pretend that whatever facade hadn't completely shattered.

"No." Each breath was harder than the next, each a step up a mountain. "But I don't know—I don't know if—"

Without another word Nora leaned over and hugged her. "How about we go back and throw everyone out of the house and it's just us? We can talk about it then or we can just sit and not talk."

Back at the house with Lee, David, and the damn mess she'd just made, with everyone looking at her and knowing. They would all know.

"Can you do that?" Her eyes couldn't meet Nora's. "Can you throw everyone out and I'll stay in the car?"

"Promise not to run away again?"

She wanted to say yes, but all she got was "Maybe."

"That's good enough," Nora replied. "I might make Beth sit on you then to make sure."

Jess nodded, she didn't have the energy to run away again.

"Do you need me to drive?"

"No." She took a deep breath. "We aren't that far."

Still, she didn't pull out, her hand hovering over the steering wheel as she wondered what she would say to her friends. It couldn't get more disappointing than her rush out the door, could it? And Lee . . . what would happen with Lee?

"Jess?"

"Right." God, it was so easy to slip back into the thoughts, wasn't it? "Let's go back."

She was so preoccupied with not listening to her thoughts that she didn't see the approaching headlights in her side-view mirror until it was too late.

LEE

LEE WANTED TO throw up—she needed to throw up. Her body shook as she sat in the waiting room, convincing herself it was just a reaction to the temperature. Waiting rooms had not gotten any better over the years. They were still too cold, too loud, and increasingly uncomfortable.

David offered her a soda, which she turned away. He insisted. "I read somewhere that sugar can help during stress. Something to do with serotonin. Plus you'll need the caffeine."

She chugged it, not feeling any calmer. She took a breath. This was all her fault. Why didn't she just tell Jess earlier? WHY? The scene kept replaying in her head: Jess finding them on David's bed, Lee's clothes on the floor, Jess backing out of the room as they struggled to get their clothes back on.

All at once parents descended on them with a flood of questions she couldn't answer. Her dad pushed through, taking hold of her shoulders. "Are you okay?"

Was she? She wasn't in the car, if that's what he meant.

"I . . ." She started to say then changed her mind. "They won't tell me anything."

Jess's and Nora's moms fixed that real quick, managing to scare even the most veteran of nurses who picked up the phone to check in.

Please. Please. Please let her be okay, please let her be okay.

Ryan was the last to arrive, giving his parents a quick hug before going straight to Lee. "Sorry, had to park like forever away. What happened?"

Lee stepped away from the adults, breaking down the whole evening, waiting for the stinging blow of Ryan's anger that never came. Instead he wrapped her up in his arms. "This is not your fault."

Her body shook, and she sobbed into his chest. "I don't know if they're okay."

"They'll be okay," Ryan replied as he wiped his own tears.

David had tried to sit by her, but she shook her head, shifting toward her dad. She wasn't mad at him, but it felt wrong to be so close to him at the moment when all she could see was Jess running out the door, over and over again. And Beth, who sat just a few chairs away, looked so much smaller than she'd ever seen her, reminding her that she'd hurt Nora too. What the actual fuck, Lee?

At four a.m. Nora came through the doors, red scratches along her arms, but otherwise just looking tired.

"I'm fine," she said as Beth, Lee, and Ryan pounced. "I promise, just some scrapes."

"She was very lucky." Nora's mother followed, running a hand through Nora's hair. "There's shitty cell service inside, otherwise we would've let you know sooner."

Minutes later Jess's mom came out, a faint smile on her face. "She's okay. Her left arm is broken from the impact, and they want to keep her under observation since she hit her head. You should all head home." She looked drawn and was rubbing her neck. "She'll still be here tomorrow, so might as well get a good night's sleep."

"When will they move her to a room?" Ryan asked.

"I don't know, Javier is with her now. Frankly we're lucky he was on call, otherwise we would still be waiting. They said maybe an hour or two till they have a free room."

"We'll stay," Lee stated. She needed to stay. If she went home right now she'd just be alone with the guilt. "If you don't mind."

"I don't mind," she replied, giving Lee a big hug.

Lee wasn't sure she deserved it.

JESS

SLEEP THROUGH THIS. Keep your eyes closed long enough, and maybe you'll wake up once everyone's forgotten about this. Maybe if you wish hard enough this could be a dream.

Her mom looked uncomfortable trying to nap in the hospital chair. They'd moved Jess sometime around five a.m. The constant in and out of nurses along with the night replaying over and over again made it impossible to sleep, but she pretended to anyway. She'd messed up pretty bad and gotten Nora hurt in the process.

So much worse than the scholarship, than running away from your own party. You got Nora hurt. How could you?

A sob broke from her throat as she tried to stamp it down, but her body was a traitor that gladly sang out everything she was trying to hide. On the bright side she did finally sleep wrapped in her mother's arms, her body giving in. They monitored her often, with a vigilance that meant either her dad or mom were responsible, most likely both. When Jess opened her eyes much later her father was in the seat, still in his scrubs, mouth open, the occasional snore escaping.

"Coño," he mumbled, placing a hand on his back before finally noticing Jess was awake. Coming to her side, he pushed her hair off her forehead. "¿Cómo te sientes?"

"Bien," she managed.

He arched a brow. She didn't believe herself either.

"Just relax if you can."

"¿Y Mami?"

"In the family waiting room con tus amigos taking a break from this Satan's chair of pain. Plus, you know how she hates my snoring."

He was trying to make her laugh, but all she managed was the ghost of a smile. She thumbed the edge of her father's scrubs.

"Sorry if I smell." He motioned to the scrubs.

Her voice broke when she looked up at her father. "I'm sorry, Papi."

He shook his head, cradling her hands in his. He wiped the tears from her face even as they kept flowing.

"I didn't see him coming."

"Lo se, I know. He didn't see you either."

"Is he okay?"

"Sí, sí. Nothing insurance can't fix." He wiped the last of the tears from her face. "I'm going to go get your madre and let her know you're awake."

"Is she angry?"

"She was scared to death," he said, "so was I. But if you're wondering if you're in trouble . . ." He paused, waiting for Jess to meet his eyes. "You are."

"I know." She should be. She should be grounded for the rest of her life for this. Why did that sound like a relief?

"But for now focus on getting better so we can get you home."

HER BODY WAS kind to her, letting her sleep more than an hour at a time. When she woke Nora's face greeted her, the afternoon sun bouncing off the brown in her eyes.

"They released you," she said. "Your parents are talking to the doctors. We snuck in to see you."

There was a small cut just below her cheek, along her jawline. It was so bright red it looked like she'd marked her face with a pen.

The bed shifted as Ryan sat on the bed to her right. "You scared the living shit out of us, Jess."

She found it hard to meet their eyes. Would she see pity or anger there?

Reaching up with her healthy arm, she touched one of Nora's cuts. "I'm so sorry, Nora." The tears came again, already hovering along her eyes, ready to fall; she wiped them away before they could do more damage.

Nora moved closer, careful not to touch Jess's cast too much. "It's okay, it's okay. I'm not the one with the broken arm."

At its mention the pain in her arm increased, tired of being ignored. She tested her fingers poking out of the cast, checking, which made the pain worse if she moved it.

"Jess . . ." Lee shifted into view—the evening replayed itself all over again—she hadn't changed after the party. Had they been here all night? Because of you, Jess.

She stared at Lee for what was probably too long, not knowing what to say, not knowing what was important. Then there was one thing that echoed in her head.

"Why didn't you tell me?" Why wouldn't you tell a friend something so important? "Did anyone else know?"

Nora and Ryan shook their heads—there was that, at least.

"I don't know." Lee's voice was small, her eyes downcast. No one could meet anyone's eyes today.

"How long were you together? Have you been together . . ."

Maybe it had just happened? And Lee hadn't figured out how to tell Jess yet. That would be it. "Two months, more or less."

"So the summer?"

Anger, sadness, confusion all mingled inside her, swirling until it was just an ugly pit of uncertainty. The only thing she could pinpoint for certain was an underlying sadness that Lee had kept something so important hidden for so long. All at once she felt tired again, her arm ached, and she just wanted to shut her eyes and move past this.

"Jess, I—"

Whatever Lee was going to say cut off as her parents came back in the room, discharge papers in hand. Behind them came David, his eyes traveling from Jess to Lee.

"Ready to go home?" Her mother smiled, presenting Jess with a set of clean clothes to change into.

"Yes."

Home to her bed. To a closed door and quiet.

"Your friends can meet us there," her mother said.

Jess shook her head. "I'm pretty tired, and I figure you guys are too. We can talk another day."

"Are you sure?" Ryan asked. He'd shifted over to where Lee stood and placed an arm around her.

"Yeah."

What would be the point? So it could make Jess feel like more of a failure? All Jess wanted to do was crawl under her covers and shut the world out. Not think of the party, or Lee, or the conversation she would have with her parents.

NORA

BETH STAYED THE night, and the next day Nora was excused from La Islita until she felt better. She wondered how long she could feign the ache along her shoulders or the pain in her arm. No one could shake Jess's accident, and it didn't help that even days after, Jess still hadn't talked to anyone, retreating into a silence no one could pull her from.

No one at school understood what had happened that night, and since Nora, Lee, or Ryan couldn't offer any explanation it wasn't long before the whispers died off. Still, when Jess came back at the end of the following week she kept to herself, avoiding all three of them.

It ached not to talk with her, not to see her messages in her phone every day. They all felt it.

"Let's give her some space," Lee said, though Nora

knew how desperate Lee was to talk to Jess. And maybe because of that, they listened.

Soon her mother decided that keeping Nora up-to-date with the remodeling plans was just what she needed to feel a part of La Islita again, even if she wasn't physically able to be there. Nora's days were filled with paint swatches, table options, and the great debate over paper place mats versus tablecloths. There seemed to be never-ending options of tiles to choose from, but only one future for Nora.

When she couldn't take it anymore she finally returned to La Islita, letting the years of muscle memory take her through days of pressing down sandwiches in la plancha and steaming milk for the café con leches.

She texted the group one night after a long stream of congratulations on the new space and gentle reminders from customers that the new store should have Wi-Fi.

Nora: Is this it? Is this really it?

Regretting it as soon as she hit send, she picked at the scabs along her arms until any reply came. Not all the scrapes had healed, and a few drops of blood pooled along her skin. She shouldn't have sent that. Just make the best of it. She'd done it before, she could do it again. But the more she thought about it, the faker it felt, a wrong note in a symphony.

Ryan: Talk to your mom, please.

Nora: It's OK. I'm just having a bad day. Ignore me.

Lee: This is your life. Emphasis on your.

Jess stayed silent as she had for the past week, her absence a gaping hole in the group. Nora's heart ached for her friend and wondered if she had let her down. Had they all let her down? Jess had always been the anchor, the one making sure they were all there for each other, but had they let her down by not being there for her?

And then it came. Jess's text lit up her phone, making Nora's heart skip. She'd texted outside the group chat, but she'd texted.

> **Jess: Hey. I know I haven't said anything since I left the hospital. But do you remember before that car hit us and we were just sitting in the car and you tried to calm me down?**

Nora waited, afraid to interrupt.

> **Jess: I haven't been calm in so long. I don't know what to do.**

Nora took a breath. Should she call her? She could see another message coming in.

> **Jess: But I let it get to that, I didn't listen when I needed to. I know you think you can just put away your dreams like they were never there to begin with, but that's bullshit and you know it. You don't deserve that. Please. Talk to your mom. For me.**

Jess, oh, Jess. Nora typed as another message came through.

> **Jess: Gotta go, but talk later.**

"Wait, no."

She tried calling, but Jess would not pick up. She read the message again, remembering that moment in the car, all jumbled with memories of broken glass and flashing lights.

In the craze of the aftermath she'd forgotten all about it. Nora needed to tell Ryan and Lee about the text, but first she'd do what Jess asked.

WAITING FOR HER mother to come home was the hardest hour of her life. She ran through scenarios, playing out each possibility, already shaking from the expected reactions. Would she be angry or just confused? There would be disappointment, of course, and that would hurt, but it was better than anger.

She heard the keys in the lock and sprang up, dancing from foot to foot.

"Sorry I'm late." Her mother tossed her purse and coat on the table. "I had to leave some samples with the contractor."

Tumble, tumble, her mind worked so slow, say something.

"Mami, can we talk?"

Passing Nora on the way to the kitchen her mother searched the fridge for something to snack on. "Sure. Let me just find something to eat. In all my running around I missed lunch."

"No." This waiting would deflate whatever courage she'd gotten from Jess's text message. "I need to talk now."

Confused, her mother closed the fridge and joined Nora on the couch.

"Okay. What is this about?"

Another breath.

Do this for Jess.

No, she could hear Jess say, do this for yourself.

"I don't want to work at La Islita after I graduate."

Nora closed her eyes against the silence and to avoid her mother's gaze.

"What do you mean?"

"I don't want this anymore."

Quiet, so much quiet, then her mother let out a breath. "No entiendo, Nora, what are you saying? Is this a joke? Because it's not funny."

"It's not, Mami." A part of her yelled to take everything back, to apologize and just move on. She didn't listen. Instead she thought of the cobbled streets of Paris, the sidewalks of New York, the stainless-steel test kitchens of the schools in California. "I want to go to culinary school. I want to learn new things. I want to study and master macarons and French bread. I want to bake what I want, regardless of whether it fits anywhere."

"Where is this coming from all of a sudden?"

She'd shrunk down without noticing and fought to keep her shoulders back, her eyes level with her mother's. "It's been a while, actually."

Her mother pursed her lips. "How long is a while? A month? Two?"

"No." It wouldn't matter, though, would it?

"And now you want to give up years of our work at La Islita, for something that only came to mind a couple of months ago? Nora . . ." Her mother sighed, pinching the bridge of her nose. "I don't have time for this. We have a remodel going on, remember?"

"I remember."

"Do you? And where do you think the money would come from for these schools? Were you going to pay for them yourself, because . . . I just don't understand where this is coming from, Nora. Changing your hair is one thing, and I accepted that, but this? This is a family business." She scrunched up her face, and Nora wanted to smooth out the worry and shock of it. "It's for the both of us. It's a legacy. You know how hard we've worked for this."

"I know. You know I know this. I grew up in La Islita, and it's been my life. And I was fine with it being my future too, but then . . ." Keep going, keep going. "I gave myself room to dream, to see the possibilities. And I know this isn't the best time—"

"The best time?" Her mother laughed, but nothing was funny. "What would be the best time to find out your daughter no longer wants the future you both planned together. What would be the best time for that?"

"I—"

"No." Her mother raised her hand, ending whatever Nora was going to say. "I don't want to talk about this anymore."

Without another word she stood and left the room, leaving Nora alone, heartbroken.

JESS

RYAN WAS ON Jess's bed and would not leave. He looped one leg over hers and wrapped a hand around the cocooned sheets that held in his friend.

Ryan's weight was comforting though she didn't tell him.

"I'm fine," she said, though he hadn't asked.

"So here's the thing," he whispered into the sheets. "I don't believe you and neither do you. But I'm not going to force you to say it if you can't, even though whatever it is you're afraid to say, you know we won't judge you, right?"

Deep down she knew, but it didn't stop the tiny little voice that wondered: What if they did?

"Lee said we should give you space, which we did."

Lee, she still hadn't spoken to Lee. Fuck, she was a horrible friend.

"But now I'm doing what you would do, Jess. I'm here to invade your space." He cleared his throat. "And I need your help destroying some sketches."

"What?" She jerked up a bit, trying to see through the fabric.

"Can you pop out of there for a second? It's getting kind of weird talking to a beige blob. You look like a giant penis."

"That's not funny." She scoffed, elbowing Ryan. "What did you mean by destroy your sketches?"

Ryan rolled off the bed with a thump. "You'll have to come out of those sheets to find out."

The bed was empty without him, and she missed the feel of his arms around her. When she poked her head out of the sheets he stood at the foot of her bed, waiting for her, hand outstretched.

She took a breath and took his hand.

They sat at the foot of her bed, a box between them.

"You want to destroy these?" Jess pulled out a sketch at random, a pastel drawing of their school.

"Transform is a better word for it—but I need to tear them up to do it."

She flipped through paper after paper of old self-portraits and pencil drawings of Jason. "Are you destroying everything?"

"Transform," he repeated. "And no, I kept a few for myself."

"Why?"

"For the dreaded self-portrait," he said, staring at one of the sketches. "It was something my grandmother said, about trying to put something broken back together again."

Jess fiddled with the edges of the stack in front of her. "That it's impossible, I remember. Broken is broken." As she spoke she crumpled the edge of one piece, then tried to uncrumple it, with little success. She couldn't imagine ripping up the pages, cutting portraits in half until they were nothing. The crumpled edge of the piece reminded her of how she felt: bent, torn, lines showing across her skin no matter how often she tried to iron them out.

"You aren't broken, Jess." Ryan reached for Jess's hand, keeping it in his as he settled closer. "And neither am I. We are something new."

"I don't feel new," her voice cracked.

"Let us help you. We love you."

"I know, I know." A sob crawled up her spine and threatened to break free. "There were so many times I wanted to say something, but I thought I could handle it, that I should handle it."

"Handle what?"

"Everything." Ryan waited, watching as she picked up another sketch, tracing it with her fingers. She followed the lines of the sketch until her mind calmed and she could speak. "I feel like I can't breathe, like I ran a marathon when I've barely gone a block. Like I'm letting people down constantly no matter what I do."

"What did your parents say? Did you talk to them?"

"I tried after the accident." They'd tried so hard, but each time she looked in their faces all she could think of was how much of a burden she was. "But not very well."

Ryan put his arm around her. "Let us be there for you. If it was happening to me or Lee or Nora you would want them to open up, right? You'd want them to get help. So why are you any less?"

Why was she any less?

Ryan nudged her. "You aren't a burden. Never think that."

They sat there for a moment, arms wrapped around each other.

"I like this new Ryan," she finally said. "Not that I didn't like the old one, of course. Where did he come from?"

"According to my ama he was always here, I just needed to get over myself." He smiled. "She didn't exactly say that last part, but pretty much."

"And Jason?"

He shrugged. "I don't know, but hopefully he's happy."

She adjusted to get a better look at his face. "That's mature."

"Yeah, well, I'm about to tear up at least a couple dozen portraits of him, so I'm not sure how mature I'm being."

He laughed. "Ready to do some damage?" Ryan handed Jess a sketch and grabbed one of his own, a pencil sketch of Jason from when they'd started dating.

Jess hesitated.

"Here, I'll start," Ryan said, ripping the portrait down the middle, then again until jagged pieces lay all over the floor. "Not destroyed, just transformed."

With a deep breath she tore the paper in half, feeling fantastic once it was done. "Okay, that was pretty good."

"Surprisingly, right?" He tore another one. "Ama is always right."

"I'm sure she knows that already."

She ripped up another portrait, watching the pieces flutter to the ground; they'd already started to form something new. She felt lighter, steps closer to putting words to emotions she would've rather buried. "Thank you."

Ryan stopped mid-rip, dropping the paper to lean over and hug her. "Don't you ever leave us again. That's not allowed. You know we need constant Jess check-ins, or we would all be lost."

"You're all stronger than you think."

"Always better together, though."

They were, she should've never worried about that.

"I owe Lee an apology." And Nora and Ryan. She should've trusted her friends from the beginning; she should've asked for help. Jess would've demanded the same from any of them. She did, often.

"You do."

"I do."

For a while all you could hear was the sound of paper being torn, of two friends laughing over old memories, transforming into something.

Scars and all.

JESS WAS NOT okay.

Breathe.

Jess needed help.

Breathe.

She would tell her friends, but first she would tell her family.

So Jess called a family meeting.

The couch cushions in their old age acted like quicksand around her as she sat. When David took the seat opposite her he didn't speak, waiting for her to speak first.

"I'm sorry."

"Me too," he replied, then moved to sit next to her. "Are you mad?"

"I'm not mad, even though one of you should've told me. You're my brother, and she's my best friend." Get to the point. "But I am sorry I didn't take it well, I haven't been taking a lot of things well lately."

"What's wrong?"

Breathe.

"I need help," she whispered.

"Dime." Her mother came around the couch, her father right behind her. Her face said they'd waited for Jess, giving her the time she needed. "We're listening."

Breathe.

"I think they are called panic attacks." She could feel her heart beating against her chest, wouldn't it be just lovely to get a panic attack while talking about her panic attacks? Just perfect. She didn't wait for them to sit. "At first I thought they were random or just like a one-time stress thing."

Her hands started to shake, and her mother reached out to hold them in hers.

"Respira, Jessica," her father instructed.

A ghost of a laugh tumbled out. "I'm trying."

She let her heart spill the worry, the thoughts, the echoes that flooded her head. That she thought it was nothing—we all have moments like this—she told herself even if they kept coming. How she thought she could handle everything even as things piled up, even as her body screamed at her that she couldn't. That she didn't want to ask for help, didn't want to let people down, didn't want to be a burden.

"Burden?" Her father shook his head. "¿Cómo puedes pensar eso?"

But she couldn't help it—there were moments where she felt like her chest was going to burst.

"You are not a burden, amor mío." Her mother held her in her arms. "And all of those things? The scholarships, the center, they are not as important as you are, do you understand me?" Jess nodded, watching the tears well up in her mother's eyes. "And I'm so sorry that I didn't see it, Mija. That I didn't think to ask. Perdóname."

"It's okay, Mami." She wasn't angry at her mother, and there was nothing to forgive.

"It's not," her mother said, "but we'll work toward that. Juntos. You are not alone in this."

They spoke through to the night, until each of them was as spent as the other. Then they made plans to speak again, and again, and again.

That night, for the first time in many months, Jess's mind was quiet.

RYAN

HE'D SPENT THE morning video chatting with his grand-mother, showing her the blank canvas and promising an actual portrait by the end of the day—or the week at least.

She'd signed off by showing him the two portraits he'd done, both up on her wall side by side. "My favorite one yet!" she said, standing next to the newest one for comparison. "Now you go do yours, and we will talk again. I'm off to the travel agent. It's time to plan my next trip!"

"So soon?"

"Soon?" She laughed. "You can't keep me down for long. Same as you."

She has so much faith.

"And maybe," she brought the phone so close all he

could see was her nose and the top of her lip, "I'll need a travel buddy."

"That would be amazing." He'd never been able to go on one of his grandmother's trips before but had a sneaking suspicion they'd make the perfect pair.

"Go," she instructed. "Remember you are who you are. Scars and all."

He'd repeated it over and over again until it felt like a mantra. He texted the group and Blake.

Ryan: I'm going in.

Nora: You can do it.

Lee: No pare! Sigue, sigue!

Jess: Yes you can!

His heart did a little dance each time Jess texted within the group now. She was going to see Lee at this very moment, and Ryan had promised to meet them later tonight. So there was no time to waste. One final text came in.

Blake: I can't wait to see it. Coffee date tomorrow?

Ryan: You're on.

The piles of torn sketches sat neatly to his right, on his left were his brushes and dollops of paint in shades of blue, black, and red. He would start with those and see what the canvas needed.

You are who you are.

He remembered the Ryan at the beginning of the year, the canvas covered in charcoal with a light at the center, and started there. He loaded the largest brush with black and circled everything but the center. Dipping a smaller brush in the deepest blue he added strokes to the darkness.

Scars and all.

He sifted through the torn pages, searching through half faces, and at one point he realized he didn't know which belonged to him and which to Jason.

Broken heart and all.

Picking three, he layered them on top of each other on the canvas, holding them in place with swaths of red and black for the moments his heart hurt the most. Then he picked two more pieces and did it again. Each piece or new color he added looked like they were coming from or going into the stark white center of the canvas.

Still, there was something missing.

He needed yellow, white, and red to form coral. Adding the bright layers in chunks along with the green of overgrown forests in tiny backyards. He crushed the last of the incense his grandmother had brought back from Taipei and blended it into the painting.

More.

He worried that the painting might slip off the canvas with the amount of material on it, so he placed it on the floor of his room and danced around it as he added layer after layer. Sky blue for Jess, Lee, and Nora and the bright futures he saw for them regardless of any storm clouds they might see for themselves. Purple for Blake, for the start of something, the hope of something. Fabric from his first baby blanket he'd kept, the rest of which became a new one for Katie.

White and gold for a trail of scars holding it all together.

When he was done there were specks of paint all over him, down to his scalp; he'd returned to the habit of running his hands through his hair. It felt right, paint was part of him after all. It belonged on his skin like the birthmarks he'd been born with.

He hovered over the painting, walking around it. He wasn't sure which way was up, but he didn't mind. There was something about the portrait he couldn't put his finger on, something it reminded him of.

Taking a photo, he sent it to his grandmother; she of all people would know.

"It's a galaxy," she replied in Mandarin.

"Is it?"

He hopped up on his bed and looked at the painting again. Of course she was right, he had painted a galaxy. The things he loved were stars in the darkness, his heartbreak pits of dark matter, his scars the interstellar dust weaving through it all.

This is who you are. Scars and all.

LEE

LEE WAS SURPRISED by how light the disc was, considering how much it held. She placed it on top of the DVD player and immediately needed something to do with her hands.

"Hi." Jess stood by her door, swallowed up in the world's largest hoodie. But she looked better, brighter than she'd been since that night. "Can I come in?"

"Yes." Lee straightened, her heart giving a quick beat. "How are you?"

"I'm sorry, Lee," Jess said, coming toward her.

"You don't have to—"

"Yes I do." Jess pulled her over to the bed, where they sat.

"I should've told you."

"I keep things to myself too, so I shouldn't judge," Jess said, her eyes puffy. Lee recognized tired eyes from too much crying.

"You can judge a little if you want."

"I don't want to." Jess shook her head, taking a deep breath. "Do you forgive me?"

"Forgive you? Jess, for what?"

"For not telling you about how the resolution was making me feel," she corrected herself, "how I was making myself feel. I said yes to everything, but . . . they were the wrong things to say yes to."

"Of course I forgive you," Lee said. Out of anyone, Lee could understand keeping things to yourself and internalizing until it was just part of your nature.

She'd never been angry, just worried. Worried she'd hurt her friend; worried she'd let her down.

"Thank you," she said with a smile that reached her eyes. "So, you and David . . ."

Lee nodded. "Me and David."

"Do you . . ."

"I like him, Jess." She felt a warm feeling in her belly as she thought of him. "I really do. I think he likes me too."

"I know he does," Jess replied. "Why didn't you tell me about it? Did you think I would get mad?"

"Maybe?" Lee shook her head. "But . . . okay, can I just be honest?"

"Please." When Jess said that, she knew she'd missed

talking to Lee as much as Lee missed talking to Jess.

"I think I was using him a little bit," Lee said, waiting for Jess to interrupt, asking Lee to clarify what she meant, but instead she nodded, asking Lee to continue. "As a way to push away the thoughts of the test, of the possible future. When I was with him everything but the present was drowned out, and I couldn't hear the thoughts anymore. Eventually it became more than just a fun distraction and I looked forward to just being with him, but I was still afraid that if I told you, or anyone, that it would just bring me back to that damn fork in the road."

Jess nodded. "I get it."

"You know my dad said my mom was really good at finding ways to be happy even in her worst moments."

"And?"

"Looking back now, it reminds me of when we talked about the fork in the road and you asked what I saw when I imagined it. And I saw one long road and one dead end."

A life with Huntington's. A life with no future.

"Now . . ." She closed her eyes and went back to that road, arriving at the fork. To the right there was life without Huntington's; it was still long and green and lush. She could see her friends, her family, and milestones, like college and a career. It was a bit too perfect, and Lee needed to work on that too. To the left was her life with Huntington's. "I can see it better, I can see it how Mami would see it." That road was bumpy and steep. "I thought it was a dead end, but it's not. It's rougher and harder, but it's still a road. I can make something of it," Lee said. Jess laced her hand with Lee's. "And I'm not alone in it."

And she could see them now, along the path, hands reaching for her: her father, Auntie Rose, Jess, Nora, Ryan, and even David. She was not alone, as her mother had not been alone. Huntington's would not take them from her.

LEE'S HAND SHOOK as she placed the disc in the player. Once in, she hopped back to the safety of her friends. Lee passed Jess the control, unable to hit play herself. Pictures were one thing, but a video quite another.

Her old house in DC came on-screen, the same couch and chairs just in a different place. Lee had almost forgotten that old house, and now the memories rushed back.

"Might be time for some new furniture," Ryan mumbled.

"Rude." Lee smacked him on the shoulder.

"It's working." Her father's voice came from the screen as the camera panned around the room. He turned it around to face him. "At least I think it is."

"I'm going to regret getting you this." Lee held her breath at the sound of her mom's voice, until she came on-screen. Her father zoomed in on her face. "Really, is being this close necessary?"

"We have to document everything for the baby."

Her mother placed her hands on her hips and looked down at her belly—a barely there bump. "I don't remember Francheska asking."

He zoomed in on the belly. "Are we married to that name?"

Her mother's hand grabbed the camera, bringing it back to her face, her lips pursed.

"I mean, it's a great name," her father said.

Lee laughed, feeling the first of the tears gathering, though her heart remained steady. She felt Ryan and Jess close around her, shoulder to shoulder. The screen blanked, then came back to a stunning close-up of her mom, the light from the camera catching her eyes and warm brown skin.

"Is this . . . yes . . . okay!" He turned the camera to beige walls then a heart monitor and finally a very sweaty Paula holding a new Lee. "Welcome to the world, Francheska Lee Carter-Perez. I'm sorry we couldn't give you a longer name."

"Hush." Her mother teased Lee's nose with her finger. "It fits her."

The camera rumbled as her father came on-screen by his wife's side, and neither of them spoke. In her mother's arms Lee shifted and fell asleep, the safest baby in the world.

"HOLA, MI VIDA." Her mother came on the screen once again.

"Hi, Mami," Lee whispered.

"I'm going to say this in English, so your dad doesn't think I'm conspiring behind his back, though he really needs to work on his Spanish, you can tell him I said that. I don't know how old you will be when you watch this, but by now you know your mami is sick and it's not something that can be cured, though we continue to pray for miracles. I want you to know que te amo. I love you and I'm proud of you, and I hope to give you as many good memories as I can. I know I will take with me some of the best memories of all time." Her mother stared off-screen, unsure of what to say next. "Your dad and I decided not to get you tested, we thought that decision should be yours, whether you decide to take it or not." She paused, a moment of anger then sadness passing over her face in a matter of seconds. "It never gets easier to know, but you can't let it stop you, Mija. My life is so much more que esta mierda, and yours will be too. I wish this message could be longer—I have so much to say, but I do have the years. Not all I wanted, but I won't waste them, I promise you. Take care of each other, mi vida. Te amo."

The silence after the video ended should've been worse. It should've sent her retreating into the darkest corners, but it didn't. The image of her mother looking straight at her through that camera steadied her heart.

She squeezed Jess's hand. "I'm going to take the test," she said. Jess nodded and squeezed back.

Her mother was not her disease. She'd lived every last second of her life with as much love and compassion as she could manage. She did not let the shadow of it drain away one second that belonged to her, and neither would Lee.

"DOOR STAYS OPEN, Francheska Lee," her father warned her, then he eyed David entering the room. "And I'm going to be popping in here at odd intervals, you hear me? So keep it PG."

"PG-13?" Lee replied, already seeing the hint of a smile on her father's face. It was well hidden, but it was there.

"Don't make me knock it down to a G," he replied.

"PG it is."

Her father made sure the door was as open as possible before leaving, giving David one final long look as well.

"When I thought about everyone knowing about us," David said, "I may have glossed over your dad's reaction to all of this. On a scale of one to ten, how soon am I going to need a new identity?"

Lee tugged at his shirt until he was much closer. "Maybe like a five."

"A five is good." David brought his lips to hers. "How does it feel?"

"The kiss? Good."

He shook his head. "Now that the world knows about us."

"A little bit new, a little bit of the same. Still great. You?"

"I'm going to miss our unsupervised Spanish lessons." He placed a hand on her cheek and kissed her again. "I'm incredibly happy."

"Did you get my message?" She kept her eyes level on his. "About the test?"

David nodded, pulling her closer. "I'll be there."

He would be there, for the test, for whichever fork in the road she went down, no matter how bumpy it got. They would all be there.

NORA

NORA WAS NOT expecting a giant Tupperware container to slide across the counter toward her as she neared the end of her shift. But there it was, and there was Jess coming around the counter to give Nora a quick hug. "I brought you some Turkey Day leftovers. Since I know you guys didn't really have time to do anything this year."

Jess was being kind. Between her mother's silent treatment and La Islita's busy schedule, they'd chosen to simply work through Thanksgiving. They celebrated by pretending her mother still wasn't hurt by Nora's revelation and passing out early.

"Thanks."

Jess pulled one more item out of her bag: a ziplock full of chocolate chip cookies. "Not Nora quality, but still

pretty good. I'm sure you can find ways of making them better."

"The secret is that the cookie batter is just a conduit for more chocolate."

She placed the cookies in her backpack as Jess put her arms around her. "Is she still angry at you?"

Nora slumped against her friend. "Yeah. She just walks around me like I'm not even here."

"Have you tried talking to her again?"

She sighed, turning to face Jess. "Can you do it?"

That made Jess laugh and Nora's mood brighten just a bit.

"You know I would," Jess said. "But why don't you tell me what you would say if you could? Like a practice run. Maybe that will help."

"That's a good idea."

"I tend to have those once in a while," she said with a smirk.

"Okay, let me think," Nora said, going through everything she wanted to say to her mother. "I should probably start with I'm sorry."

"Why?" Jess asked, making Nora pause. "Why are you sorry?"

For breaking her heart. For shattering the vision she had of La Islita. For not wanting what she wanted.

"I guess for no longer wanting the same thing? For messing everything up and making her hate me."

"I don't hate you, Nora." Her mother stood by the doorway. "How could you think that?"

Nora's heart stopped for a moment before remembering to start up again. How long had she been standing there? Jess moved closer to Nora as her mother walked up to the counter.

"It's not that hard," Nora replied. "We haven't talked in forever, Mami."

Her mother nodded, turning to Jess. "Jessica, can you give Nora and me some time to talk?"

Jess met Nora's eyes and waited for her to nod. "Call me," she said, and gave Nora another hug. "You can do this. I know you can," she whispered before pulling away.

The seconds after Jess left felt endless as her mother hadn't said anything else. Was she waiting for Nora to say something? Or putting together her own thoughts? Finally she turned and sat by the tiny table. "Siéntate, please."

"I'm not angry," her mother said, then placed her hands on her temples. "No, you're right, I was angry and confused. You can see why, sí?"

"I rejected your dream."

"Not my dream, Nora, our dream. Or at least that's what I thought it was."

"In a way it was."

"In what way? Dime." Already her voice was so much calmer than it had been that night. Maybe today she would listen?

"I . . ." How to say this and not break her heart? "I didn't know I could have my own."

"Your own what?"

"Dream."

Her mother paused, she imagined that she was running through all the years Nora had dutifully stood by her side, the perfect partner, and Nora's current words painting a completely different picture. "Keep going. I need to understand this more."

"You built La Islita from the ground up."

Her mother shook her head. "No sola."

"I was there, I know, but the soul of La Islita is you," Nora said. "So I know it's hard to understand when I say I want to move away from it."

"I always love watching you create in the kitchen. You look as happy as you do when you're with Beth."

"I still love to bake." Even now her fingernails hid traces of sugar. "But there's more outside of La Islita, and I want to be a part of it. I want to go to California or New York, I want to learn new things and try new recipes. And maybe one day I'll build something from the ground up too, or even come back to La Islita, I don't know! But it would be nice to have the option."

"You said you've been thinking about this for months. Why not tell me then?"

"I was still tied to your dream, thinking it was the only path I could have. Then when I did think it could be an option, the expansion happened and you were so happy, and I didn't want to disappoint you—"

Her mom reached for her hand until Nora was looking directly into her eyes. "No te atrevas a decir esa palabra otra vez, Nora. You could never disappoint me." She slumped back in her chair. "I may be disappointed in myself."

Her mother's eyes drifted to the papers poking out of her purse, blueprints, her shoulders sagging. She was probably thinking about the expansion and what this meant for her.

"Just because it's not my dream, it doesn't mean it still can't be yours," Nora said gently.

"Is there still time?"

"Time?"

"To apply for the culinary schools," her mother said. A rush of happiness flooded over Nora.

"Are you saying I should apply?"

"There's still more to talk about, like financials and responsibilities to La Islita. I can't promise you a yes yet, Nora. But let's just start there."

DURING HER NEXT day off Nora and Beth pored over each culinary school option, downloading applications and marking down deadlines. Nora still had time, but not a lot with Navidades coming around the corner.

She and her mother had talked again. Nora could still see the hesitation and hurt in her eyes, but she was trying at the very least. And Nora helped with that as well by promising to look at the culinary school options in Colorado.

"I can do this," she repeated to herself as she printed out her list of essays to write.

"You can," Beth agreed. "I also added those deadlines into my own phone, so you can count on me to annoy you about them."

"You can never annoy me."

"Sounds like a challenge." A quick peck on the lips from Beth was all Nora needed to blush, but she wouldn't have it any other way.

"Let's take a break," Nora said. "I'll teach you how to make palmiers with store-bought puff pastry."

Beth gasped. "Store bought? I'm not sure culinary school would approve." She laced her fingers through the loops on Nora's jeans, tugging them just before resting her hands there.

Nora relished the feel of Beth against her. "I'm sure they won't mind."

Beth snuggled into Nora's neck, watching her roll out the sheets of pastry.

"You know you did it, right?"

Nora twisted to face her. "Did what?"

"You chose your own adventure." Beth's smile took up her whole face.

"I did, didn't I?" Nora stared into Beth's eyes, the happiness there echoed in her own. Beth watched as she rolled out the puff pastry, then let the sugar fall like rain. She snuck her hand in, catching the grains on her fingers and bringing them to her lips, delighting in the sweetness. "Now if that first one was just as easy."

Beth snorted. "Yeah, not unless we drove to California."

Nora stilled. Would that be possible? In the grand scheme of things, next to Nora maybe having her own future, it didn't sound so impossible. "What if we did?"

"Did what?"

"Drive to California."

"Isn't that pretty far?" Beth said. "I mean I'm not an expert, but I'm pretty sure there's another state in between."

"Yes. More than one actually." But Nora was already looping around Beth and typing on her laptop, finding routes and figuring out logistics that would make Jess proud.

"Huh," she said when she was done. "This might just work."

FA LA LA LA LA

Nora: Happy Christmas the first!

Lee: God, Nora, I can hear you from here.

Nora: Feliz Navidad, bitches!

Ryan: I'm going to need you to bring the holiday cheer down to an 8, we just got into December.

Nora: NO. Fa la la la la LA LA LA LA!

Ryan: She must be stopped.

Nora: Feliz Navidad y Prospero Año y felicidad . . . (pause for beat)

Lee: Stop.

Nora: I wanna wish you a Merry Christmas. . . .

Jess: So, I know the trip isn't till after Ryan's show, but I'm making a list of things we might need, like extra flip-flops for the hotel room, because you never know.

Ryan: Yes, Mom. Also, I told you not to mention the show.

Lee: Which show? Is it the gallery show at the end of the week where all your art will be on display and the world will finally know that Ryan Wang Mercado is in fact a genius? Is it that one?

Ryan: No the other one.

Lee: Oh, OK, cool.

Jess: 1. Ryan, you'll be amazing. 2. I can't figure out if we can build a fire, we should buy some firewood just in case.

Lee: On a scale of 1 to 10, how hipster is buying your own firewood?

Ryan: Is it locally sourced artisanal firewood?

Jess: So that's a yes.

Lee: We're meeting you at the show, right? Do we get to go in early because we know the artist?

Ryan: Yes and no. I don't make the rules.

Lee: Fine. I guess I'll enter with the rest of the peasants.

Nora: Ohhhhh I don't . . .

Lee: DON'T YOU DARE PUT THAT IN MY HEAD.

Nora: Just one thing I need.

Ryan: ha.

Nora: UNDERNEATH THE CHRISTMAS TREE.

Lee: I'm out.

Ryan: Leeeeee, don't leave us!!!

Nora: *drum solo*

Jess: I hear my parents . . .

Ryan: Uh, yeah, I hear my parents too. I have to go paint . . . something.

Nora: You guys are no fun. I'll just save my singing for the road trip. You'll see.

Lee: You know what? I forgot I have something to do that day.

Nora: Too late. Mwahahahaha.

Lee: This new Nora is mean . . . I like her.

RYAN

HE SHOULD'VE BACKED out, he should've backed out. Was it too late to run? His eyes searched for the exit sign, but it was too late, they were opening the doors now. People started to trickle in. He recognized many faces from TAA, along with complete strangers coming to judge his work and sneer while holding free wine.

"You look so handsome!" His grandmother flooded his view, bringing him in for a hug. Did she notice how frazzled he was?

"Xièxie," he replied, fiddling with his tie, thinking for the hundredth time that he should've worn the matching blue blazer.

Behind her came his parents with Katie. "I've never seen your grandmother so pushy, we lost her in half a second."

"You're just slow. Plus I wanted to be the first to see his paintings!" his grandmother said. He crouched down so she could place a hand on his cheek. She turned to his parents. "Let's walk around, I want to see the other work."

His father sighed and offered her his arm, giving his son an apologetic glance and promising to be quick. Then it was his mother's turn to engulf him in a dual hug with Katie. When they separated her eyes were wet with tears.

While his family walked around the show, Ryan hid behind a wall, trying to get his nervousness under control. He hopped on the tips of his toes, shaking off the cold from the outside, though he was still sweating in spite of the chill. He saw a couple gingerly making their way toward his paintings and almost fainted.

"Nervous?" Blake came around the wall, wearing a bold sapphire-blue blazer with a black tie.

Ryan almost collapsed from relief that it wasn't Candace coming to tell him to stop hiding. Though Blake might be coming to say the same thing. "Can you tell?"

"Well, I'm practically shitting my pants too." Blake laughed. Ryan felt better already.

"Didn't peg you for the nervous type." Ryan ran a hand through his hair.

"I talk a big game, it hides the insecurities."

Ryan wanted to say that he doubted that, but after this year he knew even the calmest exterior could hide many things.

"Well, if it helps I think your sculptures are badass."

Blake smiled, shoving his hands in his pockets as he danced on the heels of his feet. "Thank you. And I hope you still aren't feeling like you aren't an artist, because those paintings are brilliant."

"Really?" His heart fluttered, reminding him of the question he'd asked himself not long ago. Was he ready?

"Absolutely, I might be jealous. Might be." Blake moved a bit closer, eyes level with Ryan's. His smile was so open and lovely.

Are you ready for this?

He liked Blake. He felt like himself around him, and his kiss still lingered after all this time, asking him to give it a chance. Yes, a part of him wanted to be with Blake, but another wanted more time. Time to himself. Time to shape himself after heartbreak and before another relationship.

"What are you doing after this?"

Blake shrugged. "What am I doing after this?"

"There's a family-and-friends dinner at my house, please come."

"Friends dinner, huh?" He raised his brow.

Ryan nodded, hoping that friendship was still enough for now.

Blake smiled. "Wouldn't miss it."

AT THE END of the evening, Ryan linked arms with the ladies and walked around, taking a closer look at some of his classmates' work. When he made it back to his corner, it took a beat to remember these were his pieces.

There was a swell in his chest, and it took him a moment to realize it was pride. Though he could find one thing or another he'd still tweak about each piece, he was proud of them. He could see himself in each frame. How each piece unlocked something inside him, sometimes old, and sometimes new, reminding him he was still there. Broken. Healing. Ryan.

He broke down each element of his self-portrait, pointing out the pieces of torn sketches to Jess and making sure he mentioned his grandmother's influence in all of it. And for the first time, it didn't matter to him whether anyone else thought he was good enough—if they would consider him an artist. He knew he was.

He felt Jess touch the splotches of paint along his hands.

"So?" she said, bumping against him. "How does it feel?"

"I'm not going to lie and say it feels amazing because I'm still nervous, but . . ."

"But?" Her hope echoed his own.

"I like them, I really do," he said.

"Do I get to be sappy and say I'm proud of you?"

"You may," Ryan replied. "I'm kinda proud of me too."

NEW YEAR'S EVE

NORA

NORA LICKED HER bottom lip, tasting the salt.

"Please tell me we are almost there." Nora was a bouncing ball of energy. It felt like her body would spill over with the excitement. They had to be close.

"We are not close," Jess said from the driver's seat, "we are here." She made a left turn, and suddenly the wide expanse of the Pacific Ocean was before them on the horizon.

They pulled up to Ryan's aunt's beach house, parking in the driveway but leaving their bags in the car so they could walk right to the beach. When they finally tumbled out of the car, Nora stood transfixed. There it was, so much blue, not like the sky but darker. The white waves crashed along the shore. Behind her, her friends gathered, and she felt a gentle push forward. Nora took a moment to take off her sandals and dip her feet in the sand, feeling as it spread between her toes and stuck to her skin, traveling with her as she walked forward.

"Come on!" Beth pinched her arm and shot forward, her long blond hair picked up by the gusts of wind. A beat passed, and Nora joined her, the sand scraping against her feet as she ran. She could taste and smell the salt water, the sand sticking to her lips. She passed Beth and felt the water dash to meet her, cold but welcoming. Exhilaration swam up her body, and she laughed, happiness tumbling out the farther she went.

When the water reached her knees, Nora stopped and soaked in the feel of it crashing against her, traveling around her, pulling her deeper. One by one they joined, their splashes and shouts became a song, an anthem. Ryan gathered Nora in his arms and twirled her around, tossing her back in the water. She retaliated with cold water down his back. They stripped out of their clothes, though they were soaked through, and spent the rest of the day dancing in and out.

Nora took in everything, breathing deeply, relishing the feel of the water and sand beneath her feet. She would take it with her when she left, the pull of the California ocean etched into her skin, the sway of the waves would stick with her for days.

"How does it feel?" Beth asked when they stole a quiet moment to themselves.

"It's better than the dream," Nora replied.

"Are you nervous about visiting the campus?"

Her heart fluttered. They'd managed to schedule a visit to the Culinary Institute's campus for January 2.

"No," she replied. "Not nervous. Hopeful. Excited out of my mind, but no, not nervous."

How could she be? Days ago, visiting the beach was a dream, and now she was curling her toes in the sand and dancing along the waves with Beth. It wouldn't be long before she would hear back from the schools she applied to, but she knew, maybe because of this day or the people around her, that the future she dreamed of would be more than just a dream.

"Did you think of a new resolution?" Beth curled her arm around Nora's as they made their way back to the water.

"Yes."

"And?"

"To put my feet someplace new at least once a year and kiss you as often as possible." She smiled at Beth, closing her eyes. "To fill notebook after notebook with new recipes. And to never let things be just a dream ever again."

LEE

LEE AND DAVID walked along the shore, the water kissing their feet as they did. When David reached for her hand, she did not pull away and her eyes didn't scan for who might be watching. Instead she shifted until their arms touched as they walked, until eventually they simply looped their arms around each other.

"When do you get the results?" he asked.

"I already got them."

David stopped, turning to look at her. "You did? What do they say?"

She shook her head, picturing them as an envelope on her desk, even though that's not what it was. They'd have to go in to her doctor's office for the results. "Haven't gone in yet."

"When are you going?" He heard the second question in his voice—asking if he could go with her, or at least be there for her, it brought a smile to her lips.

"After the holidays."

She tugged him back to the walk, the calming sound of waves crashing over each other seeping into her body.

"Have you decided which courses you want to take?"

"I haven't gotten accepted yet." But yes, she had. She'd plotted out a course schedule at each of the schools she'd applied to, making sure she took every genre course available and even flirting with the idea of screenwriting and directing.

He nodded. "And you applied to the school in New York?" When she nodded his grin expanded her heart. "Not that you have to go there, I'm just thinking it would be nice if we were near each other . . ."

She felt David's thumb rub the curve of her wrist and wished she could take that sensation everywhere she went. Lee had decided that her next New Year's resolution would be something as simple as taking David out on an official date. Fancy clothes and all.

"I think it would be more than nice," Lee replied.

Sometimes it wasn't easy to let herself feel happy, to push away the negative thoughts and focus on the positive. So she kept the image of the path in her head and the people along the way and the goals she wanted to achieve. She kept the feel of David's hand in hers, the touch of skin to skin, and the swell of her heart when he was near. She pictured her father's smile and his steady presence that never wavered. She saw Jess and Nora and Ryan, whose faith in her might just rival her father's. And her mother, who traveled her road with as much love as she could and nothing less than that.

Then finally herself, the lead in her own damn story, the maker of her future, the final girl, and nothing would stop her.

RYAN

RYAN DIDN'T NEED a New Year's resolution this year. After all, the spring would bring another art course and the summer featured a trip to Taipei with his grandmother.

He couldn't wait to visit her favorite shops, eat delicious Taiwanese pastries (bringing some back for Nora, of course), and test out new paints.

"That way you can carry your own art supplies," she'd said.

He watched Jess light match after match trying to start the fire. After one caught she and Ryan sat and watched as the flames consumed the wood, lifting their hands toward the sky. He watched the flames dance off her eyes and reached for his supplies to sketch her hair bleeding into the sunset like a fire goddess.

"Did you think of your resolution yet?" Jess warmed her hands by the fire.

"I don't think I need one."

"Oh really?" She pulled a bag of marshmallows from her tote, followed by chocolate and graham crackers.

"Yes, really." He motioned for her to toss it all over to him. "God bless you."

"I'm pretty sure it's a rule that you have to have s'mores by a campfire," she replied. "You know what's also a rule?"

Oh, he knew what was coming. "Let me guess? You have to have New Year's resolutions?"

"So smart," Jess said. "Plus, look on the bright side, you won't have us doing it for you this year."

Ryan shrugged and stood so he could sit closer to Jess. "That was a surprisingly good idea, though." If they hadn't given him the push he needed, who knows when or if he'd ever have started painting again. Not to mention the kiss and Blake.

"Yeah?"

"Yeah."

They tore open the supplies and started to toast the marshmallows, watching as the skin turned brown and a delicious crust formed. Off in the distance Nora, Beth, Lee, and David walked back, each hand in hand.

His thoughts traveled to Blake and the coming year. He

hadn't been ready before, and not yet, but that's what new years were for.

It brought a smile to his lips, and he thought of a new resolution for the coming year:

Kiss someone right for you.

JESS

JESS WAITED UNTIL they were all gathered around the fire to tell them.

"I have some news," she said, and they all settled, turning to her. "A decision that I came to after everything that happened this year."

The fire crackled between them, filling the silence as Jess took the moments she needed. "I'm going to take a year off."

"What?" Lee sat up.

"A gap year." Jess tugged at a strand of her hair. "After senior year, to figure things out and take my time. To be the Jess I should've been with that resolution."

Except this time she wouldn't say yes to everything, she would listen to herself, value her time, and remind herself she didn't owe it to anyone. It would be hard, but she had her friends and family and therapy, too. Her parents had insisted, and she was relieved at the idea, to have someone in her corner who would listen without judgment.

She would say yes to the things that brought her joy—like running, her friends, sometimes even bad TV. Heck, especially bad TV. She would say no to overworking her body and things she confused with productivity and achievement.

"You know what?" Ryan knocked his legs next to hers when she sat back down. "That's a perfect idea. Maybe your resolution this year should be: say yes to Jess!"

"Shit," Lee said out of nowhere.

"What?"

"That's the perfect campaign slogan," Lee said with a laugh. "It was there all along!"

Nora threw sand at Lee.

"But seriously, Jess." Lee sobered, catching her eyes. "I think that's pretty amazing and brave."

Jess shook her head. It didn't feel brave, but it felt right.

"It's brave, I promise you." Lee stood, sitting next to Jess. "And I'm happy because we need you. Not sure what we'd do without you."

NEAR MIDNIGHT, THE drinks overflowed as they laughed until their voices carried in the wind and the rhythm of the waves curled around them.

Lee and Nora danced around the crackling fire until Ryan joined with Jess. She held on to the memory until she was sure it would never fade, knowing that every moment of doubt that trickled out was not as strong as the people around her. And when she closed her eyes she could see, with every certainty, the days of happiness and possibilities that awaited them together. Always together.

REFERENCES

The information referenced regarding Huntington's Disease was cited from the Huntington's Disease Society of America. For more information on this disease, its symptoms, and how to get tested, visit www.hdsa.org.

ACKNOWLEDGMENTS

TWO YEARS AGO, after a series of highs and very-low lows, I decided I needed a change before the lows got even lower. I packed up everything I owned and stored it in my sister's basement. I then spent the next two years traveling from place to place, spending time with those I loved, refocusing on the things that mattered to my grumpy-hermit self.

I wouldn't have been able to do this if it wasn't for the support of my family, who made sure I always had a place to stay and never missed a chance to guilt me into coming to visit them. Gracias. Los amo.

To my friends Annie and Adam, who insisted I move in with them because it would be so cool, I love you both very much, even though you woke me up in the middle of the night to correct my *Warcraft* reference.

A big thank-you and lots of hugs to Janice Wang for all the late-night chats about family, life, and whatever random thing popped into our heads at the time. It has been a pleasure getting to know you more this year and I look forward to more talks soon.

Thank you to my Penguin Ladies Emily X.R. Pan, Bri Lockhart, and Kaitlyn Davis for all the support, book talk, and love.

A big book hug to my amazing friends Sylvie Larsen, Kathryn Holmes, Ghenet Myrthil, Colleen Lindsay, Benjamin Andrew Moore, Mara Delgado, Lana Pattinson, Karen Jung, Clarivel Fong, Kiana Nguyen, and many more, who read drafts or simply listened to me when I needed reassurances I wasn't messing everything up. Thank you to Shenwei Chang for their thoughtful advice and guidance.

Thank you to Patrick Murphy, who is always there, from first to final draft to the chats about branded pencils, and the long random thoughts that amount to half a sentence in the book.

To Alexandra Arnold and Rebecca Aronson, who continued to push me to dig deeper draft after draft until I very much disliked both of you for a solid day before I realized you were right. This story wouldn't be what it is without you.

Thank you to Katie Fitch for this awesome cover that makes it look like I wrote the Latinx version of *The Breakfast Club*. To Bess Braswell and Michael D'Angelo on the marketing team and Haley George in publicity for helping this book find its audience.

A big thank-you to my agent, Kerry Sparks, for always being in my corner and making sure I believe in my own publishing future as much as you do.

In addition to a nomadic lifestyle, these past two years brought with them an unwelcome health diagnosis, the result of which led me to concentrate more on my physical and mental health. So to those living with, surviving, fighting, or struggling with a disease, disorder, or illness: I see you, I'm there with you, and I love you. You are not alone.

And finally, please don't forget about Puerto Rico. The road to recovery will be very long and we need all your continued support. There are many ways to help, including donating to the Hispanic Federation's UNIDOS Disaster Relief and Recovery Program (via their website at www.hispanicfederationunidos.org) or supporting local organizations, some of which can be found via www.losambulantes.com/help-puerto-rico.